CAVES OF ICE

'GRENADE!' SIMLA YELLED, just before they detonated, and a storm of shrapnel ripped through the air. He fell backwards, ugly wounds peppering his body. Even the flak armour beneath his greatcoat couldn't stop all of the shards, and crimson stains began seeping across it as he tried to get to his feet. Hail was luckier, her partner taking most of the blast, but I could see her left arm was bleeding heavily and hung limply at her side. She leapt forward into the gap, screaming in anger, and fired her lasgun one-handed on full auto at the no doubt surprised greenskins beyond.

'Hail! Get back!' Grifen shouted, but she was too late; a volley of bolts tore Hail apart in a rain of blood and viscera, and then the orks were among us.

Also by Sandy Mitchell

FOR THE EMPEROR
The first Ciaphas Cain novel

More Warhammer 40,000 from the Black Library

• GAUNT'S GHOSTS by Dan Abnett •

The Founding
FIRST & ONLY
GHOSTMAKER
NECROPOLIS

The Saint
HONOUR GUARD
THE GUNS OF TANITH
STRAIGHT SILVER
SABBAT MARTYR

• SPACE WOLF by William King •

SPACE WOLF
RAGNAR'S CLAW
GREY HUNTER
WOLFBLADE

• OTHER WARHAMMER 40,000 TITLES •

13th LEGION by Gav Thorpe
KILL TEAM by Gav Thorpe
ANGELS OF DARKNESS by Gav Thorpe
NIGHTBRINGER by Graham McNeill
WARRIORS OF ULTRAMAR by Graham McNeill
STORM OF IRON by Graham McNeill

A WARHAMMER 40,000 NOVEL

Ciaphas Cain

CAVES OF ICE

Sandy Mitchell

For Oliver and Michael. Happy gaming!

A BLACK LIBRARY PUBLICATION

First published in Great Britain in 2004 by
BL Publishing,
Games Workshop Ltd.,
Willow Road, Nottingham,
NG7 2WS, UK.

10 9 8 7 6 5 4 3 2 1

Cover illustration by Clint Langley.

A CIP record for this book is available from the British Library.

ISBN 1 84416 070 X

Distributed in the US by Simon & Schuster
1230 Avenue of the Americas, New York, NY 10020, US.

Printed and bound in Great Britain by
Cox & Wyman Ltd, Reading, Berkshire, UK.

See the Black Library on the Internet at
www.blacklibrary.com

Find out more about Games Workshop
and the world of Warhammer 40,000 at
www.games-workshop.com

IT IS THE 41st millennium. For more than a hundred centuries the Emperor has sat immobile on the Golden Throne of Earth. He is the master of mankind by the will of the gods, and master of a million worlds by the might of his inexhaustible armies. He is a rotting carcass writhing invisibly with power from the Dark Age of Technology. He is the Carrion Lord of the Imperium for whom a thousand souls are sacrificed every day, so that he may never truly die.

YET EVEN IN his deathless state, the Emperor continues his eternal vigilance. Mighty battlefleets cross the daemon-infested miasma of the warp, the only route between distant stars, their way lit by the Astronomican, the psychic manifestation of the Emperor's will. Vast armies give battle in his name on uncounted worlds. Greatest amongst his soldiers are the Adeptus Astartes, the Space Marines, bio-engineered super-warriors. Their comrades in arms are legion: the Imperial Guard and countless planetary defence forces, the ever-vigilant Inquisition and the tech-priests of the Adeptus Mechanicus to name only a few. But for all their multitudes, they are barely enough to hold off the ever-present threat from aliens, heretics, mutants – and worse.

TO BE A man in such times is to be one amongst untold billions. It is to live in the cruellest and most bloody regime imaginable. These are the tales of those times. Forget the power of technology and science, for so much has been forgotten, never to be re-learned. Forget the promise of progress and understanding, for in the grim dark future there is only war. There is no peace amongst the stars, only an eternity of carnage and slaughter, and the laughter of thirsting gods.

Editorial Note:

This, the second extract from the Cain archive which I have pre-pared and annotated for those of my fellow inquisitors who may care to peruse it, is in much the same format as the first. The astute among you will realise that it follows my previous selection, Cain's account of the Gravalax incident, quite closely chronologically although with his usual disregard for such niceties it was actually recorded at an earlier point in the archive itself. I have chosen this section of his memoirs not only because it is relatively self-contained, requiring little background knowledge of his earlier exploits to appre-ciate, but also because the records of the Ordo Xenos contain quite a bit of detail about events on Simia Orichalcae that year and anyone with cause to consult them is certain to find the only complete eye-witness account of considerable interest. (Not least because it confirms the suspicions many of us have long harboured about the part played by certain members of the Adeptus Mechanicus in the affair, which may be useful in future dealings with them.)

It may be argued that Cain is not the most reliable chronicler of events, but I am inclined to accept his version of events as absolutely true. Here, as throughout the whole archive, he rarely gives himself credit for what, to any unbiased observer, appear to be acts of genuine courage and resourcefulness (however few and far between).

As before I have been largely content to let Cain tell his story in his own words, confining myself to annotating the original text to clarify occasional points and expand upon the wider background to the events he describes since typically he tends to concentrate almost exclusively on things that affected him personally without much regard for the bigger picture. I have also, as before, taken the liberty of breaking his account down into chapters to facilitate reading, although Cain himself didn't seem particularly bothered by such stylistic niceties. Where I've drawn on other sources they are credited appropriately; all other footnotes and interpolations are mine alone.

Amberley Vail, Ordo Xenos

ONE

WARP KNOWS I'VE seen more than my fair share of Emperor-forsaken hell-holes in more than a century of occasionally faithful and dedicated service to the Imperium, but the ice-world of Simia Orichalcae[1] stands out in my memory as one of exceptional unpleasantness. And when you bear in mind that over the years I've seen the inside of an eldar reaver citadel and a necron tomb world, just to pick out a couple of the highlights (so to speak), you can be sure that my experiences there rank among the most terrifying and life-threatening in a career positively littered with hairs'-breadth escapes from almost certain death.

Not that it seemed that way when our regiment got its orders to deploy. I'd been serving with the Valhallan 597th

---

1. Despite my best efforts to track it down, the origin of this name remains obscure. It seems fairly safe to conjecture that the world in question was famed for the presence of some statue or effigy in a past epoch, but why any-one should have chosen to commemorate this particular animal in such a way remains a mystery.

for a little over a year by that point, and had managed to settle into a fairly comfortable routine. I got on well with both Colonel Kasteen and her second-in-command Major Broklaw; they appeared to consider me as much of a friend as it was possible to be with the regimental commissar, and the kudos I'd earned as a result of our adventures on Gravalax stood me in good stead with the men and women of the lower ranks as well. Indeed most of them seemed to credit me, not entirely wrongly, with having provided the inspirational leadership which had allowed them to prevail against the vile conspiracy that had unleashed so much bloodshed on that unhappy world and provided them with an initial battle honour to which they could all point with pride.

At the risk of seeming a little full of myself, I did have some cause for satisfaction on that score at least; I'd inherited responsibility for a divided, not to say mutually hostile, regiment, cobbled together from the combat-depleted remnants of two previously single-sex units who had disliked and distrusted one another from the beginning. Now, if anything, I was faced with the opposite problem: I was charged with maintaining discipline as they became comfortable working together and the new personnel assignments started bedding in. (Quite literally in some cases, which only made matters worse of course, particularly when acceptable fraternisation spilled over into lovers' tiffs, acrimonious partings, or the jealousy of others. I was beginning to see why the vast majority of regiments in the Imperial Guard were segregated by gender.) Fortunately, there were very few occasions when anything harsher than a stiff talking-to, a quick rotation of the protagonists to different squads, and a rapid palming off of the problem to the chaplain were called for, so I was able to maintain my carefully-constructed facade of concern for the troopers without undue difficulty.

Being iceworlders themselves, of course, the Valhallans were overjoyed to hear we were being sent to Simia Orichalcae. Even before we made orbit the viewing ports were crowded with off-duty troopers eager for a first sight of our new home for the next few months and a chatter of excited voices had followed Kasteen, Broklaw and myself through the corridors towards the bridge. My enthusiasm, needless to say, was rather more muted.

'Beautiful, isn't it?' Broklaw said, his grey eyes fixed on the main hololith display. The flickering image of the planet appeared to be suspended in the middle of the cavernous chamber full of shadows and arcane mechanisms, surrounded by officers, deckhands and servitors doing the incomprehensible things starship crewmen usually did. There must have been a dozen at least of them buzzing about, waving data-slates at one another, or manipulating the switches inlaid into the age-darkened wood of the control lecterns which littered the main deck below us. Captain Durant, the officer in charge of the old freighter that had been hastily pressed into service to transport us from our staging area on Coronus Prime,[1] shook his head.

'If you like planets I suppose it's allright,' he said dismissively, his optical implants not even flickering in that direction. Of indeterminate age, he was so patched with augmetics that if it hadn't been for his uniform and the deference with which his crew treated him I might have mistaken him for a servitor. It had been courteous of him to invite the three of us to the

---

1. *Coronus Prime was a major Imperial base on the fringes of the Damocles Gulf where the Imperial forces withdrawn from Gravalax were sent for reassignment. Presumably the Munitorium decided it wasn't worth diverting a fully-fitted troopship to deploy just a single regiment, and commandeered a suitable civilian vessel for the job.*

bridge though, so I was prepared to overlook his lack
of social graces. It wasn't until some time later that I
realised that doing so was probably the only way he
would ever meet his passengers, as he showed every
sign of being as much a part of the ship's internal systems as the helm controls or the Navigator (whose
quarters were presumably behind the heavily shielded
bulkhead which loomed ominously over where we
stood.)

Cynical as I was about such things, I had to concede
that Broklaw had a point. From this altitude, as we
slipped into orbit, the world below us shone like an
exotic pearl, rippled with a thousand subtle shades of
grey, blue and white. Thin veils of cloud drifted across it,
obscuring the outlines of mountain ranges and deep
shadowed valleys which could have swallowed a fair
sized city. Despite the poor resolution, I couldn't help
searching for some sign of the impact crater where a
crudely hollowed-out fragment of asteroid had ploughed
into the surface of this pristine world, vomiting its cargo
of orks out to sully it.

'Breathtaking,' Kasteen murmured, oblivious to the
exchange. Her eyes were wide like a child's, the blue of
the iris reflecting the projected snowscape in front of us.
The clear light struck vivid highlights in her red hair,
and like her subordinate she seemed lost in a haze of
nostalgia. I could readily understand why: the Guard
sent its regiments wherever they were needed, and the
Valhallans rarely got the chance to fight in an environment where they felt completely at home. Simia
Orichalcae was probably the closest thing to their
homeworld either officer had seen since they joined up,
and I could sense their impatience to get down there
and feel the permafrost beneath their boot soles. I was
rather less eager, as you can imagine. I've never been
agoraphobic like some hivers, and quite enjoy being
outdoors in a comfortable climate, but where iceworlds

are concerned I've never seen the point of having weather, as we used to say back home.[1]

'We'll get you down as soon as possible,' Durant said, barely able to hide his enthusiasm for getting nearly a thousand Guardsmen and women off his ship. I can't say I altogether blame him; the *Pure of Heart* wasn't exactly a luxury liner, and the opportunities for recreational activities had been few and far between. The crew clearly resented their facilities being swamped by bored and boisterous soldiers, and the training drills we'd devised to keep our people busy in the few cargo holds that weren't stuffed with vehicles, stores, and hastily-installed bunks hadn't been enough to let them blow off steam completely and there had been some friction.

Luckily the few brawls which had broken out had been swiftly dealt with, Kasteen being in no mood for a repeat of our experiences aboard the *Righteous Wrath*,[2] so I'd had relatively little to do beyond telling the freshly-separated combatants that they were a disgrace to the Emperor's uniform and dish out the appropriate penalties. And of course when you have several hundred healthy young men and women cooped up in a confined space for weeks on end many of them will find their own ways of amusing themselves which raised the whole range of other problems I've already alluded to.

---

1. *Despite his frequent references throughout the archive to his being native to a hive world, Cain never specifies which one; and most of the (few) details he gives about his origins are inconsistent. The folk saying he quotes here isn't recorded in any of the anthropological databases, but that doesn't necessarily mean much; it could easily have been common in one small section of his home hive, such as a particular hab level or underhive settlement.*

2. *A serious disturbance broke out on board this troopship shortly after Cain joined the regiment, and several troopers and Naval provosts died. For further details see his account of the Gravalax incident.*

Despite the constant irritation of dealing with a host of minor infractions, I wasn't particularly eager for our voyage to end. I'd fought orks before – many times – and despite their brutishness and stupidity I knew they weren't to be underestimated. With numbers on their side, and the orks always had superior numbers in my experience, they could be formidably difficult to dislodge once they'd gained a foothold anywhere. And by luck or base cunning they had found a prize on Simia Orichalcae worth fighting for.

'Can we see the refinery from here?' Kasteen asked, reluctantly tearing her eyes from the hololith. Broklaw followed her lead, his dark hair flicking against the collar of his greatcoat as he turned. Durant nodded, and apparently obedient to his will a section of the gently-flickering planet in front of us expanded vertiginously as though we were plummeting down towards it in a ballistic re-entry.

Despite knowing that it was only a projection my stomach lurched instinctively for a second before habit and discipline reasserted themselves and I found myself assessing the tactical situation before us. The slightly narrowed eyes of my companions told me that they were doing the same, no doubt bringing their intimate knowledge of the environment below us into play in a fashion that I never could. Within seconds we were presented with an aerial view of the installation we'd been sent to protect.

'That valley looks reasonably defensible,' Broklaw mused aloud, nodding in satisfaction. The sprawling collection of buildings and storage tanks was nestled at one end of a narrow defile, which would be a natural choke point to an enemy advance. Kasteen evidently concurred.

'Place a few dugouts along the ridgeline there and we can hold it until hell thaws out,' she agreed. I was a little less sanguine, but felt it best to appear supportive.

'What about the mountain approaches?' I asked, nodding in apparent agreement. The two officers looked mildly incredulous.

'The terrain's far too broken,' Broklaw said. 'You'd have to be insane to try coming over the peaks.'

'Or very tough and determined,' I pointed out. Orks weren't the most subtle tacticians the forces of the Emperor ever faced, but their straightforward approach to problem solving was often surprisingly effective. Kasteen nodded.

'Good point,' she said. 'We'll set up a few surprises for them just in case.'

'A minefield or two ought to do it,' Broklaw nodded thoughtfully. 'Cover the obvious approaches, and lay one here, on the most difficult route. If they meet that they'll assume we've fortified everywhere.'

They might not care, of course. Orks are like that. Casualties simply don't matter to them. They'll just press on regardless, especially if there are enough of them surviving to boost each other's confidence. But it was a good point, and worth trying.

'How far have they got?' I asked. Durant swept the hololith display round to the west, skimming us across the surface of the barren world with breathtaking speed. The broken landscape of the mountain range swept past, the higher peaks dotted with scrub, lichen, and a few insanely tenacious trees – apparently the only vegetation which could survive here. Just as well too, or there wouldn't be an atmosphere you could breathe. Beyond the foothills was a broad plain, crisp with snow, and for a moment I could understand the affection my colleagues had for this desolate but majestic landscape.

Abruptly the purity of the scene changed, revealing a wide swathe of churned-up, blackened snow, befouled with the detritus and leavings of the savage horde which had surged across it. A couple of kloms[1] wide at least, it resembled a filthy dagger-thrust into the heart of this

---

1. *Kilometres: a Valhallan colloquialism Cain acquired from his long association with the natives of that world.*

strangely peaceful world. The resolution of the hololith wasn't good enough to make out the individual members of this barbaric warband, but we could see clumps of movement within the main mass, like bacteria under a microscope. The analogy was an apt one, I thought. Simia Orichalcae was infected by a disease, and we were the cure.

'Seems like we got here just in time,' Kasteen said, putting all our thoughts into words. I extrapolated the speed of the ork advance, and nodded thoughtfully; we should have the regiment down and deployed roughly a day before they reached the valley where the precious promethium plant lay open and defenceless. It was cutting it fine, but I was just thankful we'd get there ahead of them at all. Fortunately they'd crashed in the opposite hemisphere, and that had given us just enough time to make the journey through the warp to oppose them.

'I'll get everyone moving,' Broklaw offered. 'If we get the first wave embarked now we can launch the shuttles as soon as we make orbit.'

'Please yourselves.' Durant somehow managed to make his immobile shoulders convey the impression of a shrug. 'We'll be at station-keeping in about an hour.'

'Are the datafeeds set up?' I asked, while I still had some measure of his attention. He repeated the gesture. 'Not my department.' He inflated his lungs, or whatever he used instead of them. 'Mazarin! Get up here!'

The top half of a woman almost as encrusted with augmetics as the captain rose on a humming suspensor field to join us on the command dias. The cogwheel icon of a tech-priest hung from a chain around her neck. As we spoke she hovering roughly at my head height, the tunic she wore stirring unnervingly in the faint current from the air recirculators at what would have been level with her knees if she'd had any. 'The one in the fancy hat wants to know if you've wired up his gadgets.'

'The Omnissiah has blessed their activation,' she confirmed, in a mellifluous voice. Her hard stare at the captain told me his irreverence was an old and minor annoyance. 'They are all functioning within acceptable parameters.'

'Good.' Kasteen, to my mild surprise, was looking distinctly uneasy, her eyes flickering away from the tech-priest whenever she thought she could politely do so. 'We'll have full sensor coverage of the planet's surface then.'

'As long as this old blasphemer remembers how to keep his collection of scrap in orbit,' she agreed. Once again the two of them exchanged a look that confirmed my initial suspicion that their bickering was a sign of an easy familiarity rather than any genuine friction. A waving mechadendrite reached forward across Mazarin's shoulder, clutching a data-slate, which she thrust towards the colonel. Kasteen took it with every sign of reluctance, all but shying away from the mechanical limb. 'The appropriate rituals of data retrieval are on this.'

'Thank you.' She handed the slate to Broklaw as though it were contaminated. The major took it without comment, and began scanning the files.

'Waste of a perfectly good starship if you ask me,' Durant grumbled. 'But the money's good.'

'We're most grateful for your co-operation,' I assured him. A troopship would have been equipped to deploy a proper orbital sensor net, which would have been infinitely preferable, but the battered old freighter's navigational array would just have to do. Our deployment was a hurried one, made in response to a frantic astropathic message from the staff of the installation below us, so we had to make do with what we could grab instead of waiting around for the right equipment.

'You've got the easy job,' Broklaw assured him. This much was true: the *Pure of Heart* only had to stay in orbit over the refinery, feeding her sensor data into our tactical net, so we could keep an eye on our enemies from above. Given the size of the horde we'd seen, that was a comfort. It looked even larger and more formidable than my most pessimistic imaginings, outnumbering us by at least three to one. On the other hand we'd be on the defensive, which would be to our advantage. And they'd want to take the place intact, so we wouldn't have to worry too much about incoming artillery fire. The extra intelligence our orbital eye would give us would help immeasurably in deploying our defences to frustrate their attacks.

'You call this easy?' Durant asked rhetorically. A sweep of his arm took in the humming activity of the bridge. 'Having half my systems rewired, trying to hold it all together...' His voice trailed off as Mazarin floated away with a faint *tchah!* of disapproval, and something a little softer entered his body language.

'Your tech-priest seems efficient enough,' I said, trying to sound encouraging. He nodded.

'Oh, she is. Far too good to waste her time on a tub like this really, but you know. Family ties.' He sighed, some old regrets surfacing in spite of himself, and shook his head. 'Would have made a good deck officer if she hadn't got religion. Too much of her mother in her, I suppose.' Startled, I tried to make out traces of a family resemblance, but the main feature they had in common seemed to be an abundance of augmetics rather than anything genetic.

I TOOK THE first shuttle down, of course, as befitted my entirely unwarranted reputation for preferring to lead from the front. I'd be well under cover before the orks arrived and should have my pick of the quarters planetside; I wasn't expecting much in the way of comfort in an industrial facility, but whatever there was I meant to find it. In this I had a valuable ally, my aide Jurgen who had an almost preternatural talent for scrounging, which had made my life (and no doubt his own, although I was careful not to enquire about that) considerably more comfortable than it might otherwise have been in our decade and a half together. He dropped into the seat next to me, preceded as always by his spectacular body odour, and fastened his restraint harness.

'Everything's in order, sir,' he assured me, raising his voice a little so that it carried over the chatter of the troopers surrounding us, meaning that our personal effects had been stowed in the cargo bay to the rear with his usual efficiency. Despite his unprepossessing exterior, and his apparent conviction that personal hygiene was something that only happened to other people, he possessed a number of positive qualities which few people apart from me were ever able to appreciate.

From my point of view, the most important was his complete lack of imagination, which he more than made up for with his dogged deference to authority and an unquestioning acceptance of whatever orders he was given. As you can imagine, having someone like this as a buffer between me and some of the more onerous aspects of my job pretty much amounted to a gift from the Emperor. Add to that the innumerable perils we'd faced and bested together, and I can honestly say that he was the only person I ever fully trusted – apart from myself.

The familiar kick of the shuttle engine igniting cut our conversation short. It went without saying that rather than military dropships, the *Pure of Heart* was equipped with heavy-duty cargo haulers which had been hurriedly converted to meet our needs as far as possible. The end result was better than I could have reasonably expected, but was far from ideal. The front third of the cargo space had been partitioned off with a hastily welded bulkhead, and then subdivided into half a dozen decks with metal mesh flooring. Somehow Mazarin and her acolytes had managed to cram some five score seats with their associated crash webbing into this space so that we were able to disembark a couple of platoons at a time. The rest of the hold had been left open, to take our Chimeras, Sentinels, and other vehicles, along with a small mountain of ammo packs, rations, medicae supplies, and all the other stuff necessary to keep an Imperial Guard regiment running at peak efficiency.

Looking around I could see men and women hugging their kitbags, holding lasrifles across their knees, their faces half hidden by the thick fur caps worn in anticipation of the bone-biting cold on the planet's surface. Most had fastened their uniform greatcoats too. These were mottled with the blues and whites of iceworld camouflage, and I was suddenly acutely aware of what an obvious target my dark uniform and scarlet sash would make me out in that icy waste. No point worrying about it now though, so I gritted my teeth and forced a relaxed smile as the first faint tremors of the hull announced that we'd started to enter the upper atmosphere.

'Pilot's making the most of it,' I said, half joking, and raising a few grins from the troopers around me. 'Must have been watching *Attack Run*[1] in the mess hall.' Jurgen grunted something. He too was swathed in a greatcoat, but, like everything else he ever wore, it contrived to look as though it were intended for someone of a slightly different shape. He suffered from motion sickness on almost every combat drop, but that never seemed to affect his fighting ability once he was back on terra firma. I suspected he was so relieved to be back on solid ground he'd take on the enemy with a sharpened stick rather

---

1. *A popular holodrama of the time, about a squadron of Lightning pilots who shoot down an unfeasible number of enemy fighters during the Gothic War. I quite enjoyed it, although Mott, my savant, claims to have counted four hundred and thirty-seven historical and technical inaccuracies in the first episode alone.*

than have to face the possibility of retreat and being air-borne again.

This time though, he wasn't the only one. The over-loaded shuttle was being buffeted by the thickening atmosphere, bouncing around like a stone on a lake, and pale, sweating faces were everywhere I looked. Even my own stomach revolted on a couple of occasions, threatening to spray the narrow compartment with the remains of my lunch. I swallowed convulsively; I wasn't going to compromise the dignity of my office, not to mention become a laughing stock among the troopers, by throwing up. Not where anyone could see, at any rate.

'What the hell does he think he's playing at?' Lieutenant Sulla, commander of third platoon, and a sight too over-eager for my liking, scowled, which made her look even more like a petulant pony than usual.[1] Nevertheless the distraction from my somersaulting stomach was a welcome one, so I invoked my commissarial privileges and retuned the comm-bead in my ear to the frequency of the cockpit communicator to find out.

'Say again, shuttle one.' The voice was calm and methodical, undoubtedly the ground controller at the refinery landing field. The answering voice was anything but: a civilian suddenly in the middle of a war zone without a clue as to how to survive, and clearly not expecting to. Our pilot, without a doubt.

---

1. *This is the celebrated General Jenit Sulla, at a very early stage in her career. Despite the illustrious reputation she was later to achieve, Cain tends to regard her with, at best, mild antipathy throughout the archive; we can only speculate as to why. My own feeling is that he considered her tendency to decisive action unnecessarily reckless, since it put the lives of the troopers under her command (and by extension Cain's) at risk. Ironically it's clear from her own (almost unreadable) memoirs that she regarded Cain very highly, and as something of a mentor.*

'We're taking ground fire!' The edge of hysteria in his voice was unmistakable. Any moment now he was going to panic, and if he did we were all likely to die. I doubted that our overloaded engines had any tolerance left for evasive manoeuvres, and if he tried, the chances were that he'd lose control completely. As if to emphasise the point we hit another air pocket, and dropped vertiginously for a handful of metres.

There was nothing else for it: I unbuckled my seat restraints and lurched to my feet, conscious of Sulla's eyes on me. I grabbed the nearest stanchion for support. It was embossed with an Imperial aquila, which I found reassuring, and with its support I was able to take a couple of halting steps towards the cockpit.

'Is that wise, commissar?' she asked, a faint puzzled frown appearing on her face.

'No,' I snapped, not having time to waste on courtesy. 'But it's necessary.' Before I could say any more another lurch slammed my body weight into the narrow door to the flight deck, propelling it open, and I staggered inside. My overriding impression was one of flashing lights and control lecterns, uncannily like miniature versions of the ones on the starship bridge, and the bleak white snowscape passing below us at an alarming speed. The pilot stared up at me, his knuckles white on the control yoke, while his navigational servitor continued regulating the routine functions of the ship with single-minded fixity of purpose. 'What's the problem?' I asked, trying to project an air of calm.

'We're under attack!' the man shouted, raw panic edging into his voice. 'We have to pull back to orbit!'

'That wouldn't be wise,' I said, keeping my voice level, and grabbing the servitor's shoulder to steady myself as the shuttle lurched again. It just kept on adjusting controls with a complete lack of concern. Beyond the thick vision port the bleak and frozen landscape hurtled past as serenely as before. I could see no sign of enemy activity anywhere. 'We'd take hours to rendezvous with the ship if we abort on this trajectory, and we only have limited life support. You'd probably suffocate along with everyone else.'

'We have a safety margin,' the pilot urged. I shook my head.

'The rest of us do. You don't.' I let my right hand brush the butt of my laspistol, and he turned even paler. 'And I don't see any immediate danger, do you?'

'What do you call that?' He pointed off to starboard, where a single puff of smoke burst briefly. A moment later a small constellation of bright flashes sparkled for an instant some distance below and to the left. Bolter shells detonating against the ground, after some trigger-happy greenskin took a hopeless potshot in our direction.

'Nothing to worry about,' I said, almost amused. 'That's small arms fire.' The analytical part of my mind noted that the main bulk of the ork advance was still some distance away, which meant we ought to be on alert for a small scout force attempting to infiltrate the refinery (which was now looming reassuringly in the viewport), or reconnoitre our lines. 'The chances of anything actually hitting us at this range are astronomical.'

One day I'm going to learn to stop saying things like that. No sooner had the words left my mouth than the shuttle shuddered even more violently than before, and pitched sharply to port. Red icons began to appear on the data-slates, and the servitor began punching controls with greater speed and abhuman dexterity.

'Pressure loss in number two engine,' it chanted. 'Combustion efficiency dropping by sixteen per cent.'

'Astronomical, eh?' Strangely the pilot seemed calmer now his fears had been realised. 'Better strap in, commissar. It's going to be a rough landing.'

'Can you make it to the pad?' I asked. He looked tense, his lips tight.

'I'm going to try. Now get the hell off my flight deck and let me do my job.'

'I've no doubt you will,' I said, boosting his confidence as best I could, and staggered back to my seat.

'What's going on?' Sulla asked as I buckled in and tensed for the impact.

'The greenskins put a dent in us. There's going to be a bump,' I said. I felt strangely calm; there was nothing I could do now except trust in the Emperor and hope the pilot was as competent as he sounded. I considered saying something to reassure the troopers, but I'd never be heard over the noise of the crash alarms anyway, so I decided to save my breath.

The waiting seemed to take forever, but could only have lasted a minute or two. I listened to the chatter in my comm-bead while the pilot read off a number of datum points which meant nothing to me but sounded pretty ominous, fighting down the growing conviction that we weren't going to make it as far as the pad. In fact, the traffic controller seemed pretty insistent that we avoid the installation altogether, which I could well understand, as dropping an unguided shuttle into the middle of the promethium tanks would end our mission pretty effectively before it had even begun. The pilot responded with a couple of terse phrases which managed to impress me even after fifteen years of exposure to the most imaginative profanity of the barrack room, and I began to think we were in safe hands after all, and might just make it.

This impression lasted all of a dozen seconds. Then a violent impact jarred my spine up into the roof of my skull, driving the breath from my lungs. A sound uncannily reminiscent of an ammunition dump exploding echoed through the hull. I gasped some air back into my aching lungs, and tried to clear my blurring vision as the screech of tortured metal set my rattling teeth on edge. I became gradually aware, through the ringing in my ears, that Jurgen was trying to say something.

'Well, that wasn't so...' he began, before the whole ghastly cycle repeated itself another couple of times.

At last the noise and vibration ceased, and I gradually became aware of the fact that we'd stopped moving and I was still alive. I struggled free of the seat restraints, and wobbled to my feet.

'Everybody out!' I bawled. 'By squads. Carry the wounded with you!' In the back of my mind a lurid picture of overheated engines exploding into flame tried to ignite a little beacon of panic, but I fought it down. I turned to Sulla, who was trying to stem a nosebleed. For that matter I suppose we all looked a bit the worse for wear, except possibly Jurgen, as with him it was hard to tell. 'I want casualty figures ASAP.'

'Yes, sir.' She turned to the nearest NCO, Sergeant Lustig, a solid and competent soldier I had a lot of time for, and started snapping out orders in her usual brisk fashion.

The door to the cockpit burst open, and the pilot staggered out, looking as bad as I felt.

'Told you we'd make it,' he said, and threw up on my boots.

TWO

THE FREEZING AIR outside was worse than even my most pessimistic anticipation, and I'd been on enough ice-worlds before to have had a pretty good idea of what to expect. In truth, I suppose, it was no colder than Valhalla or Nusquam Fundumentibus, but it had been some time since I'd trodden the snows of either, and my memory had obviously skipped over the worst of those experiences. The bone-numbing wind seemed to flay me alive the moment I set foot on the ramp, despite the extra layers of insulation I'd put on before leaving my quarters aboard the *Pure of Heart*.

As I staggered down the metal incline, already treacherously slippery from the thin coating of snow which had settled on it, needles of ice seemed to penetrate my temples, replacing the residual headache from the crash with one a thousand times worse. I buried my face in the muffler at my throat, being careful to breathe through it in case my lungs froze, but even so the air rasped in my chest like acid fumes.

A broad plain of ice spread out before me, hazed with wind-driven snowflakes which reduced visibility to a few tens of metres, although the flurries cleared occasionally to reveal the low, grey ramparts of the encircling mountains. They stood out clearly against the lighter grey of the sky, and a moment later I realised that what I'd at first taken for some unusually regular outcrops were the towers and storage tanks of the refinery, still too distant to make out any detail.

'Seventeen injured, fourteen of them walking.' Sulla bounced up to me, the trickle of blood from her nose now frozen to her face, and saluted eagerly. 'Eight of those are ours.' The others would be from first platoon then. I nodded, not trusting myself to talk yet. It would have been a wasted effort anyway, as behind us an engine roared into life and the first of our Chimeras rumbled down the exit ramp, filling the air with the noise of its passage and the rank smell of burned promethium. Thank the Emperor for that, I thought, at least I wouldn't have to slog all the way to the refinery on foot. Sulla noticed the direction of my gaze. 'Lieutenant Voss is assessing the condition of the vehicles now.'

Her opposite number glanced up from a huddle of troopers near the ramp, a data-slate in his hand, and waved a cheery acknowledgement. That came as little surprise, as Voss tended to be cheerful about everything. He was clearly in his element now, grinning widely as the churning tracks bit into the snow, and, dear Emperor, his greatcoat was still unfastened. I immediately felt another ten degrees colder just looking at him.

'We got off lightly,' he told us, his voice crackling over the comm-beads. 'Minor damage only. Nothing we can't get fixed.'

'Should be easy enough,' Sulla agreed. 'A place like this must be crawling with tech-priests.'

'Maybe they can do something with this heap of junk too,' I said sourly, kicking a lump of snow at our downed transportation and deciding to risk talking despite the rush of razor blade air to my lungs. If they couldn't, the loss of one of our shuttles would be a major blow, severely delaying the deployment of our forces, perhaps to the point where we wouldn't be fully prepared by the time the orks arrived.

'We're in the right place at least.' Jurgen had materialised at my elbow. I was mildly disconcerted not to have noticed his approach, feeling that something was inexplicably wrong, before I realised the cold had effectively neutralised his body odour. Either that, or my nose had frozen off.

He was right about that at any rate. The pilot, who I was beginning to forgive for having soiled my footwear, had been as good as his word, bringing us down on the main landing pad after all. Not being entirely reckless he'd aimed for the outer edge though, leaving us with a kilometre or so of packed snow and ice to trudge across before reaching the shelter of the storage tanks I'd noticed before. The faint scar of melted and refrozen ice that marked where we had bounced and skidded our way to a stop was already beginning to disappear under the drifting snow.

'It looks more like a starport than a landing pad,' Sulla observed. I nodded, quite impressed by the scale of things myself, but determined not to show it.

'The shuttles from the tankers are over five hundred metres long,' I said, dredging up a half-digested fact from the largely ignored briefing slate.[1] 'And they land up to

---

1. *A quirk of behaviour Cain repeatedly alludes to in the archive. His habit of neglecting to read the background information provided to senior officers prior to deployment on a new planet is rather odd, given his caution in most other respects. (Although given the density and dryness of most munitorium documentation, it's probable that he'd developed the ability to extricate anything relevant with a quick skim of the contents, and felt little would be served by wading through it page by page.)*

twelve at a time.' Sulla looked suitably impressed. Certainly the thought of a swarm of shuttles almost half the size of the starship we'd arrived in filling the air above where we stood was an awe-inspiring one – or it would have been if I hadn't been freezing my gonads off at the time.

Any further thoughts I might have had on the subject were quickly driven from my head at that point, however, by the rather more urgent matter of a bolter shell exploding against the ceramite hull less than a metre from where we were standing.

'Orks!' Sulla shouted, rather unnecessarily under the circumstances I thought. I whirled around to look in the direction she was pointing. At least she had the common sense to do it with her lasgun, though, and opened fire on a small knot of greenskins that was closing fast, slogging through the snow with implacable ferocity.

'Are they mad?' Voss's voice crackled in my ear. 'We must have them outnumbered about ten to one!'

That did strike me as pretty stupid behaviour, even for orks, and I was just casting about desperately for the main force which must surely be flanking us when the explanation suddenly hit me. I was the only human they could see; the Valhallans' camouflage uniforms were blending them into the snowscape, as they were supposed to, and with my commissar's black and scarlet making me stand out like an ogryn in a beauty pageant, they hadn't bothered looking for anyone else. I breathed silent thanks to the Emperor for the flakes of drifting snow which obscured the others from their sight.

'Cease fire!' I snapped, seeing the opportunity for the perfect ambush. A quick glance around me made out at least three squads fully disembarked. They were lying flat in the snow which they'd scraped out into small hollows. A tactic, I vaguely recalled, which had worked well for their forefathers when an ork horde had had the temerity to attack their homeworld. 'Let's draw them in.'

Far better to cut them down at short range than engage at a distance, where we would run the risk of a survivor or two escaping to report our arrival back to the warboss.

'Good plan,' Sulla said, as though it were up for debate, and I suddenly realised that it left me the only one in immediate danger. Ork marksmanship wasn't much to worry about most of the time but even greenskins got lucky occasionally, as the downing of our shuttle had proved, so I dropped suddenly with a dramatically out flung arm and a theatrical scream. It was a performance which wouldn't have fooled a five-year-old, but I heard a whoop of triumph from the leading ork, who was carrying what looked like a crudely-fashioned bolter. The others began remonstrating in harsh gutturals, and I was able to hear enough to gather that they were arguing about who should get the credit for killing me.[1] But then if I had a coin for every time that's happened...

'Hold your fire,' I broadcast over the comm-net. Hardly necessary of course, these troopers knew what to do, but I didn't want any mistakes. The orks came on regardless, running apparently tirelessly despite the treacherous footing and the biting wind which would have sapped the strength from an unprotected man in seconds. I began mentally counting off the distance. Two hundred metres, one hundred and fifty...

The closer they got, the more detail I could make out, and the less I wished I could see. There were ten of them in all, about half carrying the bolters I'd noticed before. The others held heavy close combat blades and pistols which looked as deceptively ramshackle as the bolters. I'd seen enough examples in previous encounters not to be fooled, though. Crude as they appeared,

---

1. *Cain wasn't exactly fluent in orkish, but had managed to pick up a few phrases in the course of his adventures. Mostly insults and obscenities, of course, but it could be argued that they make up the whole language.*

the firearms were perfectly functional, and quite lethal if they should happen to hit anything. The same went for the axes, which, with the power of an ork's muscles behind them, were capable of shearing through even Astartes armour.

On they came, snarling and bickering, crude icons decorating their sleeveless vests, which alone spoke volumes for their inhuman robustness in this killing climate. Oddly, I noticed, they were all dressed alike, in dark grey, which blended better into the winter landscape than the more vivid hues I generally associated with greenskins. Then I realised the last ork in the group wasn't armed like the others. A huge calibre barrel was slung across his shoulder, the bulk of the weapon hidden behind his body. What it was I had no idea, but I was pretty sure I wouldn't like the answer.

The mystery was solved a few seconds later as they caught sight of the idling Chimera, which had been hidden from them by the bulk of the downed shuttle. Evidently intent on looting it, and arrogantly sure they could slaughter any surviving defenders, the sudden appearance of a military vehicle threw them into momentary disarray. After a quick exchange of snarls, during which the leader, who I was able to identify with a fair degree of certainty thanks to his habit of emphasising instructions with blows to the head (not unlike one of the less popular tutors during my time at the schola progenium) pointed to the Chimera. The ork with the bulky weapon swung it round to reveal a crude rocket launcher. This at least explained how they'd managed to damage the shuttle, albeit with an incredibly lucky shot. Before I could vox a warning the ork fired, a streak of smoke marking the vector of the warhead, which detonated a few metres to the left of the Chimera.

No point expecting the crew to delay their retaliation, I realised, as the next shot might get them. And sure enough the heavy bolter in the turret swung round to bracket the orks. Puffs of snow and ice were thrown up around them as the explosive projectiles detonated thunderously, tearing a couple of them apart. One of them, to my intense relief, was the rocketeer.

It was then that we saw what makes these creatures so dangerous on the battlefield. Where other, more sensible foes would have taken cover or retreated to regroup, these savages felt no urge stronger than to close quickly and neutralise the threat. With a bone-shaking cry of '*Waaaaarghhhh!*' they ran forward as one, charging headlong into a hail of withering fire.

Well, there was no point hesitating after that, particularly as one foul-smelling foot missed my head by centimetres as it passed, so I rolled to my feet and issued a general order to fire at will.

I don't suppose they even knew what hit them: suddenly struck by the concentrated fire of a couple of score lasguns, not to mention the unrelenting hail of heavy bolter fire, there was nothing much left of them apart from some unpleasant stains on the snow within seconds. Sulla ambled over to inspect the mess, and spat a small gobbet of ice into it.

'So those were orks,' she said. 'They don't look so tough.' I bit down on the sharp rejoinder that rose to my lips, suppressing it. She might as well feel confident for as long as possible. I knew from bitter experience that when the main force got here the next day it would be a different story.

'FIRST BLOOD to you, then, commissar.' Kasteen grinned at me, her red curls falling free as she took off her heavy fur cap, and glanced around the conference room in the heart of the refinery. The smile faltered a bit as her eyes flickered past the little group of tech-priests at one end of the heavy wooden table, but re-established itself as she took in the other people present: a mixed bunch of Administratum functionaries seated in strict order of precedence, and a group of men and women whose hard hands and lined faces indicated that they did most of the actual work around here.

'Luck rather than judgement, I can assure you,' I said. Kasteen had come down on the second shuttle, about twenty minutes after our advance party had made it to the shelter of the refinery hab units, and I was still feeling like a freezy stick.[1] I tightened my fingers around the mug of recaf Jurgen had found for me, feeling the warmth spread through the real ones (the augmetics felt the same as they always did, of course.) I could have done without the transparent wall at the end of the conference suite, beyond which the snow was falling steadily – a visual reminder of the chill which still had me in its grip. Nevertheless the view of the processing plant with its huge structures and belching flames was undeniably spectacular. The sheer size of it struck me for the first time, and I began to understand why it took hundreds of people to extract the raw materials from the ice beneath our feet and process it into the precious fuel.

'You call that luck?' Mazarin hummed into the room behind us, making Kasteen start. 'Bending a perfectly good shuttle?'

Perhaps there was a family resemblance to her father after all, I thought. She'd come down on the same drop as Kasteen to assess the damage, and had just returned from the landing field, thick flakes of snow beginning to melt across her head and shoulders. 'Nothing I can't fix though, praise the Omnissiah.' That was a relief, at least our deployment wouldn't be as delayed as I'd feared. She levitated across to the little

---

1. *A popular snack on many worlds with a temperate or tropical climate, particularly among juves; fruit juices are frozen solid, with a stick embedded in it to facilitate eating. It sounds bizarre, I know, but is really very refreshing.*

group of tech-priests we'd noticed before, and began to converse with them in a weird twittering language that set my teeth on edge.

'She's asking for the use of their facilities to repair the shuttle,' one of the Administratum adepts said, evidently noticing our confusion. He was a youngish man, with thinning blond hair and the pasty complexion of someone who spends too much time with a data-slate.

'You understand that gibberish?' I asked, impressed in spite of myself. He grinned.

'Dear Emperor, no. If I did they'd have to kill me.' He smiled as he said it, although for all I knew he wasn't joking.[1] 'She's just filed a request with the main depository for the spare parts.' He stuck out a hand, and Kasteen shook it formally. 'I'm Scrivener Quintus, by the way. If you need anything, come to me. If I can't get my hands on it, I'll know who can.'

'Thank you.' Kasteen smiled warmly. 'Colonel Kasteen, Valhallan 597th. This is our regimental commissar, Ciaphas Cain.'

'An honour.' His handshake was firm and direct. 'I've seen your statue in Liberation Square on Talethorn. I must say it doesn't really do you justice.'

'That'll be the pigeon droppings,' I said dryly. 'Tends to erode my natural dignity.' He laughed, with every sign of good humour, and I decided I liked him.

'Let me introduce you to a few people,' he said. He waved at the group of tech-priests, singling out a man of about his own age who was talking to Mazarin with every sign of rapt attention. 'That's Cogitator Logash. My opposite number, so to speak.' His voice dropped slightly. 'You'll get more done if you go to him first

---

1. *Almost certainly not. 'Binary,' as the tech-priests refer to their secret language, is one of their most sacred mysteries. Cracking it has long been a priority of the Inquisition, but so far even the most rudimentary syntax has yet to be established.*

instead of wasting your time with anyone higher up in the Mechanicus, if you get my drift.'

'Not unlike you and the Administratum,' I suggested, and he smiled.

'I didn't say that,' he pointed out. 'But Logash and I aren't quite so rigid in our thinking as some of the higher ranks in our respective orders.'

'You can say that again.' The man I took to be the leader of the workers joined our conversation. 'How many more of us are going to have to die down there before they sit up and take notice?' He had the hard eyes of a man used to physical toil, and his hair was grey; nonetheless he burned with a passion which seemed at odds with the coldness that permeated everything else around here.

'Technically, no one has died,' Quintus said.

The man snorted.

'Disappeared, then. Five people in as many weeks.' Quintus shrugged.

'I've done my best to get them to investigate, you know that.' The man nodded reluctantly. 'But they just argue that accidents happen. Icefalls, gas pockets...'

'I've been working here for over twenty years,' the man said. 'I know all about icefalls, and a dozen other hazards you quill-pushers haven't even heard of. And they all leave bodies.'

'But officially, without a body there's nothing to investigate.'

'That's insane,' Kasteen said. The man smiled for the first time.

'That's what I keep telling them. But the lad here's the only one with a functioning brain, apparently.' He stuck out a hand. 'I'm Artur Morel, by the way. Guild of miners.' His grip was firm.

I have to admit, all this talk of death and mysterious disappearances had me spooked. If we were going to fight a battle I didn't want to be looking over my shoulder the whole time, and I resolved to have a longer talk with him at the earliest opportunity. We'd already encountered one ork scouting party after all, and if there was another one already lurking in the mine we'd have to clear them out as a matter of priority.

But first things first: we had a war to plan. Mazarin left the room with Logash trotting along behind her, evidently detailed to sort out her requirements, and the highest ranking Administratum adept, a white-haired woman called Pryke, called the meeting to order with every sign of enthusiasm.

Needless to say, it turned out to be interminable. The facility seemed to be equally dependent on the three factions present to keep functioning, or at least that's what Pryke fondly imagined, although I'd have laid a small wager that putting the Administratum drones out in the snow to keep the orks amused while we prepared our defences would have had a negligible effect on the promethium output. Every point she raised was politely challenged by Magos Ernulph, the senior tech-priest, who would remind everyone that without his people to perform the appropriate rituals the plant would simply grind to a halt. Of course without Morel's miners to provide the raw materials it would do so anyway, but the guildsman was tactful enough not to drag things out even further by pointing this out, for which I was extremely grateful, especially since my stomach had started to realise how empty it was.

Fortunately Kasteen had a much lower level of tolerance for idiots than I did, so it was with some relief that I saw her stand to interrupt the ageing bureaucrat in mid flow.

'Thank you all for your input,' she said crisply. 'It's clear that you all have particular insights to offer, which we will be calling upon as and when we see the need.'

'I think my colleagues will require a little more than that,' Pryke rejoined. 'May I suggest you provide us with daily progress reports?' Ernulph nodded in agreement, his blank metal eyes turning on the colonel. She ignored him, with an effort only I knew well enough to discern.

'You may not. We're here to fight a war, not push files around.' There was an edge to Kasteen's voice now which every officer in the regiment had learned to be wary of. Pryke bristled.

'That's just not good enough. There are procedures to be followed...'

'Then let me relieve you of them,' Kasteen snapped. 'This facility is now under martial law.' The result was hugely enjoyable, I have to admit. Pryke went scarlet, then white, then scarlet again. Ernulph probably would have done too, if he'd had enough organic bits left to manage it. Both stood at once, shouting excitably.

'You can't do that!' Ernulph boomed, his voice apparently magnified by some implanted amplivox unit. It was a cheap trick, and one which remained resolutely un-terrifying to anyone who'd been shouted at by a daemon as I had.

'Yes she can,' I confirmed quietly, my voice carrying all the more effectively for not being raised like all the others. 'A field commander has the right to declare martial law at any time with the approval of the highest ranking member of the Commissariat present. Which is me. And I do.' I stood, and gestured to the plant outside, and the barren snowscape beyond. 'By this time tomorrow all you'll see out there is orks. We're your only hope of not ending up dead or worse. So shut up, keep out of our way, and let us do our job.' Morel and Quintus, I noticed, were openly enjoying their colleagues' discomfiture.

'This is unacceptable,' Pryke said, her voice tight with outrage.

'Live with it,' Kasteen said. 'Unless you prefer the alternative.'

'I most certainly do.' Pryke glared at both of us.

'Fine.' I drew my laspistol, and dropped it on the table from just the right height to produce a nicely resonant thud. 'Under the powers bestowed upon me by the commissariat in the name of His Divine Majesty, I serve notice that any civilian obstructing His forces in the defence of His realm will be subject to summary execution under article seventeen of the rules of military justice.' I raised an interrogative eyebrow at Pryke and the tech-priest. 'You were saying?'

'I withdraw my objections,' she said tightly. Ernulph nodded too.

'On reflection, the colonel's assumption of authority seems entirely the best course of action,' he conceded.

'Good,' I said, leaving the gun where it was – no harm in concentrating their minds a little further. 'Colonel. You have the floor.'

Editorial Note:

There can be very few readers who will be unaware of the enormous importance of the promethium production facility which Cain describes, both strategically and economically. Since its retention or seizure was so vital an objective for the contending armies, I felt a little extra information on this amazing substance wouldn't come amiss. Unfortunately I haven't been able to lay my hands on very much, as such things remain the jealously-guarded province of the Adeptus Mechanicus, so this is the best I could do.

From *Our Friend Promethium*, Imperial Educational Press, 238th edition, 897 M41.

FROM THE EMPEROR-BLESSED fighting machines of the Astartes to the most humble spaceport cargo-hauler, it can truly be said that the Imperium runs on promethium. This might seem amazing enough on its own, but this miraculous substance gives us so much more than just the power to feed the animating spirits of our vehicles. The alchemical by-products of its production provide the raw materials to create a vast array of everyday necessities, from dyes, plastics and pharmacopoeia to the synthetic protein bars which make up the bulk of the proletarian diet on some of the drearier forge worlds.

But it's the combustibility of promethium which allows its most holy use. From the flamers which scourge the unholy with the purifying fire of the righteous to the alchemical constituents of the explosives which blast them into oblivion, it's this most blessed of substances which keeps us safe and preserves our homes from the depredations of the alien, the mutant, and the heretic.

Promethium itself can be produced in a variety of ways, and from an astonishing number of sources. Among the most common are the atmospheres of gas giant planets, subterranean deposits of ancient organic materials, and certain kinds of rare ices found only on the coldest of worlds...

[Of course it's the illustrations which are the real charm of this little book, particularly those of its narrator, Pyrus the flame. Even now I can't help smiling at the expressions on the faces of the heretics he's burning on page twenty-eight, just as I did as a child all those years ago.]

THREE

'SIEUR MOREL. I'D like a quick word with you if you can spare the time.' I judged my movement precisely, so that to the casual observer it would look as though we'd reached the door of the conference room together purely by chance. The grizzled miner turned in my direction, assessed the situation with keen intelligence, and nodded, dismissing his staff with a casual wave. They filed out along with the tech-priests and the quill-pushers, Ernulph and Pryke, still simmering nicely leaving us alone with Kasteen and Broklaw.

The major had joined the conference shortly after Kasteen dropped her little bombshell, taking over the tactical debriefing of the refinery staff. Now the two of them were huddled over data-slates refining their strategy for the defence of the plant. Ernulph, Pryke, and their respective hangers-on had turned out to be quite helpful after the sight of my sidearm had cleared the air, no doubt reflecting that the orks might very well get

43

them if they didn't do all they could to help, and if the greenies didn't I most certainly would.

A handful of troopers were bustling in and out of the conference suite, setting up map boards and a large urn of tanna leaf tea. It looked as though this was going to be our command post, at least for the time being. (Kasteen claimed it was an excellent vantage point from which to direct the troops, but I suspected she just liked the view from the window.) I found the gradual transformation from civilian decadence to the purposeful military atmosphere quietly reassuring; how the miner viewed it I had no idea, or interest, come to that.

'Of course. How can I help?' Morel asked. I poured myself a bowl of tanna tea, and offered him one. After a moment he took it, sipped cautiously, and appeared to approve, although the Valhallan brew isn't to everyone's taste.

'Earlier you mentioned some of your miners had disappeared in mysterious circumstances. Would you care to elaborate?' An expression of mild surprise crossed his grizzled features. I suppose after being stonewalled by the other factions here for so long our interest was unexpected.

'Five people, in just over a month. It might not sound much out of a workforce of six hundred, but believe me it matters to us.' He shrugged. 'Of course the Administratum and the Mechanicus don't give a damn. Just trot out the same old line about the losses being within acceptable statistical parameters.'

'What's your opinion?' I asked. Morel sipped his tea, formulating a response, and I forestalled him. 'I want your gut reaction. Don't feel you have to be polite.' He laughed, and looked at me with renewed respect.

'Just as well. Diplomacy isn't exactly my strong point.' He sipped again. 'Something's definitely wrong down there. Don't ask me what, though.'

'Then we need to find out,' I said. Kasteen broke off from her conversation with Broklaw long enough to nod.

'Quite,' she said. Broklaw nodded too.

'Absolutely. No point in fortifying the place if the trouble's already inside with us.'

'You think we've got orks in the tunnels?' Morel paled at the thought. Whatever he'd thought the problem might be, this clearly wasn't it. I shook my head doubtfully.

'It's possible. Although sneaking around picking people off one at a time isn't exactly their style.'

'And I don't see how they could have got here that soon,' Kasteen added, with a glance at the hemisphere map pinned to the wall close to her seat. 'It's taken them over six weeks to get here from the crash site. If an advance party was taking your miners they'd have had to have got halfway round the planet within a few days of their arrival, and we've seen no sign of any rapid deployment capability.'

'Unless they teleported,' I suggested. 'It has been known.'[1]

'We're not jumping to conclusions are we?' Broklaw mused. 'Could it just be an unfortunate series of accidents after all?'

'That hardly seems likely.' Morel stared at the plan on the opposite wall. The straggling and meandering lines looked like nothing so much as a detailed diagram of a plate full of noodles. A map of the tunnels beneath us, I realised, where the precious veins of ice which could be transmuted into promethium had been hauled out for countless generations.[2]

---

1. *Ork units were deployed by teleporter on several occasions during the Armageddon campaign, for instance.*

2. *Only about half a dozen, in actual fact. The processing plant on Simia Orichalcae was relatively new.*

'Can you show us where the missing miners vanished from?' I asked. That might give us some kind of clue. Morel nodded, picking up a stylus from the desk, and marked the points in rapidly; I realised he must have done this before, no doubt hoping to find some connection himself. I stared at the rumpled sheet of paper, translating the lines in my mind into a three dimensional image, and trying to get a feel for the space.[1] If there was a pattern to be discerned, however, it eluded me.

'Have you spotted something?' Kasteen asked hopefully, aware of my tunnel rat's instincts from my reports on the Gravalax incident. I shook my head.

'There's no obvious connection between these points,' I said. I tapped one with a fingernail. 'This gallery's a dead end, for instance. An assailant would have to get past an entire shift of workers unobserved.'

'And that's just not possible,' Morel confirmed. Which begged another question that Broklaw was obliging enough to ask.

'Unless one of the refinery staff is responsible...' he began, but trailed off as Morel's face darkened.

'If you're planning to accuse any of my people of murder, you'd better have some damn good evidence.'

'No one's accusing anyone of anything,' I soothed, biting back the unspoken *yet*. 'You've brought a potentially serious security breach to our attention, and we're trying to get to the bottom of it, that's all.'

'If it saves any more of my people I'm glad to help,' the miner said, somewhat mollified.

'I'm glad to hear it.' I gazed at the map of the mine workings again, as though deep in thought. 'But I don't think we'll solve the problem talking about it over a bowl of tea.'

---

1. *As I've noted elsewhere, Cain had an uncanny affinity for the layout of underground passageways, probably as a result of his early upbringing on a hive world.*

'Then what do you suggest?' Kasteen asked. I sighed with every appearance of reluctance and shook my head.

'I'll just have to go down there and take a look around,' I said.

Now if you've been reading my memoirs with any degree of attention it's probably struck you that this apparent willingness to put myself in harm's way is somewhat uncharacteristic, to say the least. But try to see things from my point of view. For one thing, if I hung around here while the defences were being prepared there was a pretty good chance I'd end up in that bone-chilling cold again, and I was most reluctant to do so. Not to mention the fact that there was a horde of green-skins on the way. True, they weren't expected to arrive in force for another twenty-four hours or so, but that hadn't held back the advance party we'd encountered already, and who knew how many more of them might be lurking out there waiting for an unwary target to show itself?

Tunnels, on the other hand, were an environment I felt right at home in, and I could match my fighting skills in a dark confined space with anything we might find down there. And it wasn't as if I was going in alone either; anything used to taking on solitary unarmed civilians was in for a big surprise if it tried jumping a squad of troopers with lasguns. So all in all I was pretty confident that whatever might be lurking in the dark lower levels, it wouldn't pose nearly as much of a threat to my continued well-being as hanging around outside like a chunk of deep-frozen ork bait. (In this assumption I was, as it turned out, both quite correct and catastrophically wrong. Of course I had no reason to suspect at that point what our investigation would ultimately lead to.)

I'VE SEEN SOME sights in my time, and it takes a lot to impress me, but I have to admit that even today, after more than a century, the ice caves of Simia Orichalcae stand out in my memory as a sight to behold. I don't know what the troopers made of them, but to a born and bred tunnel rat like me they were quite spectacular. Though broad mining galleries ran off into the distance beyond the reach of our luminators, it was never quite dark, as the ice surrounding us reflected the light back so that it rippled away in a faint blue sheen as far as the eye could see.

And the walls glittered, every single irregularity in the surface reflecting and refracting the beams, so we moved through an ever-scintillating constellation of ephemeral stars. Our boots crunched gently on frost-packed floor, and our breath puffed visibly with every exhalation, but down here, away from the flensing wind, I found the temperatures tolerable enough. They were certainly no worse than those in the average Valhallan billet when they could get the air conditioning to work, and I was used to that. It was even warm enough for Jurgen's characteristic odour to have returned, albeit in a slightly muted fashion, for which we were all grateful. I'd requested Lustig's squad for backup, as after our adventures on Gravalax I was confident in their abilities, and I found the familiar faces and the sergeant's taciturn presence a welcome boost to my spirits. I'd declined the offer of a guide from among the miners as I was confident in my own tunnel sense, and if there really were orks down here the last thing I wanted was some hysterical civilian getting in the way in the middle of a fire fight.

The early stages of our descent had been through the bustle of the upper workings, where miners and servitors hurried through broad, well-lit thoroughfares reminiscent of the streets of a Valhallan cavern city, and mobile ore bins full of shimmering ice shoved everything else unceremoniously out of the way. But as we penetrated further into the complex, into the lesser-used passages, they grew narrower and less well lit, until the only illumination was what we carried with us. From time to time we heard sounds of activity from the main galleries, where Morel's colleagues were still hacking the precious ice away with the aid of tools which looked alarmingly like the meltas we used as weapons, but after an hour or so of steady descent even this had faded away.

'What are we looking for, exactly, sir?' Sergeant Lustig asked. I shrugged.

'Emperor knows,' I said. 'Just something unusual.' His squad was spread out in a standard search pattern, with everyone in visual range of at least two other troopers. I wasn't going to have any more mysterious disappearances if I could help it, particularly if one of them was likely to be me. The sergeant's broad face creased in a grin.

'Well that narrows it down,' he said, glancing round at our surroundings. Coming from an iceworld as he did, I suppose he found them bordering on the mundane. In a way, that's what I was counting on; between the Valhallans' feeling for ice and my hive boy's affinity for enclosed spaces, whatever was down here was bound to have left some traces which would strike one or another of us as odd.

'Penlan here.' The voice of one of the troopers hissed in my comm-bead, followed a moment later by the attenuated sound of her actual speech overlapping the transmission like a distorted echo. She could only be a hundred metres or so away. 'I've got something. Looks like tracks.'

'Hold your position,' I ordered, and worked my way towards her silhouette. She was backlit by the luminator she'd taped to the barrel of her lasgun. Jurgen trotted at my heels, his own weapon levelled and ready for use. Experience had taught both of us you could never be too cautious in circumstances like this.

'What do you make of it, sir?' Penlan asked, turning towards us. As she did so, she brought the patch of discoloured skin on her left cheek where she'd taken a glancing las hit on Gravalax into the beam of Jurgen's luminator. Her expression was as puzzled as her voice, brown hair falling into her grey eyes from around the rim of her hat.

'Damned if I know,' I said, not relishing the doubt. She shone her light directly on the marks she'd found, deep gouges in the frozen floor, which indeed looked uncomfortably like claw marks. After more than a decade and a half in Imperial service, during which time I thought I'd encountered pretty much every malevolent life form in the galaxy, I should have been able to recognise them. The fact that I couldn't was deeply disconcerting. Even the mark of ork boots, which I'd been half expecting, would have been preferable.

'They look a bit like genestealer tracks,' Jurgen said uncertainly. He was partially right: they'd been gouged out by what looked like powerful talons, but the spacing was all wrong to be the work of a 'stealer. 'Or 'nids, maybe?'

'I don't think so,' I said. 'The weight distribution's all wrong.' Which given the hive fleets' ability to conjure new and unpleasant creatures out of thin air wasn't exactly a certainty, but if there was a bio-ship or two in the sector the chances of them getting this far into Imperial space undetected were negligible. I pointed that out too, and pretended I hadn't seen the momentary flicker of visible relief on Penlan's face. The two original regiments which now made up the 597th had fought the tyranids shortly before I joined them, and both had been all but annihilated. Come to that, I'd seen more than enough of the 'nids to last me more than a lifetime by this point too.

'We'd best press on,' I decided after a few moments' reflection. Somehow the confirmation that there was something down there made it easier to do that than go back, however strong the impulse to retreat I now felt. I knew from experience that an unknown enemy is always a bigger threat than one you've identified, and, in truth, nothing much had changed. I still had a crack squad of veteran troopers between me and anything malevolent lurking up ahead. Not to mention Jurgen, whose peculiar gifts had saved my hide on more than one occasion, even though neither of us had been aware of their existence until our encounter with Amberley and her entourage on Gravalax.[1] Lustig nodded, and gave the order to move on.

The mood was, if anything, even more sombre after that. The occasional outbreaks of joking and banter between the troopers sounded hollow now, uncomfortable, and soon petered out into silence punctuated only by the terse monosyllables of report and response. The trooper on point, Penlan still I think, began communicating by hand signals wherever possible, and resorted to the comm-net only when absolutely necessary. Almost without thought we'd slipped into the assumption that we were now in hostile territory.

I found that comforting. A healthy dose of paranoia goes with my job, of course, but it was nice to know that everyone else was as jumpy as me for once, with the possible exception of Jurgen, who never seemed particularly put out by anything which didn't involve aerodynamics. Almost without thought my hands went to my weapons, loosening the chainsword in its scabbard and drawing the laspistol. No point in not being prepared, I thought.

'If there's anything down here we must be right on top of it,' Lustig muttered. I nodded. We were only a few dozen metres from the end of the gallery by now, and the dead end I'd spotted on the map. The chances of whatever had left those tracks staying behind to be bottled up by our advance were remote in the extreme, I knew, but still my mouth went dry, my stomach cramping with the

---

1. *Very early on in my association with Cain and his aide, it became obvious that Jurgen was a blank: a staggeringly rare attribute which made him immune to daemonic possession or psychic attack.*

anticipation of combat, my imagination running wild with images of rampant Chaos spawn.

'That's it. Dead end.' Penlan's voice had an unmistakable edge of relief, which rippled around the rest of the squad like a breeze through summer grass. I exhaled, feeling my muscles relax, unaware until then of how tense I'd become.

'Take a look round,' I said, starting forward to join her. Jurgen stayed at my shoulder as always, and behind me I heard Lustig issuing orders with his usual calm efficiency. He was deploying the rest of the squad to secure our perimeter. Good. That meant no unpleasant surprises while we were poking around.

'Frak all that I can see.' Penlan moved carefully, sweeping her luminator ahead of her. The beam picked out a blank wall, where the tunnel had simply been abandoned when the seam of refinable material had run out. Then it swept on to pick out a jumble of ice boulders over to the right. The palms of my hands started to tingle as they always did when my subconscious alerted me to something untoward. Penlan started towards the heap of rubble.

'Be careful,' I started to say, as the realisation began to seep through to my forebrain. The tumbled pattern of ice blocks looked familiar, scattered like the debris from an underhive roof fall. I swept my own luminator beam towards the ceiling, where a crack began, no thicker than a hair, before widening to the width of my fist as it reached the wall. From there the fissure grew exponentially, terminating in the pile of frozen rubble.

It still didn't feel right to me. For the debris to have fallen in that pattern, the wall itself must have been undermined. A faint, but ominous cracking sound echoed through the chamber.

'Penlan!' I shouted. 'Get back!' But I was too late. She was half-turning towards me, an expression of puzzlement on her face, when the floor gave way beneath her and she vanished from sight with a single startled shriek.

'Penlan!' Lustig started forward, until I restrained him with an arm across the chest; there was no knowing how far the treacherous deadfall extended. 'Penlan, report!' Static hissed in our comm-beads.

'Watch that first step, sarge.' Her voice sounded winded, but if she could crack jokes she couldn't be that badly hurt. 'It's steeper than it looks.'

'Better move carefully,' I counselled the sergeant. 'No telling how unstable the rest of the floor is.' I inched forward cautiously, Jurgen at my side, just enough to shine the beam from our luminators down into the hole. It seemed sufficiently solid. From here I could see that a thin crust of ice had formed across the gap where the roof fall had breached the ceiling of a chamber below us. A chamber, I suddenly realised, which didn't appear anywhere on the map.

'That froze over recently,' Jurgen said, with the certainty of an iceworlder. I edged a little closer to the hole, from where I could see Penlan. She'd fallen about five or six metres, but most of that, thank the Emperor, had been down a steep slope rather than a sheer drop. A friction-gouged channel in the ice showed where she'd slid most of the way. Seeing my face appear in the gap, she waved.

'Sorry about that, sir,' she said. 'My foot slipped.'

'So I see.' I got Jurgen to direct his luminator around the chamber she was in. It was roughly circular, no more than a few metres wide, and I began to suspect that it might have been a natural ice pocket. It was easy to imagine a solitary miner falling the way Penlan had, and being less lucky about landing. The gap they'd left behind them could have frozen over before the search party arrived. Perhaps Morel's mysterious disappearances had been accidents after all. 'Does that hollow look natural to you?'

'Maybe.' Penlan shone her own beam around, then stiffened, aiming the lasgun. 'There's another tunnel here. I can't tell how far it goes.'

'Sit tight.' Lustig appeared at my elbow, a coil of climbing rope in his hands. He began looping it round himself, and threw the end down to Penlan. She grabbed it, slung her lasgun, and began to swarm up the rope. After a second she hesitated.

'Sarge. There's something down here. I can hear movement.' After a second or so I heard it too. The scrape of claw against ice, moving fast, and the loud panting of a predator which has caught a fresh scent. I joined Lustig, grabbing the rope, and hauled until the muscles in my back cracked.

'Get her up!' I shouted. Jurgen ran to help too, and between us we dragged Penlan a good three metres up the ice face. From there her boot soles caught some purchase, and she was able to scramble her way up the wall. I dropped to my knees, feeling the cold bite through the fabric of my trousers, and extended a hand down into the darkness. 'Grab it!'

Penlan did so, a firm grip clamping round my wrist, and I tightened my grip on hers. We'd nearly made it, when something seized the dangling rope below her and jerked it hard.

'Frak!' Lustig and Jurgen dropped suddenly, pulled off balance, and Penlan's weight dragged me down. For a moment I thought we'd make it, but the ice beneath me had too little traction, and for a long, agonised moment I felt myself slipping. My hand tightened reflexively around her wrist, instead of letting go which would have been far more sensible, and before I knew it I was plunging forwards into the shadowy pit.

I landed hard, the breath driven from my lungs, a dozen small pains flaring across my body where I'd bounced on the way down. Penlan groaned beside me, face down and winded. Just as well, a small analytical part of my mind told me, or the slung lasgun might have broken her back.

'Commissar!' Bright light shone down on us, the luminator taped to Jurgen's lasgun, and I heard the distant

echo of running feet as the rest of the squad responded
to our plight. They wouldn't be quick enough, I thought,
as the creature – whatever it was – rushed out of the
darkness. I had a brief, panic-stricken image of claws and
jaws too large and terrifying to be real, and as I scrabbled
frantically backwards. My hand fell against the lasgun on
Penlan's back. Without thinking I twisted it round, finding just enough play in the sling, and fired without even
aiming properly.

Either luck or the Emperor was with me, because she'd
left it on full auto. As my panic-spasmed hand locked on
the trigger a hail of las bolts sprayed the chamber, blowing chunks of ice from the walls and deafening us with
the roar of ionising air and ice flashing into steam. The
creature screamed and fled, even more terrified than I
was, and as the power cell died and relative silence
descended on our ringing ears, Penlan stirred.

'I've got to stop doing that...'

'I'd appreciate it,' I agreed. A degree of understanding
returned to her eyes.

'What happened?'

'The commissar saved your hide,' Lustig said. I was suddenly aware of the ring of faces around the hole over our
heads. No point mentioning that it was purely by accident, of course, so I made a show of mild embarrassment,
and patted the frost from my greatcoat.

'Better get the medic to check you over,' I said, just to
reinforce my caring image.

I took a glance around the chamber. It looked bigger
from down here, and the hail of las bolts had melted a
number of small pits into the walls. Something seemed
to be embedded in one, and I tried to focus on it, to
stop my head spinning. Then my brain finally inter-
preted what I was seeing, and I regretted my curiosity at
once.

'Looks like we found our missing miner,' Penlan said,
with what I felt was rather unseemly relish.

'Almost,' I agreed. It was a human hand, severed at the wrist, the stump scored with vicious bite marks.

'What was that thing?' Jurgen asked, his habitual phlegmatic tone a welcome calming influence.

'I haven't a clue,' I admitted, scooping my laspistol up from the floor where it had fallen. As I did so I noticed a thick smear of ichor on the ice. The sight cheered me remarkably, not least because if I'd managed to wound the creature it was unlikely to come back for a while. 'But it bleeds.' I thrust the sidearm back into the holster on my belt with a sense of grim satisfaction. 'And if it bleeds, we can kill it.'

FOUR

'AND YOU DON'T have a clue what it was?' Broklaw asked. I shook my head. In the three or four hours since we'd returned from the depths of the mine I'd been asked that question often.

'None. But you wouldn't want one as a house pet, believe me.' A few of those present in the command centre chuckled dutifully. Besides myself and the major, Kasteen was the only other person seated on what I couldn't help thinking of as the military side of the conference table. Facing us was Morel, whose interest in the situation was undeniable and whose reaction had fallen somewhere between shock at the news that his worst fears were founded and grim satisfaction that his forebodings had been vindicated. Alongside him sat representatives from the Administratum and the Adeptus Mechanicus. Around us the rest of our senior officers continued to monitor troop positions and intelligence reports, ignoring the little knot of civilians in our midst as best they could as they bustled in and out with data-slates and mugs of tanna.

Remembering Quintus's advice I'd requested that he and Logash be our liaisons with their respective orders, and was pleased that this decision had proven to be wise. The young scrivener was as affable as I remembered, and Logash had turned out to have a quick wit and a courteous manner at marked odds with the defensiveness of his superior. To Kasteen's evident relief he had few visible marks of augmentation as well, beyond a pair of faceted metal eyes, which caught the light as his head moved, and although the Emperor alone knew what his robes concealed, she was able to keep her revulsion in check. (When I asked her why she found the tech-priests so disturbing she just shrugged, and said, 'They're weird, that's all.' She never reacted that way towards me, or anyone else in the regiment with augmetic replacements, so I guess it was just the sense she got from them of having voluntarily, if not eagerly, surrended part of their humanity.)[1]

'I've taken a look through the Codex Ferae,' Logash volunteered, 'based on the commissar's description of the beast. I'm pretty sure whatever it is, it isn't native to Simia Orichalcae.'

'Then how the hell did it get here?' Morel asked. Logash shrugged.

'Maybe the orks brought it with them.'

'That's highly unlikely,' Kasteen said, taking a little too much satisfaction in contradicting the tech-priest. But he took it in his stride and gave way to her greater expertise.

'You'd be a better judge of that than me.' He shrugged again. 'Maybe it stowed away on one of the tanker shuttles then.' Quintus nodded in agreement.

---

1. *A common reaction to members of the Adeptus Mechanicus. Personally it's their air of smugness I find most off-putting. And isn't it about time the Ordo Hereticus started asking some pointed questions about this Omnissiah cult of theirs?*

'They're certainly big enough for something to hide in undetected. I remember a couple of years back a few of the miners thought it would be funny to smuggle in some...'

'Who cares how it got here?' Morel broke in. 'The question is, what are we going to do about it?'

'Go back down there and kill it,' I said. Morel nodded with grim satisfaction, but Quintus's eyes narrowed a little.

'I don't want to sound as though I'm doubting your sense of priorities, but surely the orks are the real threat. Can't this thing wait until you've seen them off?'

'It's not the creature we're worried about,' Kasteen said. 'It's the unmarked tunnels the commissar found down there.'

'Probably burrowed by the beast,' Logash said. He pulled a data-slate from the recesses of his robes, and started scribbling notes with a luxpen embedded in the tip of a finger. 'That might account for the size of the claws the commissar saw...'

'It doesn't matter who dug them,' I pointed out. 'What matters is that they're a potential hole in our defences.' As if to underline my words a bright flash cut through the flurrying snow outside the window, followed almost at once by the concussive thud of explosive detonation. The orks had obligingly arrived on schedule and were busily throwing themselves (or more probably their gretchin cannon fodder) against our outer defensive line with a gratifying lack of success so far. Luckily, Mazarin and her acolytes had managed to get the damaged shuttle flying again in a matter of hours, and the rest of our deployment had gone without a hitch, so we'd been more than ready to meet them despite my fears.

'I take your point,' Quintus said. 'What do you suggest?'

'I'm going back down there,' I said. 'With a squad of troopers. We'll map the tunnels as we go, and kill the creature when we find it.'

'You're leading the group personally?' Logash asked. I nodded.

'Commissar Cain is by far the best man for the job,' Kasteen explained. 'He has more experience of tunnel fighting than anyone else in the regiment.' Not from choice, I might add, but if it kept me out of the cold and away from the orks, I wasn't about to object.

'I'd like to come too, if I may,' Logash said. I think I'm hardly exaggerating when I say the rest of us simply stared at him in blank astonishment. 'Xenology's a bit of a hobby of mine. I might be able to identify what we're looking for.'

'This is a search and destroy mission, not a stroll around the zoo,' Kasteen said irritably. Logash looked a little crestfallen, I thought she was being unnecessarily hard on the boy. At least he was trying to help, which was more than his superiors were willing to do, and it didn't seem too good an idea to squash that enthusiasm. Besides, I had no objection to presenting the beast with another potential meal, to stand between me and it. (Of course if I'd known just how much trouble he was going to turn out to be I'd have left him behind, or even shot him on the spot, but regrets are a waste of good drinking time, as my old friend Divas used to say.)

'It would be at your own risk,' I told him. 'And you'd be under military authority. That means you do what you're told at all times. All right?'

'Fine.' He nodded eagerly. 'Do I get a gun?'

'Absolutely not,' Kasteen and I said simultaneously.

AFTER SEEING THE civilians out, Kasteen, Broklaw and I returned to the business of fighting the war. Our strategy seemed to be working, at least for now, keeping the main line of the ork advance bottled up in the neck of the valley quite nicely. The peculiar nature of an iceworld, and the Valhallans' understanding of how to exploit it, were paying handsome dividends, as the latest sensor downloads from the *Pure of Heart* were making abundantly clear. I gazed at the blurry image in the tactical hololith. It looked like someone had dropped it on the journey up here from the landing pad, as the three-dimensional representation of the battlefield would occasionally jump a few centimetres to the left, blank out, and reset itself. I reflected ruefully that perhaps we shouldn't have been quite so eager to get rid of Logash. (Who had practically skipped out of there, eager to be off, and prattling about various unpleasant life forms our intruder probably wasn't.)

'Never a tech-priest around when you need one,' Broklaw murmured, obviously thinking the same thing. He cast a sidelong glance at the colonel who pretended not to have heard.

Thanks to the frozen landscape we'd been able to fortify in depth with an ease which would have been impossible practically anywhere else. I was looking (when the blasted hololith would let me) at an extensive network of trenches and firing pits which would have taken weeks to dig in more normal terrain, but which had been hollowed out in mere hours by adroit use of our heavy flamers and multilasers. Of course half the troops manning them would have frozen to death by now if they'd been anyone else, but these were Valhallans, and the bone-chilling temperatures outside were just like a holiday resort so far as they were concerned. I'd even had to break up a couple of snowball fights before the orks turned up to spoil the party.[1]

'So far so good,' I said, quietly satisfied with the conduct of our troopers. The line was holding nicely, and the view from orbit showed that the ork advance had pretty much ground to a halt in the face of this unexpected resistance. So far as I could tell, the topography of the

---

1. *From which we can infer that, despite his reluctance to step outside, Cain had visited the front line at least once by this point, probably after his return to the surface.*

valley was working to our advantage as well as we'd hoped, with the broad front of the ork advance funnelling into the mouth of it and running right into our killing zone. Of course being orks this didn't diminish their enthusiasm, quite the reverse. Some flashes of gunfire on the outer fringes of the mob indicated that fratricidal firefights had broken out as the groups farthest from the fighting had run out of patience and had started blasting their way through their own comrades to get to us. Well that was fine with me, the more of them who killed each other the better I liked it, but there were still plenty left where they'd come from.

'What's that?' Broklaw asked, pointing at a blip some way behind the bulk of the ork army. Whatever it was it was massive, and moving slowly but inexorably towards us. A heavy sense of foreboding sank into my stomach as I stared at it. I had a horrible suspicion as to what it might be, but prayed fervently to the Emperor that I was wrong. (Not that I thought for a moment that He might actually be listening, but you never know, and it relieved the stress.)

'According to this, it's huge,' Kasteen said, a hint of confusion in her voice. Rather than verbalise my fears, which would somehow make them more concrete, I voxed Mazarin aboard the orbiting starship to request a more detailed analysis. That way I could continue to cling to the hope that I might be wrong for a few more precious minutes.

'Single contact, about two hundred kloms... kilometres to the west,' I said. 'Can you give us a little more detail?'

'If the Omnissiah wills it,' the tech-priest said cheerfully, and busied herself for a few moments with the appropriate rituals. After a short pause her voice returned, with a slightly harder edge to it. 'It's a single artefact, approximately eighty metres in height. Self-propelled, with a high thermal signature which indicates combustion processes of some kind. Metallic shell, mainly ferric in composition.' Her voice faltered. 'I'm sorry, commissar, I don't have a clue what it is. I can meditate on it, but...'

'There's no need, thank you,' I said. 'You've just confirmed what I suspected. It's a gargant.' Kasteen and Broklaw stared at one another in horror. The orkish equivalent of a battle titan, the approaching construct might be crude but it would certainly have enough firepower aboard to punch through our defensive lines without even so much as slowing down. 'Any suggestions you might have about vulnerabilities we can exploit would be gratefully received.'

'I'll analyse the data and see what I can find,' she promised.

'We can't ask for more,' I said, and turned back to the other officers. We studied the hololith together, brows furrowed. 'I reckon we've got less than a day before it gets here...' I began, then Mazarin's voice interrupted me again.

'Sorry to break in, commissar, but the captain would like a word.'

'This isn't exactly a good time,' I said, then changed my mind. If things went horribly wrong, which they looked very like doing at the moment, the *Pure of Heart* was my best chance of getting out of the system with my hide intact. And annoying Durant would be a seriously bad idea. 'No, put him on.'

'Why's my ship crawling with groundlings?' the captain asked, his voice tinged with an asperity which didn't seem entirely affected. 'I've just got rid of your troopers and now you're shuttling up half the population of this miserable iceball.'

'We're sending up rather more than half,' I said, trying to sound reasonable. 'I thought the Administratum here had cleared it with you.'

'You mean Pryke?' A phlegmy sound of disgust rattled the speakers of the vox unit. 'Impossible woman, doesn't listen to a word you say. How in the Emperor's name did you manage to get her to co-operate with you?'

'It was surprisingly easy after the commissar threatened to shoot her,' Kasteen said, with a hint of a smile. Durant seemed speechless for a moment.

'Harrumph. Worth a try I suppose.' A faint tinge of amusement entered his tone. 'But that still doesn't answer my question.'

'We're evacuating as many of the civilians as we can,' Broklaw explained. 'Especially the workers' families. They'll be a lot safer with you than they are down here.'

'And we can fight more effectively if we're sure they won't be getting underfoot,' Kasteen added, a little more candidly.

'Under your feet, you mean.' The captain sounded mollified. 'I suppose we can stick them in a couple of the cargo holds now they're not cluttered up with your military junk.'

'That would be appreciated,' I said.

'No problem. I'm sure the Administratum can afford their fares.' He broke the connection abruptly.

Of course there was another, unspoken reason for evacuating the workers from the plant, although none of us wanted to think about it. If we were unable to hold the place, and I was a lot less sanguine about that now than I had been twenty minutes ago, the orks would want to make use of it. No point in leaving them a pool of highly skilled slave labour which would maintain promethium output at the current high levels. Their own meks would figure out the process eventually, of course, but they wouldn't be nearly so efficient. And with any luck we'd have had time to launch a counter attack or call the Astartes in to sterilise the place before they got the plant up and running again.

I stared at the hololith, and the almost imperceptibly moving blip of the gargant. We had nothing in our inventory capable of fighting something like that: no tanks, no artillery, and most especially no titans of our own. Broklaw noticed the direction of my gaze.

'Cheer up,' he said. 'We'll think of something.'

'Better make it quick,' Kasteen said.

Editorial Note:

It is with profound apologies that I append the following excerpt, but feel that some wider perspective on the tactical situation than Cain's typically self-centred one may prove of interest. I just wish I'd been able to find something a little more readable. If you find the prose style (or more accurately, lack of one) as painful as I do, feel free to skip it.

Extracted from *Like a Phoenix From the Flames: The Founding of the 597th*, by General Jenit Sulla (retired), 097.M42.

THE GREEN TIDE broke against the bulwark of our defences as surely as an ocean wave against a harbour wall. For such we were, protecting the little islet of civilisation at our backs from the monstrous sea of barbarity which threatened to wash it clean. To the pride of all, it was us,

Third Platoon, Second Company, which had been given the all-important task of holding a hastily-constructed redoubt at the very centre of our forward line, and not a woman or man of us shirked that responsibility. Crouched below the parapet of a rampart of ice I scanned my tactical data-slate, heedless of the bolter shells bursting against it to shower me with a refreshing powdering of frozen dust, noting with satisfaction the disposition of the squads under my command. As I'd come to expect, all were positioned with perfect precision, and I permitted myself a moment of pride in the level of battle-readiness they showed.

'Here they come!' someone shouted, a voice shaded, to my great satisfaction, by exultation rather than fear, and a quick glance over the frozen rampart confirmed it. A horde of orks was running towards us, yelling in their barbarous tongue, and I gave the order to hold fire. On they came, trampling the corpses of the dead we'd already left strewn across the virginal icefields, kicking up powdered snow as they came, so that it seemed as if the front ranks were wading waist-deep in mist. Like the wave that had assaulted us before they seemed scrawny specimens, quite unlike the heavily-muscled monstrosities which Commissar Cain had so resourcefully defeated after our shuttle was grounded,[1] but they died no less easily as I divined when they came within close range of our lasguns. 'Fire!' I ordered, and a devastating wave of las-bolts tore into the front ranks. Dozens fell, and more behind them as the casualties tripped those who followed after: forthwith the emplaced lascannons and multi-lasers we'd carefully sited finished the job, putting out a withering crossfire which ripped them to pieces. After a moment of

---

1. *Almost certainly the weaker subspecies known as 'gretchin,' a distinction Cain was well aware of, as his earlier remark makes clear.*

indecision the survivors broke and fled in all directions, leaving a few more normal-sized specimens who seemed to have been directing them cruelly exposed to our sight and firepower; and this was to prove their death warrant, as they were summarily cut down by a second barrage.

'Like shooting rats in a box,' the young corporal next to me remarked. I reproved her, but could scarce keep the satisfaction from my own voice.

'I doubt they'll give up that easily,' I said, and of course I was right. The frontal attack, as I had half suspected, was a diversion, and the roar of engines heralded a flank attack by a squadron of curious vehicles which resembled motorcycles with tracks replacing the rear wheels. Heavy weapons, bolters I assumed, were slung from them on outriggers, and opened up with a roar which almost drowned the noise of their engines.

'Fire at will,' I ordered, and the snow around them erupted with the concentrated firepower of our doughty host. 'Death to the enemies of the Emperor!'

I must confess my heart swelled at the answering cheers of the heroes under my command, and the conviction of our inevitable victory buoyed my spirits to such an extent that, despite our peril, a smile forced its way onto my face.

FIVE

OF ALL THE experiences which have befallen me in a century or more of service to the Golden Throne, creeping through a network of darkened tunnels in search of a foe which could be lurking almost anywhere is one I could very well have done without becoming so familiar with. I don't know why, but show me an enemy of the Emperor and chances are I can point to the nearest hole in the ground with the near certainty of finding their lair festering away down there. Chaos cults, genestealer swarms, mutants, you name it, they all seem to scurry for the darkest corners they can find; and then, of course, someone has to go in after them and winkle them out.[1]

---

1. Cain is exaggerating a little here, but it's certainly the case that a significant proportion of the heretical and unclean gravitate naturally to undercities and similar habitats. Then again, given the hostile nature of many worlds, both Imperial and xeno, the population may have had little option but to burrow underground to survive, which at least partially explains the prevalence of such labyrinths throughout inhabited space.

And, far more frequently than I'd like, that someone turns out to be me. Partly, I suppose, that's due to my inflated reputation (when something dangerous needs doing who better than a hero of the Imperium to get stuck with it?), but in truth I suspect that, as Kasteen told Logash, in most cases I really am the best man for the job. (In theory at any rate, my old hiver's tunnel sense brings a definite advantage, but in practice enthusiasm for the job is most definitely absent, you may take my word for that.)

In this case, though, while not exactly pleased to be back in the network of tunnels, it was rather more attractive than the alternative. True, there was our mysterious beast to worry about, but I'd already wounded it once and didn't anticipate it putting up much of a fight, not with a full squad of troopers to back me up, and the indispensable Jurgen, who'd managed to scrounge a melta from somewhere. He'd done the same on Gravalax, and we'd both found cause to be thankful for his foresight. Indeed, after that little incident he'd become quite partial to that particular item of equipment, and tended to bring it along whenever we might meet heavier resistance than we anticipated. As it turned out I was to have occasion to be even more grateful than usual for this little habit of his. But in all honesty if I'd known what we were going to find down there I would have charged the orks, even the gargant, with a broken chair leg rather than set foot in those caverns again.

As it was though, I remained in blissful ignorance, and even felt relaxed enough to joke with my aide as he fell in at my shoulder, preceded as always by his distinctive bouquet.

'Did you remember the marshmallows this time?' I asked, echoing Amberley's jest when she caught sight of the melta he was carrying on Gravalax. He smiled sheepishly.

'Must have slipped my mind, sir.'

'No problem. We'll just have to find something else for you to toast,' I said.

'I'm not sure that would be wise,' Logash said, hurrying to join us, and looking somewhat askance at the heavy thermal weapon. 'That would pretty much vaporise the creature.'

'Along with a fair sized chunk of the wall behind it,' I agreed. Meltas are designed to punch through tank armour, and using one to eradicate a single creature might seem like overkill to most people, but so far as I was concerned there was no such thing. Especially when you were dealing with something the size of the beast I'd glimpsed before.

'Then we might never know what it was,' Logash objected. I shrugged.

'That's a disappointment I could learn to live with,' I said, then took pity on his crestfallen expression. 'But I'm sure it won't come to that. Jurgen's choice of weapon is purely for worst-case contingencies.'

'I see,' he said, nodding, and clearly trying to imagine what those contingencies might be. Well, he was going to find out soon enough.

'We're here,' the pointman said, his voice tinny in my comm-bead. The squad sergeant, a stocky young woman called Grifen, called a halt, and Logash shut up, eager for a sight of our quarry. I would have preferred to be accompanied by Lustig and his team, as they'd been down here before, but Penlan was too stiff from her healing injuries to tackle any more ice faces and I didn't want to be backed up by an under-strength squad. Besides which, as veterans, they were needed at the front line, especially with the approaching menace of the gargant.

Grifen's squad had seen little combat so far, and the sergeant herself was newly promoted, so this little errand had seemed like an ideal chance to break her into command without too much pressure (ironic, as things turned out.) Her troopers seemed competent enough,

and had got over their impulse to gawp at the ice forma-
tions and the sparkling reflections in the first few
minutes, settling into the routine of a xeno hunt with
reassuring efficiency.

I looked down the tunnel to where the beams of our
luminators reflected back from the tumbled heap of ice
shards which marked the boundary of the hole I'd fallen
into before. It was as eerily beautiful as ever, and despite
the grimness of our errand I found myself savouring the
sight as I turned to speak to Grifen.

'This is it,' I said. 'The end of the map. Once we pass
this point we're in unknown territory.'

'Understood, sir.' She saluted crisply, without
betraying her nervousness to anyone less skilled than
I was at reading body language. She began to issue
orders to her squad. 'Vorhees, on point. Drere and
Karta, cover him. Hail, Simla, watch our backs. We're
moving as soon as the commissar gives the word, so
look alive, people.' Despite her inexperience she was a
good motivator, and I began to feel a little easier
about our travelling companions – most of them,
anyway...

'Are there any tracks?' Logash asked eagerly. Grifen
looked at him with an air of vague surprise, as though it
had slipped her mind for a moment that we were being
accompanied by a civilian. She shrugged.

'You're the expert. You tell us.' Anyone else, I suppose,
would have had the sense to realise he was being
snubbed, but Logash, like most of the tech-priests I've
come across, had the social skills of a bath mat.[1] Instead
of subsiding like any normal person he nodded eagerly,
and started waving an auspex around as though it were
an incense burner.

---

1. *Probably something to do with all those augmetics. It must be difficult to
interact with mere humans when you feel you've got more in common with
a beverage dispenser.*

'There are some interesting striations in the ice layer,' he said, 'which could be frozen-over claw marks. Still too vague to make a clear determination, though...'

I caught the sergeant's eye, and raised my own brows in a pantomime of tolerant exasperation. She smiled back a little nervously, not quite sure how to respond to a commissar with a sense of humour, and no doubt in awe of my reputation.

'I think if your people are ready we might as well move on,' I said, already sure they would be, and she gave the order with alacrity.

'Vorhees, front and centre. Let's get ourselves a new trophy for the mess room wall.' Logash shot me an unhappy look, which I ignored, and the pointman dropped nimbly through the hole in the floor.

'I'm down,' he said, his voice still attenuated in the comm-bead. 'No sign of life.' The rest of his fireteam[1] followed him, rappelling into the darkness below. The glow of their luminators was visible now, diffusing through the ice floor like the first faint echo of the dawn breaking somewhere a klom or two over our heads,[2] rippling like an aurora borealis.

'Our turn,' I said, with a cheerfulness I hoped no one would realise was forced, and stepped confidently up to the gap, trying to suppress the memory of my vertiginous plunge into the unknown the previous day. I bounced down the slope, the support of the rope more of a comfort than I'd realised, and found my boot heels crunching against the hard-packed scattering of ice crystals on the floor before I even knew it. The chamber was just as I'd remembered it: featureless save for the tunnel

---

1. *The Valhallan 597th divided its squads into two fireteams of five troopers each, a common, though unofficial, practice in regiments experienced in urban warfare.*

2. *In fact, according to the schematics, the lowest level of the mines was almost three kilometres below the surface at this point.*

mouth we'd come to investigate. But it was crowded with troopers this time. A moment later Jurgen slithered down next to me. The heavy melta slung across his shoulders pulled him over to one side, but he regained his balance and hefted it properly back into position. The small knot of troopers around us took a step or two away.

Logash came next, clinging too tightly to the rope so that he descended in a series of jerks and wild parabolas. The Guardsmen and women watched his progress with unconcealed amusement and the expectation of an igno-minious tumble to come. To his credit he made it though, letting out his breath in a wild rush as he reached the floor of the cavern.

'Are you all right?' I asked, reaching out a hand to steady him. He nodded.

'Yes. Fine. I'm just not very good with heights, to be honest.' He caught sight of the splash of ichor from where I'd shot our quarry and went scuttling off to exam-ine it without another word. Soon I heard him muttering in disappointment at the way our boot prints had dis-turbed any tracks the thing might have left.

I looked up to check the progress of Grifen and the remaining four troopers, who were all descending with-out any problems. When I looked back the little tech-priest was arguing furiously with private Vorhees. I strode over to investigate, wondering once more whether bringing him was turning out to be more trouble than it was worth.

'What's going on?' I asked, trying to sound reasonable. Vorhees had the young tech-priest held firmly by the upper arm, evidently restraining him. The trooper jerked an irritable head at the mouth of the tunnel down which the creature had disappeared.

'He tried to get past me,' he said. I shone my luminator into the darkness, the beam catching a thousand glitter-ing highlights from the irregular walls. Then I turned to glare at Logash.

'I thought I made it clear you were to stay close to Jurgen,' I said. My aide had accepted the ad hoc bodyguarding assignment as phlegmatically as he did every other order, and I suppose Logash could be forgiven for being less than enthusiastic about it. That wasn't his main concern at the moment though. He jerked his arm free of Vorhees's restraining grasp with a degree of petulance which reminded me of a sulky juve, and pointed at the tunnel floor in the pool of light from my luminator.

'I was looking for tracks,' he said, clearly wanting to say a great deal more. 'The ground in here's too trampled to tell anything from.'

'Right. Fine,' I said. I turned back to Vorhees. 'Keep him in sight. He goes no further than five metres.' I returned my gaze to Logash. 'That should be enough for you, right?'

'Oh yes, indeed.' He trotted a couple of paces into the tunnel, spot lit by the beam of the luminator Vorhees had taped to the barrel of his lasgun, and squatted down to wave the bloody auspex around. Sure he could still hear me, I turned to grin at Vorhees.

'Maybe we'll catch it quicker if we leave some bait out.'

'Worth a try,' he agreed, with a smile of his own. Logash ignored us, already wrapped up in his data-divining rituals. After a few moments he walked back to join us, still muttering under his breath as he studied the display of the little machine.

'Well?' Grifen demanded. 'Can you tell what it is yet?' Logash looked confused.

'Well, there are indications. If we were anywhere else I might take a guess. But the habitat's all wrong...'

'Then just give us what you can,' I encouraged gently. Grifen nodded, flicking her black hair out of her eyes as she tried to make out the runes on the screen, but they were all tech-priest gibberish and none of the rest of us could make head or tail of it. Logash shrugged.

'It definitely burrowed these tunnels,' he said. 'There are claw marks on the walls and ceiling as well as the floor.' A flicker of apprehension rippled around most of the troopers. The narrow passage was high enough to stand up in without stooping, even for me,[1] and if not quite wide enough for two abreast had at least enough room for us to be able to see past the man in front (and shoot, too, which was more to the point.) The creature must have a considerable reach – that much was obvious.

'Well, we're not going to find it by standing here,' I pointed out, more to steady the troops than anything else. 'And we still have to map these tunnels.' So we set off into the dark, our nerves taut with fearful anticipation.

I WAS MORE at ease down here than any of my companions with the possible exception of Jurgen, who simply accepted the situation as he did everything else, with taciturn stoicism. These tunnels were different from the ones I was used to, however. They turned and meandered apparently at random, with innumerable branching corridors which came to a dead end or turned back on themselves to rejoin the one we'd just left, or split into further radial passageways. I had several occasions to thank the Emperor for my sense of direction, without it I'd have been disorientated within moments, but the subconscious instinct which lets me know roughly where I am and how far I've come in an underground environment proved as reliable as ever.

'It's a frakking maze down here,' one of the troopers, Drere I think, muttered under her breath. Grifen silenced her with a few well-chosen words, in the manner of sergeants the length and breadth of the galaxy. Logash

---

1. *Cain was just under two metres in height, and was generally among the tallest in any given group.*

was travelling in the middle of the group next to me, as I hoped to keep a respectable number of heavily-armed troopers between me and the creature whichever direction it approached from. Logash agreed, heedless of the sergeant's admonishment.

'Surprisingly extensive for so recent an excavation,' he added. Just then the palms of my hands started tingling, in the way they do when my subconscious warns me of something my forebrain has yet to grasp.

'How recent?' I asked. Logash pointed out something on the screen of the auspex, which I couldn't see clearly.

'A few weeks,' he said. 'A couple of months at the most.' In other words, about the same time the orks turned up, and that was just too much of a coincidence. Not that I believed for a moment it was some kind of squig[1] we were after. The chances of that were extremely remote, as anything the greenskins had brought with them would have arrived at the same co-ordinates. But the space hulk which had brought them to the system (and, to my intense relief, dropped back into the warp again within hours) could have carried any number of other horrors in its bowels, and if that were so it wasn't unlikely that something else had seized the opportunity to make planetfall at the same time.

I made a mental note to ask Quintus to look through the sensor logs of the refinery's orbital traffic control system when we got back. The chances were the blaze of warp energy emitted by the hulk's emergence, a

---

1. *A generic term for a bewildering variety of organisms apparently associated with orks. Opinion in the Ordo Xenos remains divided as to whether they represent true symbiosis, or are simply an entire genus of unpleasant creatures sufficiently close to the greenskins' peculiar metabolic processes to flourish in close proximity to them. It is undeniable that they do seem to accompany most orkish infestations, however. Where Cain picked up the word is conjectural, presumably from the same source as the rest of his smattering of orkish.*

thousand times stronger than that of a starship, would have swamped them, but there might be a clue there we could disentangle given time.

Any further opportunity I might have had to muse on the matter was abruptly curtailed as I felt a faint tremor through the soles of my boots. My palms tingled again, foreboding flooding through me. The narrow passageway seemed even more claustrophobic than before, although that's not a sensation I'm normally familiar with either. The faint tremor intensified, and I stopped trying to identify it. I felt a yielding impact against my shoulder blades as Grifen walked into me, and halted in her turn.

'Commissar? What is it?' she asked.

'Quiet!' I looked back and forth down the tunnel, craning my neck to see as best I could past the troopers on either side of me. The light from our luminators receded in both directions, still striking dazzling highlights from the deep blue surface of the ice around us. 'Something's coming!'

'Nothing here,' Vorhees said, his voice crackling over the comm-net from a hundred metres or so up the tunnel.

'Nothing back here either,' Private Hail chipped in, her voice tense. I can't say I blame her for that, the rearguard is the second most vulnerable position in the column. Everyone stared at me, probably wondering whether the commissar had gone bonkers. Except for Jurgen of course, who had doubtlessly made up his mind on that score years before. But all my hiver's instincts insisted I was right, something was coming, even if we hadn't seen it yet...

Sudden understanding punched me in the gut. The creature we were hunting was a burrower! It didn't need to come at us along an existing passageway. No doubt it had detected our presence in some way, probably picking up the vibrations of our footfalls, and was heading straight towards us by the most direct route.

'Jurgen,' I shouted. 'Give us some elbow room!' Divining my intentions the troopers nearest to us scattered back along the passageway. Logash was hauled away protesting by Grifen, who couldn't be bothered trying to explain. His voice was drowned out abruptly by the hiss of the melta as Jurgen fired at the wall, instantly flashing a dozen cubic metres of ice into steam, which condensed almost instantly in the subzero temperatures, filling the narrow passageway with mist.

He was just in time, too. An instant later the newly frozen wall burst in on us in a hail of glittering ice shards, and the living nightmare I'd encountered before was among us.

By sheer foul luck I was the closest to it, and I barely had time to draw a weapon before it was upon me. This close up a gun would have been all but useless, so I drew my chainsword almost without thinking, and made a block with the instinctive lack of thought that comes from assiduous practice. It was lucky I had. An impossibly long arm, tipped with the talons I'd glimpsed before, swung at me as I thumbed the selector to maximum speed. It would probably have disembowelled me if I hadn't deflected the blow. The blade whined, cutting deep through plates of chitin which wouldn't have seemed out of place on a tyranid, and the thing howled with rage and pain.

I was vaguely aware of Jurgen standing aside to make room for some of the other troopers, whose barrel-mounted luminators spot-lit the confrontation. They were hoping they could get in a shot which wouldn't vaporise me along with the monster I fought, but the hope was a vain one. We were locked in too close, and circling too fast, for anyone to have a hope of getting a clear line of fire.

(It's moments like this, incidentally, which point up the wisdom of fostering the illusion that I cared about the common troopers. I have no doubt at all that, were I the type of commissar who relies on intimidation rather than respect to get the job done, and there are all too many of those around, most of the grunts would have taken the shot anyway and cheerfully reported that the creature got me first. It's a lesson I try to pass on to my cadets, in the hope that the less bone-headed among them might actually get to enjoy a reasonably lengthy career, but it's probably a wasted effort.)

I drove in under the thing's barrel chest, which barely came up to my chin, and tried to avoid the huge mandibles which snapped at my face as I ducked. Bizarrely the thing's unnaturally long arms were jointed about two-thirds of the way up its length, so the closer in to it I remained the harder it would be for it to reach me. Well that suited me fine. I swung the humming blade at its thorax, feeling the teeth bite home, and was rewarded with a spray of ichor and foul-smelling viscera. It screamed again, opening the mandibles impossibly widely, and bringing its head down to snap at me.

That was precisely what I'd been hoping for. The tactic worked well on some of the larger tyranid bio-forms, so I was ready and waiting, thrusting the tip of my trusty chainsword up through the open maw to chew its way contentedly through what passed for the creature's brain. I snatched my hand away quickly, fearing the reflex closing of those terrible jaws, and opening up a wide gash which split the side of its head open from the inside. A jet of blood and cerebral fluid sprayed the wall, which hardened to ice within seconds.

That was enough; the creature fell, making me scramble backwards in an undignified fashion to get out of the way, crashing into the ice at my feet. Thin flakes of powdered ice, condensed from the steam, rose into the air, and fluoresced like miniature galaxies in the light from our luminators.

'That was amazing,' Grifen said, clearly torn between protocol and the urge to pat me on the back. The murmur of voices among the troopers told me that she wasn't the only one to be impressed. Only Logash was looking at the creature rather than me, his face an almost comical mask of confusion.

'There's your specimen,' I told him, returning my trusty chainsword to its scabbard. 'Do you think you can identify it?'

'It's an ambull' he said, shaking his head in bafflement. 'But it can't be. They're native to Luther Macintyre IX...'

'Never heard of it,' I said. 'But it wouldn't be the first time a species jumped planets.'

'That's not the point. Ambull colonies are already known on dozens of worlds.' The young tech-priest looked completely bewildered. 'But they're all desert-dwellers, like their native stock. This creature shouldn't be on an iceworld at all.'

'Maybe it got lost,' one of the troopers suggested. His comment was accompanied by derisive laughter from his squad mates. I didn't join in. Something was badly wrong here, that much was evident, even without my tingling palms to underline the fact. And as I looked at the creature I'd slain, I noticed something else that wasn't quite right.

'Where are the lasgun wounds?' Jurgen asked, putting my thought into words an instant before I could. 'I definitely saw you hit it the last time...'

'It's a different one,' I said, looking to Logash for confirmation. 'That means there must be another one of these things down here with us.'

'More likely several,' he confirmed eagerly. 'Ambulls tend to form extended social groups.'

Better and better, I thought sourly. But if only I'd known, there was far worse still to come.

Minutes of the meeting of the Committee for the Defence and Preservation of Simia Orichalcae From the Orkish

Incursion (by the Grace of His Majesty), convened this day 648.932 M41 (just too early for a decent breakfast.)

Those Present:

Colonel Regina Kasteen of the 597th Valhallan, a fair and gallant warrior, acting military governor of the Simia Orichalcae system.

Major Ruput Broklaw, her second in command, equally gallant but not remotely as fair.

Artur Morel, professional hole-grubber.

Magos Vinkel Ernulph, senior tech-priest, with too much metal where his brain should be.

Codicier Marum Pryke, the Emperor's gift to the Administratum, at least in her own mind.

Me.

Assorted sycophants and hangers-on.

Order of Business:

Defence of the refinery (actually the only thing we discussed.)

Proceedings:

Colonel Kasteen called the meeting to order. Then she called it to order again. Major Broklaw fired his bolt pistol into the ceiling, and the meeting came to order.

Colonel Kasteen put forward a plan for disabling the gargant, and hopefully eliminating a significant number of the besieging orks into the bargain. This relied on the fact that the mining tunnels extended some way beyond the perimeter of the refinery proper; given the immense weight of the thing it should be possible to collapse the galleries underneath it with sufficient quantities of explosive.

Magos Ernulph wanted to know just how close to the refinery the explosion would be, pointing out that the promethium tanks were almost full, and that if things went wrong the entire refinery could be reduced to a smoking crater.

Major Broklaw pointed out helpfully that in that case none of us would be around to complain about it.

Codicier Pryke raised the point that a significant credit value was attached to this installation, and that its destruction would result in a 0.017 per cent fluctuation in the mean commerce averages of the sector. She went on to suggest that an alternative strategy should be found. Colonel Kasteen said she was welcome to go outside and ask the orks to go away if she thought that would help.

Morel offered the assistance of his miners in determining the optimum placement of the explosive charges, citing their expertise with the local geology, which the colonel appreciated (she has a very nice smile.)

As no one had any other suggestions for disabling the gargant, Ernulph conceded that we might as well blow the place up ourselves before the orks do it.

I raised the matter of Commissar Cain and his scouting party, asking how they were likely to fare if they were still underground when the mine was blown up. Kasteen and Broklaw evinced a degree of concern on this point, admitting that their chances of survival under those circumstances would be slim. Broklaw added that he was sure they'd be back by then, as the commissar had something of a knack for avoiding such difficulties. I suggested voxing them with a warning, but apparently they were too deep underground now to get a message through.

No doubt wherever he was, though, he'd be having a better time of it than we are.

SIX

I'M SURE I wasn't alone in brooding over Logash's off-hand announcement as we penetrated deeper into the maze of passages that made up the ambull den. The thought that we shared these tunnels with an indeterminate number of heavily-armoured predators wasn't exactly comforting, and we pressed on with renewed caution. The labyrinth was remarkably extensive, as the tech-priest had noted; if we'd had to walk every metre of it we'd still have been down there when the Emperor stepped off the throne,[1] but fortunately that wasn't going to be necessary. Between my hiver's instincts, Logash's knowledge of xenology, and the readings of his auspex we were beginning to get a pretty good idea of the layout of the place.

---

1. *Such beliefs became remarkably widespread as the turn of the millennium approached. Cain wasn't superstitious enough to place any credence in such folk tales, of course, but like many others used the phrase metaphorically to mean the start of M42, which of course at that point was still sixty-eight standard years in the future.*

'Any idea how many more of those things there are down here?' I asked him, once I was sure we were out of earshot of any of the troopers (except Jurgen, of course, whose discretion I knew I could rely on absolutely). No point in spooking them any further if the answer was as bad as I feared. Logash looked pensive for a moment, as though communing with some inner voice. (Which he may well have been, I've known plenty of tech-priests with augmetic data stores plugged into what's left of their brains. But he may just have had indigestion.)

'Judging by the extent of the tunnel system, and assuming that your guess they arrived on the same space hulk as the orks is correct...' he began. (Which it wasn't, as we were shortly to find out, but the timing was the same so it didn't make any practical difference in the end.) He was interrupted by a fusillade of lasgun fire further down the tunnel, and a babble of shouting voices that overlapped into nothing but multitudinous echoes in the confined and twisting tunnels. I activated my comm-bead.

'Grifen. What's going on?' I asked.

'Contact. Another creature.' Her voice was crisp and steady, so the situation seemed under control. I hurried forward, not wanting to be too far from the bulk of our firepower if any more of the beasts were attracted to the sounds of combat.

'No more than half a dozen,' Logash finished, panting in my wake. No doubt he felt the same urge, only stronger than I did, as he was the only member of our party who was completely unarmed. Whether he still had enough meat on him to actually interest an ambull was a moot point, of course, but I declined to consider it at the time. 'Probably fewer by now,' he added, as the firing stopped.

Well, that was a relief. These creatures weren't all that tough, compared to some of the things I'd faced, and the news that we weren't likely to run into too many more of them was undeniably welcome.

The carcass of our latest victim was lying a few metres further on in a wider tunnel that opened out from the one we followed. It was surrounded by chattering troopers and riddled with the cauterised craters of las-bolt impacts. Vorhees was breathing heavily, trembling from the reaction, and shrugging off the attentions of the squad medic. The front of his flak armour was deeply scored, visible through the rents in his greatcoat. I gathered from the conversations around me that the ambull had just managed to get within arms' reach of him before he finally succeeded in dropping it.

'Well done,' I said, clapping him on the back; it never hurt to show the troopers I cared – even if I didn't. He grinned weakly at me.

'Persistent little frakkers, aren't they sir?' I nodded.

'Take a bit of putting down,' I agreed. Which of course indirectly reminded everyone I'd taken mine down hand-to-hand. I glanced at the carcass, wondering if it was the one I'd shot before, but Vorhees had made such a mess of it blazing away on full auto that there wasn't really enough left intact to tell.

'Fast, too,' Vorhees agreed. It seemed that the thing had come at him along the main tunnel almost as soon as he'd entered it. He'd just been able to bring his weapon up before it was on him.

'Interesting,' Logash said. He was looking at the walls of the tunnel, and messing around with his auspex again. After a moment he turned back to me. 'I think we've found one of the main runs.' Well it certainly seemed a lot wider than the tunnels we'd been following before.

'Which means?' I asked. The tech-priest shrugged, his white robe beginning to look distinctly grubby now, I noticed. Hardly the most practical garment for tunnel fighting, but evidently it hadn't occurred to him to get changed before setting out. Either that or he didn't have anything else to wear in any case.

'The main chamber should be at one end of this passageway.' He glanced uncertainly up and down it. I considered his words carefully.

'Main chamber meaning...?' I asked. Logash responded with the eagerness of the enthusiast.

'The central nesting site, or den. Ambulls are social creatures, with strong familial instincts, and tend to congregate when not out hunting or...'

'Vorhees,' I said. 'Which direction did the creature come from?' Logash looked a little hurt at being abruptly cut off (just as he felt he was getting to the interesting bit no doubt). The trooper jerked a thumb past the rapidly cooling chunk of meat, which was now surrounded by a garnet-coloured nimbus of frozen blood.

'That way,' he indicated. My sense of direction kicked in, and I absently noted that it was almost directly towards the ork siege lines. A sense of grim foreboding settled across my shoulders.

'If it was returning to the lair it would have been carrying prey of some kind to share with the others,' Logash chipped in helpfully.

The pool of light from our luminators revealed nothing apart from the dismembered ambull. There was the answer. We weren't going to be able to complete our reconnaissance mission without passing through a cavern full of these monstrosities. Wonderful. But bowel-clenching as the prospect appeared, I liked the idea of a horde of orks pouring through these tunnels to slaughter the lot of us even less.

'Close up,' I ordered. 'Be ready to concentrate your firepower.' Grifen nodded, and went to shout at Hail and Simla, who were blunting their combat knives by trying to hack the ambull's head off. Up to that point I thought she'd been kidding about taking a trophy back with us, but it seemed at least two of her troopers had taken her literally.

'Move out,' she ordered. 'By teams, covering the commissar and the cogboy[1].' Logash showed considerably more common sense than hitherto by pretending he hadn't heard her. I must confess to feeling a little better, though, knowing everyone else would be watching my back. (In case you were wondering why Grifen should care about my welfare, and Logash's – I was deemed to be the best judge of the value of any intelligence we might gather, and Logash... well, let's just say Kasteen didn't want to have any more dealings with the Adeptus Mechanicus than she already did.)

So we moved out cautiously, heading towards the centre of the maze, our senses alert for any sign of movement in the darkness. We'd debated dousing a few of our luminators in the hope that we'd make ourselves less obvious, but according to Logash it wouldn't make any difference as the creatures could see in the dark anyway. He started to explain how,[2] but it made no sense to me and I soon stopped listening.

Second team still had the lead position. Grifen was already showing a veteran commander's common sense when it came to hanging back enough to keep an objective eye on the whole squad, although Karta (the ASL[3]

---

1. *A less than complimentary slang term for tech-priests, apparently derived from their symbol of office. It is common among Guard troopers, along with several others, most of which are considerably more offensive.*

2. *According to the Magos Biologos they can see heat rather than light. Rather an odd concept, I have to say, but having looked through a tau blacklight system recently I can attest from personal experience that such a phenomenon can be achieved by technosorcery, so I suppose it's not beyond the bounds of possibility that it might also occur in nature.*

3. *Assistant squad leader, a lower-ranking NCO trained to take command if the sergeant becomes a casualty. Where a squad has been divided into fireteams (which, as has already been noted, was standard practice in the 597th) the ASL will normally take command of the second team when it becomes detached from the first, and the direct control of the sergeant.*

and corporal in charge of the fireteam) had rotated Vorhees back to where the medic could keep an eye on him, and had put Drere on point. It made a kind of sense, I suppose, as Vorhees was still pretty twitchy after his close encounter with the ambull, but I'd have been inclined to leave him where he was; if he was going to be trigger happy I'd rather have him where there was nothing but targets in front. I was behind him in any case though, so it was all one to me.

Jurgen, Logash and I trotted along in the middle, keeping a cautious distance between the leading team and the one covering our backs, because if either made contact I wanted to be well out of harm's way. Of course I was still uneasily aware of the ambulls' ability to carve their way straight through the ice to get at us, but I kept my ears open and my paranoia cranked up to maximum, and so far I hadn't noticed any of the telltale vibrations which might betray the approach of another of the beasts.

'So what do they taste like?' Jurgen asked. I stopped tuning out Logash's prattling to gather that his monologue on the subject of the ambulls' life cycle, social structure, and habitat had finally yielded some useful information. Apparently there had been a number of attempts to domesticate the things as a handy source of meat on desert worlds.[1]

'Rather like grox, I'm told.' Logash looked a little uncomfortable, and I clapped him on the shoulder.

'Excellent,' I said. 'We'll send a scavenging party back to recover the carcasses once we've cleaned out the nest.' All the refinery had to offer in the way of cuisine was a dozen different varieties of soylens viridians, which had already begun to pall, despite being fresh from their own

---

1. *With a conspicuous lack of success, if truth be told. Their burrowing abilities make them almost impossible to confine, with the inevitable result that the colonies which tried soon found themselves overrun with dangerous predators.*

vats. Of course, we'd brought our own supplies along, but a nice fresh steak would lift my spirits nicely, I thought. Besides, the creatures had been eating the miners, so it seemed fair enough to return the compliment.

'Good idea, sir,' Jurgen said with relish. Logash looked a little green for someone so heavily augmented. Maybe he was a vegetarian, if he still bothered eating at all.

'I can hear movement,' Drere said, her voice slightly flattened by the comm-bead in my ear.

'Close up. Prepare for contact.' Grifen issued the order with calm authority, and I found myself at the centre of a small knot of troopers as first team caught up with us. We picked up our pace, fell in with them, and began closing on the lights from the luminators of second team.

'There's a cavern here.' Drere's voice tightened a little, the tension she must have felt transmitting itself through the gently hissing comm-bead in my ear.

'Hold position,' Karta said, his own voice calm, but with audible effort. 'Wait for the rest of us.'

'Confirm that,' Drere said, a faint edge of relief entering her voice. The dancing lights ahead of us were closer together now, I thought, refracting more brightly through the crystal shards which rimed the irregular walls of the tunnel. 'I'm not about to stick my... Emperor's guts!'

A lasgun opened up, bright muzzle flashes strobing down the reflective tunnel, and the luminators ahead of us bobbed more wildly than before as their bearers broke into a run. We followed suit, our boot soles crunching on the ice crystals underfoot. Logash slipped from time to time as he lost traction. The Valhallans, of course, had no such difficulties, and I'd picked up enough expertise in running on ice from them over the years to avoid my own feet slithering out from under me. I drew my laspistol.

'Janny!' Vorhees shouted, and a second weapon opened up in support. A moment later there was a shriek which echoed through the tunnels, raising the hairs on my arms, and a howl of feedback through the comm-bead which made my teeth ache.

'Medic! Trooper down!' Karta yelled, and by that time the rest of us had reached the scene of the carnage. The tunnel had indeed opened out into a large central chamber, about thirty metres across, and with a handful of other passageways visibly piercing the walls at irregular intervals. Drere was down, steaming blood starting to freeze in a slick hard plate over a gaping wound in her torso. Her face was pinched and white from the shock. Vorhees stood over her, pouring lasfire into the monstrosity which had evidently inflicted the damage, driving it back, screaming in rage and frustration.[1]

The cavern was a positive maelstrom of whirling bodies and wild firing. Luminator beams and las-bolts strobed as the troopers swung the muzzles of their weapons to meet the nearest perceived threat. It was no place for me, I decided, standing aside to let Grifen's team join the mêlée. I held an arm across Logash's chest as though I intended to keep him from harm. (In actual fact, of course, if one of the beasts had come anywhere near us it could have had him and been welcome; and if I'd known just how much trouble he was shortly to cause us I'd probably have thrown him to the closest and bidden it *bon appetit*.)

The reinforcements pitched in with a will, targeting the seething mass of enraged monstrosities which were boiling out of the shadows at us. There were too many to count, or at least that's how it seemed at the time. When the ice chips finally settled it transpired that Logash's estimate hadn't been all that far out, with a mere five of

---

[1]. *It's not entirely clear from this final subordinate clause whether Cain is referring to the ambull or the trooper; sometimes he lets his immersion in his memories run ahead of comprehensibility. After some reflection I've elected to let his wording stand, as under the circumstances either or both seem equally likely.*

the creatures stretched out on the floor. But if you had asked me to take a stab at the numbers amid all that confusion I'd probably have said dozens.

'Pick your targets! Fire for effect!' Grifen yelled, her actions matching her words. She squeezed the trigger methodically, placing single shots on the head of the nearest ambull with commendable accuracy, aiming for the eyes and maw. A las bolt burst against the roof of the thing's mouth, blowing a large chunk of brain matter backwards which clung to the frozen wall, solidifying like an obscene outgrowth as the creature toppled backwards. It hit the floor with a concussion which I was certain I could hear even over the cacophony of combat.

'Omnissiah protect us!' Logash was shivering in shock, which surprised me with all that metal in him. Evidently looking at holos of exotic species in the comfort of his chambers was rather more fun than having the blood-soaked reality trying to tear his face off.

'Over there. Eight o'clock.' Jurgen swung his hand in a familiar gesture, lobbing a frag grenade over the heads of the nearest monsters to burst among the ones clustered at the back. (Juveniles just out of the nest, according to Logash when he had a chance to examine them, but they looked dangerous enough to me, pushing forward as maddened by bloodlust as any of the others we'd encountered.)

A scream to my right snapped my head round just in time to see a pair of hideous mandibles close around the arm of the medic with a loud crunching sound which spoke of broken bones or worse. As the creature lifted him off the ground I turned, chainsword shrieking, and leapt forward to lop through the distended jaw. He fell heavily, clutching his wounded arm, and scrabbled for a self-injector from his pouch with his uninjured hand. That should have been enough to establish my participation in the battle and allow me to go back to babysitting Logash, but of course the thing came at me. I swung the weapon again, cursing myself for my stupidity. Jurgen hefted the melta uncertainly, unable to get a shot without killing as many of us as the creatures, and I had a moment to wonder if I'd ever get the chance to suggest he settle for something a little more manageable like a hellgun or a flamer next time. Then a line of bloody craters stitched themselves across the ambull's chest.

'Thanks!' I called to Karta, and administered the *coup de grace* to my staggering foe, lopping the head from its shoulders as it fell to its knees. (Probably unnecessarily, but it was a suitably theatrical gesture for a hero of the Imperium to make, and the surrounding troopers seemed to appreciate it.)

Abruptly I became aware of the sudden silence around us, was broken only by the ticking of the re-freezing ice and the groans of the wounded.

'Casualties?' I asked, playing up to my caring image. Grifen made a rapid assessment.

'Two serious. A few cuts and bruises among the rest, but they'll live.' She turned her attention to the medic, who was treating Drere as best he could with his one good hand. He was assisted by a grim-faced Vorhees.

'How is she?' I asked, walking over to them.

'She'll be fine,' Vorhees said flatly, clearly in no mood to accept any other outcome; the memory of him calling her given name as the fight started came back to me, and I smelled trouble. The nature of their relationship, clearly more than purely professional, was pretty obvious. And if she died he'd no doubt blame himself for not having been on point instead of her. Or Karta for switching their positions. Either way, it was clear his mind was no longer on the mission objectives. 'Won't she, doc?'[1]

---

1. *A traditional nickname for the squad medic in most guard units. Most aren't qualified doctors, of course, being trained simply in primary aid techniques designed to stabilise casualties long enough to get them back to a properly equipped aid station or chirurgical facility.*

'Sure she will,' the medic said, the doubt in his voice obvious to everyone but Vorhees. 'Stick in an augmetic lung and a new liver, she'll be good as new.'

Provided we got her back in time. I hesitated. Our mission was far from over, but we'd seen no sign of any ork presence in these tunnels, and the greenskins weren't exactly subtle. Come to that, they wouldn't have left any ambulls alive down here either. Chances were the tunnel system was fully secure, and there was nothing more to be gained by completing the sweep.

On the other hand, I haven't made it through to my second century by being complacent. We needed to be certain the orks didn't know the tunnels were here, and even the slightest doubt could fatally undermine our plans for the defence of the refinery. But that certainty could only be bought with time; time Drere clearly didn't have if we were going to get her back in time to save her life.

I hate choices like that. There are no good outcomes, all you can do is pick what seems to be the least bad, and so I dithered. The certainty of safety, or the potential loss of my carefully nurtured image as a leader who cared about the troopers he serves with? The illusion that I was one of them had saved my life many times as they repaid the loyalty they believed I held for them.

It was Jurgen who broke the deadlock in my vacillating mind. As instructed, he'd stuck close to Logash, who, predictably, was ignoring the carnage around him. He was now pottering around the chamber waving his auspex about and digging chunks of ice out of the walls with his augmetic fingers for reasons entirely beyond me.

'Commissar. You'd better take a look at this.' As usual my aide's voice betrayed no excitement, but I knew him well enough to recognise the undercurrent of urgency in his tone. I walked over to the corner where the tech-priest was crouched, grubbing in the ice like a holidaying infant in the coastal sand.

'What have you found?' I asked, then got a good look over Logash's shoulder and wished I hadn't.

'It appears to be a midden,' he said, his voice curiously like a juve comparing scrumball statistics. He picked up a fragment of bone, which looked uncomfortably human in origin.

'A what?' Jurgen asked, his brow furrowing.

'A spoil heap,' Logash explained. 'Ambulls are quite organised, disposing of their waste in a specific part of the den...' I took a step backwards as it occurred to me just what the discolorations in the ice that he was so blithely digging through consisted of. The tech-priest prattled on. 'With proper analysis we should be able to determine what they were eating...'

'We know what they were eating. The miners.' Grifen came over to join us, and lowered her voice. 'Drere's in a bad way, commissar. Do we go on, or go back?' It was clear which alternative she preferred.

'I doubt that would have represented a sufficient food source,' Logash said, still digging, absently responding to the only part of her remark which interested him. He began to work something large out of the ice. 'What have we here?'

'It's a skull,' Jurgen responded helpfully, unable to identify a rhetorical question if one sat up and bit him. I glanced at it, idly wondering which of the luckless miners this was, then froze as something about the shape triggered warning bells in my mind. The cranium was low browed and heavy, the jaw prothogonous, and as Logash brushed the obscuring ice away jutting tusks became visible protruding from the lower mandible.

'From an ork,' I added unnecessarily.

So I had my answer. Whether or not the greenskins were aware of it, there was a way down into this labyrinth somewhere beyond their lines, and any other choice I might have made was now moot. I turned back to Grifen.

'We go on,' I said.

SEVEN

THE NEXT DECISION I had to make was the all-important one of how best to maintain morale. I didn't think any of the troopers would actively defy a commissar, even Vorhees, whose concern for Drere looked like outweighing pretty much every other consideration, but simply abandoning our wounded wasn't going to be an option. It would leave everyone demoralised, wondering if they'd be the next to be left to die.

That's not a thought you want your troopers to start brooding on. It makes them jumpy and sloppy, and the next thing you know they're so concerned with preserving their own skins they're losing focus on the important stuff: fulfilling the mission objectives, and preserving mine.

I made a big show of consulting Logash where everyone could hear me.

'Are we likely to run into any more of these creatures?' I asked. He frowned uncertainly.

'Possibly,' he said at last. 'But I doubt it. We seem to have a breeding pair and their offspring here, and given the average size of a family group...'

'I'll take that as a no,' I said firmly, cutting him off before he could bog us all down in extraneous detail. 'Which means we can safely divide our forces.' As I'd expected, a flicker of interest passed around the faces surrounding me, except of course for Drere and the medic, who were too busy bleeding to take much notice. And Jurgen, who rarely showed much sign of interest in anything apart from porno slates.

'Divide how?' Grifen asked. I indicated the wounded, and Vorhees hovering anxiously over his recumbent girlfriend.

'Second team's down to three effectives, and it'll take two of those to carry Drere,' I said. Vorhees's head came up like a hound hearing a ration pack being opened, a spark of hope kindling in his eyes. 'That'll leave one to take point, and pick off any of the creatures we might have missed.' Grifen nodded, understanding and relief mingled in the gesture.

'You're sending them back,' she said, a statement rather than a question. I nodded.

'The sooner the better,' I added, before turning to Karta. 'Better get moving, corporal. We're counting on you.' Not that I gave a frak, you understand, but it sounded good, and it passed the buck nicely; if anyone died before making it to the medicae at least it was out of my hands now. Karta saluted.

'We'll make it,' he asserted, and peeled off to organise his people.

'Am I to understand we're moving on at half strength?' Logash asked, clearly wondering what in the warp I thought I was playing at. I indicated the skull he'd dug up.

'First team, Jurgen and I are,' I said. 'There's obviously a way down here from behind the ork lines, even if the greenskins haven't noticed it yet, and we're not going back until we've found it and plugged the hole in our defences.' Needless to say I wasn't expecting to actually encounter any of the brutes, or run into anything else down here capable of harming us now that we'd slaughtered the ambulls, or I'd never have dreamed of doing such a thing. At the time, though, I was just trying to find a reasonable excuse to linger down here for a while and avoid the gargant.

'I see.' Logash considered it carefully, taking on that half-lost look again. 'Then I assume I should continue to accompany you.'

I hadn't actually considered it, to be honest. I'd have welcomed the chance to get rid of him if the thought had occurred to me, but on reflection he would only slow the wounded down if he tagged along with them, and I supposed his auspex might come in handy. All in all it was marginally preferable to keep him with us, I decided.

'I suppose so,' I said, leaving Jurgen to keep an eye on him, and turning back to watch the wounded depart. I had a final word with Karta, making sure Kasteen would hear about the ork skull we'd found and reinforce the mine entrance until we got back. Then we wished them the Emperor's speed and watched the bobbing lights from their luminators recede up the tunnel.

'Well,' Grifen said after a while, summing up what we all felt. 'Best get to it then. No point waiting around, is there?'

Despite my confidence that we were alone down here, we moved out in full combat order. Hail was on point, her lasgun held with the casual readiness of the veteran, and I found the sight reassuring. Simla followed her. The two of them worked well together, sharing an intuitive understanding which probably meant they had a personal association going as well; only to be expected in a mixed unit, of course. Behind him was Lunt, the squad heavy weapon specialist, who carried a flamer. That was something else I was pleased to find ahead of me rather than behind, although he had shown enough restraint to refrain from using it during the fight in the ambull den, relying instead on the laspistol he wore holstered at his belt.[1] (Just as well, really, as he'd probably have barbecued his squad mates as easily as the animals.) Tall and heavy-set, he carried the weight of his twin promethium tanks with ease, the liquid within them sloshing quietly as he walked.

I came next, along with Logash, Jurgen and Grifen, who kept a little behind us and as far from my aide as possible, while Trooper Magot, a small redheaded woman with disturbingly hard eyes, took up the rear. Out of the entire squad she was the only one to address Grifen as 'sarge' instead of 'sergeant,' and moved with the easy grace of an experienced soldier. (I learned later that they'd served together for some time, and she'd requested a transfer to Grifen's squad when her friend was promoted; beyond that I felt it prudent not to enquire.)

Despite everyone's unspoken apprehension we encountered no more of the ambulls, which came as an immense relief believe you me, and the only footfalls we heard were our own. Like everyone else, I kept my ears open for the harsh guttural sounds of ork voices and the crunch of iron-shod boots in the rime ahead of us, but the only noises to be heard were the almost subliminal creaks and pops of the slowly-shifting ice. We must have been moving for some time, I recall, as the vox messages from second team had faded to inaudibility by this

---

1. *Although not prescribed by regulations, many support weapon troopers and vehicle crews carry a back up sidearm in case they have to abandon their heavy equipment or it malfunctions in the heat of the battle. (Of course if a flamer malfunctions there isn't likely to be all that much left of the trooper carrying it, but Lunt was evidently an optimist.)*

point, when Logash stopped to examine the walls of the tunnel.

'How very curious,' he said.

'What is?' I asked, caution taking precedence over the surge of irritation I felt when his metallic elbow jabbed into my ribs as I stumbled into him. By way of reply he scraped a handful of ice from the wall. It crumbled, to reveal the dark grey surface of some kind of rock behind it, still grooved with the marks of the ambull's claws.

'We're below the ice layer. Actually down into the bedrock of the planet. Quite fascinating.'

'I'm glad you're finding the trip so entertaining,' I said, but the tech-priest was almost as impervious to sarcasm as Jurgen, and nodded in response.

'Not quite the word I'd choose, but it certainly beats recalibrating the interociters,' he said cheerfully. I had no idea what he meant, of course, so I smiled and suggested we get moving again. Unfortunately getting his legs going didn't slow down his mouth, and he prattled on about the underlying geology of the mountain range at inordinate length.

'Mountains are just there, aren't they?' Jurgen asked after some time had passed, blinking in befuddlement. Logash shook his head.

'To our limited perception of time, yes. But on a geo-logical timescale, which is to say on the order of millions of years, a planet's crust is as fluid as a pan full of stew on the stove.' Well he understood which metaphors would appeal to Jurgen, I had to give him that. 'The lower strata rise to the surface, and are gradually worn down again by the processes of erosion.'

'So what you're saying,' Jurgen said slowly, 'is that these mountains are like a very large carrot?' I kept my face straight with an effort, although a strangulated snort escaped from Magot who was behind me.

'In a manner of speaking.' Logash was clearly unsure whether Jurgen was taking the frak or not. 'Floating on the surface of the pot. A few million years ago this whole area would have been an open plain, or the bottom of an ocean.'

'How can you have an ocean when everything's frozen?' Jurgen asked, all innocence. But Logash nodded as though pleased with a promising student.

'A good question.' He went on after a moment's thought, ignoring my aide's expression of pleased surprise. 'In its early history this would have been a far more hospitable world. But it's just too far from the sun, and it cooled down gradually. Where we are now is on a continental shelf, which is why we've penetrated as far as the bedrock. The ice goes down for tens of kilometres just out from the mountain range, which would have been an island chain in those days. Or perhaps this was a coastal plain which flooded as the oceans froze and increased in volume.'[1]

'There's something up ahead,' Hail reported a moment later, and I hurried forward to join her, grateful for the excuse to get away from the endless babbling. That may sound harsh, but believe me, after several hours of nonstop logorrhoea you'd have felt the same. As I did so I felt the palms of my hands begin to tingle.

'What is it?' I asked, joining her. She was halted next to the entrance to a side tunnel and peering round it. The luminator taped to the barrel of her lasgun skipped its cone of light around the walls and floor.

That was when it hit me. Unlike the irregular ambull tunnels we'd been following, this corridor was squared off, composed of regular lines and angles beneath its coating of ice. There was no telling who might have built it, of course, or anything else for that matter, as the frozen epidermis effectively obscured every detail.

'Lunt,' I ordered after a moment's thought. 'Get up here.' The hulking trooper ambled across to us, and

---

1. *Almost certainly the latter, given Cain's subsequent discovery.*

aimed his flamer down the mysterious passageway, seeking a target. It stretched into the distance, swallowing our luminator beams as though they were the most tenuous of candle flames. After a moment he triggered the weapon, sending a gout of burning promethium down the corridor ahead of us, blasting the shadows from the corners and replacing them with flickering orange spectres. Steam hissed and water dripped from the walls as the pool of burning accelerant roared away on the floor, melting the ice around it.

The hairs on the back of my neck rose. It's an odd sensation, and one I've seldom felt. Grim memories from years before came flooding back as I recognised the obsidian architecture surrounding us, finely polished stone of absolute blackness seeming somehow to suck the light into itself, all the darker and more forbidding for the faint reflective sheen which coated it.

'Omnissiah preserve us,' Logash breathed at my elbow, and for a moment I thought he'd recognised it too. But the words that followed betrayed an ignorance that was almost blissful. 'We must make a full record of this at once. We had no idea that the planet was once inhabited...'

'Everyone out,' I commanded. 'Break out the demo charges and prepare to seal this now.'

'Commissar?' Grifen looked a little confused. I suppose she might have been forgiven for wondering if I'd gone a bit siggy[1], but by that point the last thing on my mind was how I appeared to the other ranks. 'Those are

---

1. *A colloquial reference to the Guard medicae sanitorium in the Sigma Pavonis system where troopers suffering from mental illness and combat fatigue are sent for assessment and rehabilitation. The less chronic cases are returned to duty after treatment, while the more severe ones can receive long-term care, sometimes for years. Co-incidentally, the system's other claim to fame is as a manufactoria of combat servitors, many of which find their way into Inquisitorial service.*

supposed to be used to seal the tunnels off from the orks.'

'There are worse things than greenskins,' I said. Grifen looked a little sceptical at this, what with the orks being the Valhallans' ancient blood enemy and all that (don't get me wrong, they'd happily pile into any of the Emperor's enemies who happened along, but give them a choice and they'd kill greenies every time), but took my word for it.

'Are you mad?' Logash raised his voice, clearly determined to challenge me. 'The knowledge contained in there could be priceless. We don't know why this structure was built, or by whom...'

'I do,' I said and pointed to one of the walls, where a curious arrangement of lines and circles was partially visible through a curtain of half-melted ice. It was illuminated by the dying flames of the promethium pool. 'The necrons built it.'

The name didn't mean anything to most of them, of course. Only Jurgen had encountered them before aside from myself, and that far less up close and personal than the terrors I'd escaped from on Interitus Prime. But the troopers seemed willing to take my word for it, at least. If only I could say the same for the tech-priest.

'But you can't just blow up a discovery of this magnitude!' Logash was practically beside himself. 'Think of the archeotech that must be down there! Destroying it would be a crime against the Omnissiah!'

'Frak the Omnissiah,' I said, finally shutting him up. 'I swore an oath to serve the Emperor, not a bucket of bolts, and that's exactly what I intend to do. Have you any idea what would happen if there are dormant necrons down there and we did something to disturb them?'

'I'm sure your soldiers could deal with them whatever they are,' Logash replied stiffly.

'Well I'm not,' I said without thinking. Then I remembered who else was there and carried on as though I'd meant to say more all along. 'I'd back this regiment against everything from eldar to daemons, but even the best soldiers in the Guard couldn't stand long against a full-scale necron incursion. These things aren't even alive as we understand the term. They can't be reasoned with, they can't be intimidated, and if they have the numbers on their side they simply can't be stopped. They'll just keep coming until every living thing on this planet is dead!' I was uncomfortably aware as I finished that my voice had risen in pitch. I fought it back to a semblance of calm.

'You're not being rational about this,' Logash said. 'If there were active necrons down here they would have killed the ambulls, surely?'

'Just for starters,' I said. My old nightmare of orks pouring through these narrow passageways bent on plunder and destruction seemed positively comforting now. I fought down memories of those blank metallic faces, fashioned in the semblance of skulls, advancing through a hail of hellgun fire as though it were a refreshing spring rain, and shuddered in horror. Logash might have a point, I supposed, the temple or whatever it was might well be abandoned, but then we'd thought that on Interitus Prime as well. And look how that had turned out. Entering so unhallowed a place was simply too dangerous to contemplate, and if Logash and his pals were that keen to take such an insane risk they could damn well do it once the orks were taken care of and we were long gone.

Not that I intended waiting around on this iceball until we'd got rid of the greenskins. Finding a necron artifact changed everything, and our best course of action was simply to evacuate our forces back to the *Pure of Heart*, turn the whole matter over to the Inquisition, and have done with it. I might even get to renew my acquaintance with Amberley, which would at least be one blessing in the affair – assuming she didn't drag me off on another suicidal escapade in the name of the Ordo Xenos of course.

Grifen didn't need telling twice, and was already breaking out the demo charges. Once again my undeserved reputation was working to my advantage, and she no doubt thought that anything bad enough to leave a hero of the Imperium in need of clean undergarments was something she didn't want to meet.

'You can't do this! I simply won't let you!' Logash practically screamed like a petulant child as Simla and Hail placed the charges. He stepped forward as if to interfere. Jurgen barred his way with the melta, and shook his head.

'Best to keep out of the way, sir,' he said. Logash raised a hand to the barrel, as though about to slap it out of the way. I was suddenly uneasily aware of how much strength he might have in his augmetic limbs, and Emperor alone knew what other little alterations the baggy robe might conceal. I stepped forward, ostentatiously loosening the laspistol in the holster at my belt.

'Might I remind you,' I said levelly, 'that this world is currently under martial law. That means you're as subject to my authority as any member of the Guard, and I'm fully within my rights to deal summarily with any attempt to interfere with the protection of this installation.' He took my meaning at once, but with ill grace, and subsided. He glared at me with an expression of malevolent disgust completely at odds with the demeanor of cheerful idiocy I'd come to expect. I suppose I might have found it intimidating if I hadn't been glared at by experts in my time (and trust me, until you've hacked off a daemon you've got no idea of what a real glare is), so I returned his gaze levelly until he broke eye contact.

'Typical meatbag[1] behaviour,' he sneered, failing miserably to regain any dignity. 'Just trample on anything

---

1. *A derisive Adeptus Mechanicus slang term for the unaugmented, who they hold in noticeable contempt. Which, to be fair, is generally reciprocated.*

you don't understand. You're no better than the orks.'
Considering he was surrounded by heavily armed Valhallans it wasn't exactly the most tactful thing he might
have said, but to their credit the troopers continued
working with undiminished efficiency, merely breaking
off for a second to stare sullenly at him. He must have
realised he'd overstepped the mark, though, because he
was quiet after that, apart from occasional barely audible
mutterings about meatbag barbarians.

'If it's any consolation,' I reassured him, 'we're not
destroying anything.' Not from choice, mind, but if the
necron architecture I'd come across before was anything
to go by the strange black stone would simply be too
resilient to be seriously damaged by the meagre quantities of explosive we had at our disposal. 'We're merely
sealing it off as a precaution. Once the refinery's safe you
can grub around down here to your heart's content.' Just
so long as I was at least a sector away by that point.
Logash still looked sulky, but slightly mollified.

'Fire in the hole!' Magot bellowed, with rather too
much relish for my liking, and we retreated to what I
hoped would be a safe distance before she hit the deto-
nator.

The explosion was satisfactorily loud, bringing down a
chunk of the corridor ceiling, which proved to be composed of cubical blocks of the strange black stone
roughly the length of my forearm. They tumbled down
in disarray, followed by chunks of ice and bedrock that
formed a solid-looking seal over the mouth of the corridor, reducing the ambull run we'd been following, to
half its original width for a dozen paces or so.

'Shady!' Magot said, with evident satisfaction. 'I'd like
to see anything get past that.'

'No you wouldn't,' I said. Solid as the blockage
seemed, if there really were necrons beyond it they
wouldn't take long to dig their way out. Those metal
bodies were tireless and implacable, their weapons and

equipment so powerful they made the most sophisti-
cated toys of the Adeptus Mechanicus look like
sharpened sticks. I forced the image of ancient horrors
out of my mind again.

'Well if that was the way the ambulls got an ork down
here it's pretty well sealed,' Grifen said. I nodded. It
seemed likely, but I supposed we had to be sure. With an
effort I dragged my mind back to the mission at hand.

'We'll make a final sweep and head back,' I decided, to
everyone's relief. 'We have to report this. It takes priority
over everything.'

'Commissar!' Simla called, from the other side of the
spoil heap. 'Take a look at this!'

Cursing, I rounded the pile of rubble, homing in on
the light from his luminator to find the sharp-featured
trooper crouching over something metallic which had
evidently been frozen into the floor of the tunnel and
dislodged by the explosion. A crudely made bolter of
some kind, the barrel sheared off by what looked like
claw marks.

'An ork shoota,' I said unnecessarily. 'It must have been
dropped by the one the ambulls killed while they were
dragging it back to the den.' Simla nodded.

'So it must have come from further up the tunnel.'

Great. The hole in our defenses was still wide open. I
dithered for a moment, but in the end there was really
no other choice. The necron threat, though terrible, was
only a potential one, and had been contained for the
time being. But the orks remained a clear and present
danger, and would do so until we'd completed our mission. Slowly and reluctantly I stood.

'Sergeant!' I called. 'Move them out. We're going on.'

Editorial Note:

Again I must apologise for inflicting another example of Sulla's overly purple prose on my patient readers (except for those of you who, quite understandably, may choose to skip it.) I do so because events were still moving along on the surface of the planet even as Cain made his disturbing discovery in the depths of the mine. And, as before I feel it important to present a little more background detail than Cain's typically self-centred narrative provides.

We pick up her account of events at a point where her platoon had been rotated back from the front lines for rest and recuperation, after taking a number of casualties while repelling a series of increasingly determined ork assaults.

Extracted from *Like a Phoenix From the Flames: The Founding of the 597th*, by General Jenit Sulla (retired), 097.M42.

I'M PROUD TO say that despite the loss of so many gallant comrades in arms, whose sacrifice will ever be remembered,[1] our morale remained high and our determination resolute. Though the greenskins were undeniably a nuisance, we had sent them packing on every occasion they troubled us, and it was almost with a sense of reluctance that we pulled back from our beleaguered redoubt and gave it into the care of Lieutenant Faril and the eager warriors under his command.

Wiser heads than ours had made the decision to relieve us, however, so there was no point in appealing it, and so we picked up our wounded and joined the trickle of tired but still resolute soldiery and headed back to the main refinery complex for a hot meal and a few hours of sleep. We were secure in the knowledge that the fray was far from over and that we would shortly once again have our chance to wreak the Emperor's vengeance on the greenskin barbarians who had had the effrontery to encroach on His sacred dominions.

As we trudged through the snow the sky above us was bright with the trails of the shuttles from our sturdy transport ship, and I reflected how beneficent fate, or the guidance of His Glorious Majesty, had so arranged matters that even now, as we faced and bested His bestial foes, His loyal subjects were being taken to the safety which our doughty vessel afforded. Indeed, the truth of the soldier's maxim, 'The Emperor Protects,' had seldom been made manifest to me with such crystal clarity.

It was while I was reflecting thus, and enjoying an unexpectedly lavish meal of the soylens viridians which the tech-priests who ran this palace of wonders had so generously provided from their own resources, that Colonel Kasteen summoned me to the command centre.

---

1. *Though not, apparently, their names, as she doesn't bother to record them.*

Upon my arrival my attention was immediately seized by the hololithic display, which the colonel was consulting along with Major Broklaw, Captain Federer of the engineering contingent, and a civilian I was given to understand had something to do with the mining operation here.[1]

As I listened to the plan which the colonel began to unfold, I was stunned by its boldness and elegance. For it was nothing less than to lure the loathsome greenskins into a trap which would surely annihilate both them and their awesome engine of war which, even as we spoke, was edging ever nearer. How fitting it seemed to use the creatures' impetuosity and overconfidence to lure them to their own destruction!

As I considered the plan in detail the keen intelligence behind the order to pull my platoon back became instantly apparent to me. By replacing the weary units at the front with fewer numbers of fresh soldiers our forces could maintain the illusion of remaining at full strength, at least for the few hours necessary to prepare our trap, while we could continue to gradually reduce the number of defenders. When the time came we could easily pull the remainder back to lure our enemies in, covering our own forces' retreat from our positions on either side, and catching the orks in a withering crossfire which ought to distract them for long enough to detonate the mine.

From the sombreness of Colonel Kasteen's demeanour I had expected to be given the honour of acting as the lure in this most cunning of stratagems, but it seemed even greater glory was to be ours. The colonel explained that within the hour she had received a message from the gallant Commissar Cain, who even as she spoke was continuing his heroic reconnaissance of the lowest levels of

---

1. *Undoubtedly Morel.*

the mine, to the disturbing effect that it was possible the greenskins had found a way into the tunnels. Though all were confident that a hero of his stature would easily repel any of the bestial foe incautious enough to venture there, it was felt necessary to provide an armed escort for the sappers and miners who were to prepare our trap; and since Second Squad of my own platoon had ventured into those very tunnels no more than a day before, with the commissar himself, we were the obvious choice for this vital assignment.

I must own up to it, my breast swelled with pride as I contemplated the honour of the task with which we had been entrusted, and assured the colonel that we would indeed prove worthy of her confidence.

EIGHT

NEEDLESS TO SAY the decision to continue our assignment was far from universally popular, although no one apart from Logash voiced any dissent. Grifen and her team were professional enough to understand the necessity of ensuring the safety of our comrades, not to mention ourselves, and so we pushed on in uneasy silence. The only sounds were the crunching of our boot soles in the thick frost that still coated the tunnel floor and the tech-priest's *sotto voce* imprecations. Besides which, no one in our party could have been more reluctant to proceed than me, you can depend on it. Every instinct of self-preservation I possessed urged me to flee the caverns at once, and find some excuse to board the first shuttle back to the relative safety of the *Pure of Heart*.

'Commissar?' Jurgen asked, and I suddenly became aware that I was murmuring one of the Catechisms of Command under my breath, something I swear I'd never done consciously since leaving the schola. Just goes to show how spooked I was.

'Nothing,' I said hastily, hawking a gob of rapidly cooling phlegm into the encircling darkness. 'Just clearing my throat.'

'Oh. Right.' He nodded, in his usual imperturbable fashion, and walked on, melta held ready across his body. Logash gave me a nasty look.

'"Fear is the mind killer," eh?' he asked, which at least told me his hearing was preternaturally augmented. 'I think you've already proved that today.' I could hardly believe it: here we were, caught between two of the nastiest foes you could ever hope not to meet, and he was still sulking about not being allowed to loot the bloody tomb.

'At least I've still got enough of a mind to know I ought to be scared,' I snapped back. We glared at each other like pre-schola juves whose vocabulary is too limited to prolong an exchange of verbal abuse, and for all I knew we'd have descended to shoving and finger-poking if Hail hadn't cut in on my comm-bead.

'I can see light up ahead.'

A shiver of apprehension shot through me. We were still deeply underground, and although the tunnel floor had been rising gently for the last couple of kilometres my natural affinity for these conditions told me we should be nowhere near the surface.

'Hold position,' I ordered, my irritation with the truculent tech-priest already forgotten, and hurried forward to join her. Jurgen's familiar odour followed, and we overtook Lunt and Simla. The big heavy weapons specialist watched as we passed, and began to ready his flamer, which now we were in front it was rather less comforting than his show of initiative might otherwise have been.

As we approached Hail's position I clicked off my luminator, and a moment later Jurgen did the same. As was my habit I closed my eyes as we did so, knowing my dark vision would adjust a little faster, for such things can mean life or death in these situations and all too often do. To my relief Hail had doused her own light, either from training or common sense, so there was nothing to impede my perceptions as I moved up to join her.

'Over here, sir.' The whisper came from one of the deeper shadows, into which the woman had blended almost invisibly. Her skin was very dark, almost the colour of recaf, and she used this natural advantage to the fullest.[1] As she moved her silhouette came into focus, backlit by a soft, greyish radiance from somewhere further down the tunnel. I sighed with relief. I'd been dreading the sight of the sick, greenish glow which had permeated the necron tomb I'd penetrated before, and the realisation that whatever we were coming to had nothing to do with them hit me with an intensity akin to euphoria.

'Any sign of movement?' I asked, and Hail shook her head, a barely-visible motion in the darkness which I sensed as much as saw.

'Nothing yet,' she said.

'Good.' I stood still for a moment, letting my tunnel rat's senses attune to this change in our environment. As my eyes adjusted fully the pale glow seemed to strengthen, a faint, irregular disc about the size of my thumbnail throwing the darker stone around it into stark relief. And there was a faint current of air on my face too, sharp with the smell of cold and heavy with damp. Impossible as it seemed, it looked very much

---

1. *This was extremely unusual for a Valhallan; perhaps as a result of living underground they generally tend to the lightest of complexions. Hail's colouration is the norm on many other worlds in the sector, however, where the white skin typical of her homeworld would seem equally unusual, so it's probable that an ancestor or two of hers settled there after relocating for some reason.*

like a fissure to the surface. 'I think this is it,' I concluded.

'Surely we're far too far underground?' Logash queried at my elbow. Lost in my reverie I hadn't noticed him tagging along, and I started momentarily, to his unconcealed amusement.

'Could be the bottom of a crevasse,' Jurgen volunteered. It sounded plausible to me, and he had grown up on a world like this, so I nodded.

'That would explain our dead ork,' I said. 'It just fell down into the tunnels here.' Maybe the fall had killed it and the ambull who brought it home just got lucky, although in my experience it would take more than dropping a few hundred metres down a hole to finish off a greenskin for sure, especially if it landed on its head.

'So this whole expedition has been a colossal waste of time,' Logash concluded. I shook my head.

'Far from it. If one ork found the hole, others could, and they can climb down a rope just as easily as any other species.' That's not entirely true, of course, they're clumsy brutes at the best of times, but they're determined and resilient, and sometimes that's enough.

'Best go on and check it out then,' Hail said, more for the pleasure of contradicting the tech-priest than supporting me I suspected, but the display of solidarity was welcome nevertheless.

'I think so,' I said, and moved on, the others taking up their positions around me as we continued on towards the gradually intensifying glow. As we got closer the faint current of air grew stronger, and the almost tolerable low temperatures of the tunnels began to drop rapidly, so that I found myself shivering again even through the thick weave of my greatcoat.

'Smells like snow,' Grifen said cautiously. 'We must be getting close.' I was prepared to take her word for it, after all she knew snow and ice the way I did tunnels. I was mildly surprised to see even the stoic Valhallan pulling her greatcoat just a little tighter. If I could trust her instincts as strongly as I believed, that didn't augar well.

In the event we were even closer than we realised. We turned a corner, skirting an outcrop of some deeply-veined rock I didn't bother listening to Logash identify, and the full force of the blood-chilling cold I'd experienced after the shuttle crash hit me in the face along with a weak shaft of sunlight which seemed almost dazzling after the gloom of the tunnels.

'Emperor's bowels!' I said, pulling my scarf up over my mouth and nose, feeling sharp shards of pain skitter through my abused lungs. Somehow, incredibly, the ambull tunnel had broken the surface, hundreds of metres deeper than should have been possible. But we were undeniably outside again.

'Interesting,' Logash said, not even shivering, Emperor rot his augmented hide. Snow whirled in around us, stinging our eyes, and obscuring everything in front of us from sight. He pondered for a moment. 'Perhaps a small valley, cutting into the mountains...'

I considered it, overlaying a rough estimate of our position on the orbital images I'd seen in the *Pure of Heart's* hololithic bridge display. It was perfectly possible that we'd come right through the heart of the ridge forming one of the sides of the valley protecting the refinery complex, and found ourselves at the bottom of a defile of some kind that cut into it from the other side.

If so, that was both good and bad news. Bad in that there was indeed a way through the tunnels which breached our defences, but on the plus side we would be a long way from the main body of the besieging orks. The only ones this far down the other side of the ridge would be stragglers or scouting parties like the one we'd encountered before.

Even shivering as I already was, the thought was enough to send an additional chill through me. There was no telling how many such groups had struck out ahead of the main advance,[1] and if one had already discovered the tunnel entrance and reported back the entire army could be on its way to take advantage of it. Well, perhaps not that many, but a large enough force to cause us some real problems if they got loose behind our defensive line. (Not that it was going to hold for a second once the gargant arrived, of course, so I was just having to thumb my palm[2] that Kasteen had come up with some strategy to deal with it while we were running around in the tunnels.)

'Tracks.' Magot was kneeling on the ice a few metres back from the curtain of whirling snow, staring at it intensely. I couldn't see a thing myself, but once again I found myself putting my full confidence in the Valhallans' natural affinity for these dreadful conditions. Grifen moved to join her, squatting beside her friend.

'Looks like,' she agreed. 'Ork boots, I'd say.'

'How many?' I managed to ask, through the muffling scarf and my rapidly numbing facial muscles. Magot shrugged.

'One pair?' She didn't sound terribly sure. 'The floor's chewed up around here something awful.'

'One ork,' Logash confirmed, scanning the floor with his metal eyes, a hint of impatience entering his voice. 'And ambull tracks. The greenskin must have wandered in, disturbed it, and ended up as lunch.'

'Only one ork?' I asked. 'You're absolutely sure?'

---

1. *Not that many, in all likelihood. 'Kommandos' as they're known (a loan word from some human culture according to the Ordo Diologus, as orks aren't able to conceptualise anything to do with subtlety for themselves) are quite rare among the greenskin forces. Most lack the patience or, to be blunt, intelligence for anything other than a brute force frontal attack. Which makes these occasional exceptions a danger out of all proportion to their limited numbers, as they generally succeed in taking their targets completely by surprise.*

2. *A good luck gesture Cain appeared to have retained from his early childhood, wherever that was actually spent.*

'Of course,' Logash said. 'It's completely clear to anyone with the right eyes to see these things.' Normally I'd have found the hint of the typical tech-priest arrogance returning to his voice irritating, I admit, but at the time it almost came as a relief. I assumed it meant he was getting over his sulkiness. But I had more pressing concerns to consider.

'Then what happened to the others?' I wondered aloud. Orks were obnoxious and quarrelsome, but they were curiously sociable in their own brutal fashion, and our solitary ambull victim wouldn't have been out here alone. True, his friends wouldn't waste all that much time looking for him once they noticed he was missing, but they might still be in the vicinity. And that meant they could stumble in here just as easily as their erstwhile companion.

'A good question,' Logash conceded. 'I suppose you'll want to scout around and make sure there are no more of them outside?'

Well actually that was the last thing I wanted to do, but it was necessary, and I couldn't back down in front of the troopers now that someone had verbalised the thought, so I nodded.

'It's the only way to be sure,' I agreed, managing to conceal my reluctance tolerably well I believed. I was not quite sure whether I detected the ghost of a vindictive smile on the tech-priest's face.

Conditions outside were even worse than I could possibly have imagined. The snow continued to flurry all around us, driven by a wind keener than an eldar wych's flensing knife, and I found my eyes shutting reflexively before I was a handful of paces from the cave mouth. With a thrill of panic I realised I couldn't open them again: the wind-driven tears had frozen on my face and sealed them closed. I was just about to give way to the impulse to retrace my steps (a sure way of stumbling to my death down a crevasse or terminal hypothermia away from the vigilance of my companions), when a reassuring arm settled across my shoulders. I inhaled Jurgen's acrid odour gratefully, as though it were the bouquet of a fine vintage, mildly surprised to find that my nose was still working.

'Hold on, commissar.' Something settled across my face, and the stinging in my eyes abated a little. I blinked them clear, forcing them stickily apart, feeling the partially-melted ice crystals slither round the corners of my eye sockets. Jurgen's face came blearily into focus, the portion of it between his scarf and thick fur hat obscured by a pair of snow goggles identical to the ones I now realised were protecting my own sight. 'That should do it.'

'Thank you Jurgen,' I managed to force out through practically immobilised face muscles. His scarf twitched as though concealing a smile.

'Lucky I usually carry a spare.' That was the closest he would ever come to uttering a reproof, but he had every right to do so of course. The goggles were standard kit in a Valhallan regiment, and I had a pair of my own packed away somewhere in my quarters, but it had never occurred to me I might need them in the depths of the mine where whiteout conditions weren't exactly common. So once again I had cause to thank the Emperor for my aide's streak of thoroughness.

To my complete lack of surprise every trooper in first team had donned a pair as well, but, like Jurgen, these conditions were common to them. Warp it, judging by their body language, most of them were actually enjoying these hellish temperatures.

'Chill enough for you, sir?' Magot asked cheerfully, seemingly genuinely unaware of just how intolerable I was finding it.

'Wouldn't mind a pot of tanna about now,' I conceded, deciding the best approach was game but suffering a little more than I was willing to admit (rather than a hell of a lot more.) That way they'd keep a closer eye on me without resenting it.

'Wouldn't mind a brew myself,' she admitted, before trotting away to take her turn on point.

'This is all a complete waste of time you know,' Logash grumbled. I swear I would have missed him entirely if he hadn't spoken: his white robe was almost invisible in the swirling snow, and only his pale face and metallic eyes appeared wholly in focus. He appeared to hang in the air in front of me like an extreme version of Mazarin's levitation act. 'If there were any more orks around they'll be kilometres away by now. Or frozen to death.'

He was a fine one to talk, I thought, barely even seeming to notice the sub-zero temperatures. Once again I found myself wondering precisely what that robe concealed.

'They're a lot more resilient than you might think,' I pointed out, and Lunt nodded in passing.

'My grandfather found one frozen in a glacier once, back home, left over from the invasions. When they got it back to their camp and thawed it out it came back to life and tried to kill them. It's true, that's what he said.'

Him and every other Valhallan's grandfather, of course, 'The ork in the ice' is one of the most popular folktales on the planet, but I doubted that Logash would know that, so I nodded confirmation.[1]

'So I'd keep looking over my shoulder if I were you,' I added. I can't be sure, but I think Lunt winked at me, enjoying winding up the outsider and treating me as if I was Valhallan myself. Of course I've spent so much of my career

---

1. *And like many folk tales, there may be an element of truth to it. Although there's no way to be sure, there are still occasional reports of solitary orks being sighted in the Valhallan wilderness, sometimes even backed up by bodies. Chances are these are just corpses left over from the invasion preserved by the cold, but you can never take anything for granted where these creatures are concerned.*

serving with them I often find that I've picked up something of their speech patterns, dietary preferences, and so on. I suppose it's not all that surprising that they seem to have adopted me as one of their own in many ways[1].

'We're in a defile, all right,' Grifen told me, glancing around at the barely visible topography. 'You can tell by the pattern of the snowflakes.' They just looked like a swirling wall of white to me, but I nodded as though I understood. I didn't actually need to know, of course: one of the most important principles of leadership is knowing when to rely on the judgement of your subordinates. But it's always a good idea to look interested.

'Can you tell which way the orks would have gone?' I asked. She nodded.

'They won't have left any tracks we can follow in this blizzard, but that way,' she gestured in what looked to me like a random direction, 'is closed off by the head of the valley. My best guess would be downslope.'

'Fair enough,' I decided. 'We'll check as far as the mouth of the defile. If there are any greenskins out here we'll find them. If not we can pull back and collapse the cave behind us.'

'That might be difficult,' she pointed out. 'We used most of our demo charges to seal the... whatever it was back down the passage.'

'We'll think of something,' I said, with more confidence than I felt. The constant swirling of the snow was making me feel vaguely nauseous, the cold was cramping my stomach muscles painfully, and my head felt as though someone was squeezing it in a vice. The sooner we got this over with the better. 'Jurgen's still got the melta, and I'm sure our cogboy friend will be able to point out a few weak spots in the ceiling.'

---

1. *Actually, given the relationship between most commissars and the troops they serve with, this is pretty remarkable. As so often in his memoirs, Cain gives himself far too little credit for his own achievements.*

'I suppose you're right,' the sergeant said, and I glanced around, expecting some response from Logash, but the surly young tech-priest had vanished into the storm as thoroughly as though he'd never even existed.

NINE

'WE'RE GOING TO have to search for him,' I said, resenting every extra second that was going to mean staying out in the bitter cold. For good measure I filled my lungs with the burning air, and called the tech-priest's name as loudly as I could. To no avail, of course, as the screaming wind and the muffling snow combined to stifle all but the loudest noise. Fortunately, I had more than my own lungpower to call on, as the comm-bead in my ear was still tuned to the general squad frequency, and I lost no further time in appraising everyone else of the problem.

'We've lost the tech-priest,' I broadcast, suppressing the impulse to add a number of qualifying adjectives. 'Anyone seen him?'

To my complete lack of surprise a chorus of negatives was the only response.

'At least it'll be quieter on the way back,' Magot added, with rather more candour than tact. That was hardly the point, though, however much I might have agreed with her.

'Complete the sweep,' Grifen ordered, with just enough emphasis to discourage any more flippancy, and the troopers responded, sounding off in turn with a noticeable lack of enthusiasm. She turned back to me. 'If he's ahead of us we'll run into him. And if he's behind we should pick him up on the way back.'

I have to admit to feeling rather less sanguine on that point than she seemed to be. He was, after all, effectively invisible to us in the swirling snow, and I didn't think we stood a chance of finding him under these conditions in any way other than stumbling over him by accident. But if anyone could pick up his trail I supposed it would be the Valhallans, so I nodded in return.

'Better get moving then,' I said, echoing her words of a couple of hours before.

It wasn't that simple, of course. As I've already mentioned, the wind was sweeping up the defile, which was liberally strewn with grey, jagged rocks. These loomed up suddenly out of the swirling blanket of snow, promising a moment of respite from the razor-edged wind which, time and again, proved to be merely a delusion. The irregular topography simply broke the onrush of air into flurries and eddies which dashed handfuls of snow into these pockets of illusory shelter, adding a sudden unexpected lash of stinging ice crystals to an already miserable experience. The only consolation, if that was the right word, was that what little exposed skin I still had was completely numb by this time.

I slipped and slithered down the slope behind Grifen, grateful for the stolid presence of Jurgen behind me; several times he reached out a supporting hand just in time to prevent me from sprawling face down in the knee-deep snow. The Valhallans remained completely sure-footed, but any amusement they may have felt at my floundering progress was well concealed. Glancing back I could see that the furrows we'd left behind us were already beginning to fill with the ever-shifting drifts, and that without my companions' sure instinct for these ghastly conditions we would almost certainly never find the cave mouth again. That, at least, was something of a relief, as the chances of any greenskins stumbling across it were beginning to look reassuringly remote.

On the downside though, any tracks Logash had left would be obscured as completely as our own, so once again it seemed we weren't likely to stumble across him by any means other than sheer blind luck.

At least with all those augmetics I supposed he wasn't likely to freeze to death, in the short term at any rate, but right now I was beginning to think that was a very mixed blessing.

I had, by this time, lost sight of all my companions save for the reassuring presence of Jurgen, their camouflage greatcoats blending so perfectly into the snowstorm that they were effectively invisible. For that matter so was I; my dark commissar's uniform being so coated with the wind-driven flakes that I resembled one of those misshapen effigies children throughout the galaxy sculpt with the onset of winter. (On Valhalla, building snowmen is something of a cross between a serious art form and a competitive sport, with some quite astounding creations to marvel at, but that's beside the point.)

I was just on the verge of deciding that this was futile and ordering everyone to turn back, letting Logash take his chances with the elements as best he could, when Magot's voice crackled over my comm-bead.

'Contact, ninety metres down slope.' I could hardly see an arm's length in front of my own eyes, but she sounded confident enough. I was still trying to force my numb lips to form a reply when Grifen's voice cut into the net.

'Is it the cogboy?'

'Negative.' Magot's voice was tense. 'I can see a lot of movement down there.'

That could mean only one thing, of course, and I was already scrabbling for my laspistol with numb and nerveless fingers when she spoke again, confirming it.

'Greenies. Lots of them.'

'How many?' I asked, keeping hold of my weapon Emperor knows how, my fingers feeling thick and swollen in the cold. Luckily the augmetic ones were working as well as ever, at least enabling me to maintain my grip on the stock, but whether I'd be able to squeeze the trigger with my very real and probably frostbitten index finger would be problematic at best.[1]

'Hard to tell,' Magot replied. 'They're well spread out.' That was hardly surprising under the circumstances, the terrain being less than conducive to their normal habit of charging forward in a disorganized mob. 'But a dozen at least.'

'Contact.' Simla cut in too, and with a sudden thrill of horror I realised he was over to the left side of the defile, three hundred metres at least from Magot's position. No way he was seeing the same group. 'I've got seven. No, eight. Maybe more.'

'Me too,' Hail added, from our right flank. 'Looks like a full squad from here.'[2]

'Pull back,' I ordered. That made at least thirty, probably more, too many for us to take out here even with the Valhallans' ability to make use of the terrain and weather conditions to mount an effective ambush. It also confirmed my worst fear (apart from the thought that the

---

1. *Since Cain makes no subsequent mention of any medical treatment, we can infer that this is either exaggeration for effect or hypochondria rather than an accurate diagnosis.*

2. *Presumably meaning a group the size of an Imperial Guard squad, as ork mobs can vary greatly in size, and wouldn't recognise the concept of any formation as organised as this in any case.*

necrons were stirring down in the darkness beneath our feet.) The comrades of the dead ork we'd found had indeed made contact with the bulk of their army, and were on their way back with a full-scale raiding force intent on exploiting the gap they'd discovered in our defences. 'We have to secure the cave whatever happens.'

'Confirm that,' Grifen said, overriding whatever objections her subordinates might be on the verge of expressing. Not that I really expected any, but Valhallan antipathy to the greenskins ran deep, and the temptation to take a pot-shot at them before withdrawing must have been acute. To their credit no one gave way to it though, so I began to breathe a little more easily as we made our way back up the slope towards the welcome refuge of the cave. With any luck we'd be able to slip away before they even knew we were here.

I must confess that the thought of getting out of the bone-numbing wind was so strong, and so all-pervading, that I quite lost track of my surroundings. I stumbled through the snow like an automaton, following in the tracks ploughed by Jurgen, intent only on putting one leg in front of the other. The image of the tunnel mouth and the respite from the cold it represented loomed ever larger in my thoughts, driving out everything but the determination to keep my numbed and frozen limbs moving. So it was with a shock of genuine surprise that I heard the unmistakable report of a bolter round detonating against an outcrop of rock a few metres away.

Spurred by a sense of imminent danger I dropped out of my fugue state at once, bringing the laspistol in my hand around, seeking a target. A hulking shape loomed out of the snow, bounding forward with incredible speed, swinging a crudely-fashioned axe. So eager was it to spill my blood it seemed to have forgotten the primitive bolt pistol clutched in its other hand. I fired by reflex, finding that my panic-spurred finger was able to tighten on the trigger just fine now that the question was a practical one, blowing a hole through its torso. The creature staggered and came on, then dropped to the ground, already cooling, as a second las bolt took it from the side.

'Sergeant.' I acknowledged Grifen's assistance with a nod, and she gestured with her left hand, the right still holding her lasgun ready to fire.

'This way,' she said. I stumbled in her direction, sure that Jurgen would be with me as always, and in this I was soon proved correct. The unmistakable hiss of the melta opening up behind me made me turn, just in time to see my aide cut down a small group of the creatures that had evidently been following the first with a single ravening blast of thermal energy. After a moment spent scanning our surroundings he lowered the weapon and began slogging through the knee-high drifts towards us as implacably unconcerned as though he were out for an afternoon stroll. Maybe by the standards of his home-world he was.

'Up here, commissar.' Lunt reached down from atop a tangle of rocks, grasping my outstretched hand, and lifting me bodily to the top without any apparent effort. Grifen scrambled up after us, barely slowing down, and a moment later Jurgen heaved himself over the rim, the bulky weapon now slung to facilitate climbing, and preceded as always by his unmistakable odour.

'I thought this would be a good spot to regroup,' Grifen said. I glanced around, feeling almost warm now that we were partially sheltered from the relentless wind, and nodded approvingly. She'd chosen an elevated position surrounded by tumbled boulders, from which we could look down on the tunnel entrance from an elevation of a couple of metres or so. That was good thinking: if the orks had made it there ahead of us after all there was no sense in walking up to the cave mouth wearing a big sign saying 'shoot me I'm here.' As I strained my eyes through the whirling snow I wasn't able to discern much, but as

I've said before I'd trust her instincts where the green-skins were concerned.

Hail and Simla had made it to our refuge too, I was pleased to see, each raising a hand in greeting as Jurgen and I appeared before going back to scanning the horizon over the sights of their lasguns. I was just about to try contacting Magot and asking her position when a flurry of las-bolt detonations and a bellow of orkish pain somewhere off to our left answered that question quite satisfactorily. The diminutive redhead appeared in person a few moments later, grinning with malevolent amusement.

'There was this greenie over that way making a latrine stop,' she reported gleefully, 'so I shot him right up the...'

'Is it dead?' I interrupted. She nodded, still enjoying the approbation of her comrades, who seemed to think this was as hilarious as she did.

'Deader than Horus,' she confirmed. Good. Her tracks would have been all but obliterated by now, and with any luck the orks wouldn't have a clue where we were or how many of us they faced. Unless they found and interrogated Logash, of course, in which case it was credits to carrots they'd learn everything they needed to know in pretty short order. That left me with only one choice.

'We're pulling back to the cave as soon as we know it's clear,' I said. 'And prepare to collapse it behind us.'

'What about the tech-priest?' Grifen asked, clearly not terribly concerned, but sticking to the letter of her mission brief with admirable tenacity.

'He'll just have to fend for himself,' I said. Catching her look, I added 'I'll take the responsibility.' It went without saying, of course, that went with the scarlet sash.

'It's your call, commissar.' Well, she was right about that, but I could see abandoning a human to the mercy of the orks wasn't going to go down too well with the rank and file, even if he was an annoying little grox-fondler who'd brought it on himself, so I went all solemn.

'It goes against the grain I know,' I said. 'But our first duty is to the Emperor, the regiment, and our mission. The colonel has to know about the necron presence here. It changes everything, and until then the lives of all our comrades are at risk.'

Everyone nodded solemnly at that, apparently perfectly happy to hang the little tech-priest out to dry now I'd been able to make it seem like a noble sacrifice, and we prepared to move out.

As I glanced back down slope, straining my eyes through the swirling blanket of snow for some sign of another party of orks, I thought I caught a glimpse of something moving smoothly and silently through the frozen landscape. I inhaled, intending to call out, then dismissed the impulse as the blur of apparent motion vanished in the kaleidoscope of white. Chances were it was only wishful thinking on my part, I thought, and even if it was Logash he'd never hear me over the howling of the wind. Later, when I had the leisure to reflect on that moment, I was to shudder at how close I had probably come to dooming us all.

'It seems clear enough,' Grifen said, after a few more moments spent observing the cave entrance. So we moved cautiously towards it, putting our trust in the obscuring snow and what little concealment the rocks afforded. The troopers were well disciplined, I found, moving by stages as though we were already in combat, waiting until one of their comrades was in position to provide covering fire before moving to the next place of refuge. I did the same, falling into the rhythm with the instinct born of long practice.

At length we were ranged around the mouth of the cave. I stepped into it gratefully, feeling the barbed wind let go of my flesh, and gasping with the agony of returning circulation. For a moment or two my entire body felt

as though I'd been hit by a flamer, then the pain subsided from unbearable to merely excruciating. Even so
my survival instinct remained strong, and I was able to
override the discomfort for long enough to sweep the
tunnel before me with the beam of my luminator, keeping the barrel of my laspistol in line with it. (Under most
circumstances, of course, there's no better way to make a
target of yourself than that, but I was backlit by the tunnel mouth in any case so it wouldn't make any difference
to an assailant lurking in the dark. If anything I might
dazzle them for long enough to get a shot off.) As it happened there was nothing waiting to shoot me, and after
a second or two I relaxed.

'All clear,' I called, and Jurgen joined me at once, his
melta pointing away down the tunnel before us. Bearing
in mind what we'd have to pass to get back to our comrades that eased my mind as much as was possible under
the circumstances. I turned back to check on the rest of
the troopers, who had all taken up positions behind what
cover they could find in the immediate vicinity of the
cave mouth. Grifen turned to wave at me, from behind a
small boulder, and then froze at the unmistakable sound
of bolter fire crackling towards us on the wind.

'What the hell?' she asked, seemingly forgetting for a
moment that she was still broadcasting on the whole
squad net rather than the command channel. Lunt
grinned, readying his flamer.

'Sounds like a difference of opinion to me.' He could
have been right, of course, greenskins have a definite
propensity to settle disputes in the most basic of ways,
but the sheer volume of fire I could hear argued against
it. It sounded like a full-scale firefight to me. Well, good
if it was, the more of each other they slaughtered the better. On the other hand... I strained my ears for the sound
I most dreaded, the unmistakable ripping noise of a
necron gauss weapon, but if it was there to be heard it
was swallowed by the wind.

'Maybe they've found the cogboy,' Hail said slowly, clearly not relishing the idea. I nodded, sharing the same mental picture of the tech-priest fleeing blindly through the snow, howling greenskins in pursuit, firing their ramshackle weapons excitedly as they ran. That seemed unpleasantly plausible.

'Shouldn't we try to help him?' Simla asked. I shook my head, with as much reluctance as I could feign.

'I wish we could,' I lied. 'But we'll never get to him before they do. And unless we want his sacrifice to be in vain we have to report back what we've found.'

'The commissar's right,' Grifen said. 'Pull back, and prepare to blow the entrance.'

Before anyone could move, though, hulking silhouettes could be discerned through the swirling snow, charging towards us with the berserk fury of their kind. By some freak of the weather conditions the eddies of snow were lighter here, affording us an uncomfortably clear view of them as the visibility increased. Crude bolters barked, and chips of stone flew from the outcrops of stone surrounding the cave mouth. Grifen levelled her lasgun.

'Fire at will,' she said.

'Wait!' I ordered, an instant later, and thank the Emperor everyone had the presence of mind to obey. 'Just stay down and don't move!' It had suddenly struck me they weren't firing at us; the bulk of the bolter impacts were off to our left, and it seemed to me that they weren't charging the cave so much as fleeing towards it. And that, my tingling palms and a sudden spasm of the bowels told me, probably meant only one thing. The Valhallans froze, melting into the icy landscape in the way only they could, and even knowing where they were I found them hard to pick out.

A second later my worst suspicions were confirmed, as a vivid green beam, the colour of a festering wound, ripped through the air with the all too vividly remem-

bered sound of tearing cloth, striking one of the orks full
on. In less than a second he seemed to dissolve; skin,
muscle, and skeleton whipping away to vapour, leaving
only the echo of a howl of inhuman agony to mark his
passing.

'Emperor on Earth!' Grifen breathed, horror suffusing
her voice, and I have to admit to trembling with terror
myself. The beam swept on, transfixing another victim,
and was joined by another, then another.

The orks scattered, and began to fire back, a little more
accurately now that their assailants had so considerately
revealed their positions. The swirling snow parted,
revealing the sight I had so dreaded, and yet had dared
to hope I might be spared after collapsing the entrance to
the tomb: eerie metallic warriors, striding silently forward, their carapace sculpted to resemble skeletons.
These were surely death incarnate come to claim us all.

'So that's what they look like up close.' Jurgen, imperturbable as ever, his faith in the Emperor's protection
still absolute despite taking a bolt to the head on
Gravalax, raised the melta, sounding no more than
mildly curious. Then again, given some of the horrors
we'd faced together over the years, I suppose he just
thought it was business as usual. One thing I can say for
Jurgen, despite his unprepossessing appearance, he had
reserves of courage greater than any man I've ever met.
Either that, or he was just too stupid to understand the
magnitude of the dangers threatening us.[1] I raised a
hand to forestall him.

'Wait,' I breathed. 'Our only chance is to avoid being
seen.' That I could attest to from personal experience, my
natural propensity for running and hiding being the
only thing that had saved me on Interitus Prime when
everyone else had been slaughtered. To my relief Jurgen

---

1. *I must confess to remaining undecided about that myself, despite having
fought alongside him on a number of occasions.*

nodded, but kept the heavy weapon aimed, ready for use if it should prove necessary.

The orks had gone to ground by now, taking cover behind the nearest rocks, shooting back at the necron warriors with their usual lack of accuracy. Inevitably the sheer weight of firepower began to tell, however, a number of shells finding their targets regardless. As I'd seen before, the implacable metal warriors simply shrugged off the impacts, the detonations against their metal hides seeming to do no more than discolour whatever unholy alloy they were made of.

A few of the shots were more effective than the rest, though, more by luck than judgement. As we watched, one of the ork bolts detonated against the power pack attached to the weapon of the leading automaton, and an instant later an explosion ripped apart both the weapon and the necron carrying it.

At this the orks set up a great roar of triumph, and a few of the more incautious broke from cover to race forwards, apparently intent on tackling their gleaming metal assailants in hand to hand combat. Inevitably most died, ripped apart by the gauss flayers, but incredibly a couple closed the distance, swinging their crude, heavy axes as they did so.

One was unlucky, or too slow, his target turning with eerie precision to spit him on the combat blade mounted on the end of its weapon. Thick brackish blood poured from a gash which opened the creature from groin to shoulder blade, and the necron shook the eviscerated body from the end of its weapon with an air of weary disdain. The gutted ork fell heavily to the snow, where a slowly-spreading pool of blood began freezing into a thick, icy scab.

The other greenskin parried the blow aimed at it, and whirled around to strike at the necron's neck. Crudely-forged metal met aeon-old sorcery in a blinding flash of discharged energy, and the unliving warrior's head fell heavily to the snow. The ork's triumph was short-lived, however, as the concerted beams of the two surviving necrons ripped it to vapour in a heartbeat.

'Never thought I'd be rooting for the greenies,' Magot said quietly, sentiments I imagined we all shared. The surviving orks stood their ground with the brutish defiance of their kind, pouring inaccurate small arms fire into the area around the skeletal metallic figures, blowing gouts of snow and ice up around them for the most part, but still inflicting a number of hits which, for the first time, appeared to give the walking nightmares some pause for thought. More distant weapons fire could be heard over the wind now, speaking of other, equally desperate battles, and I allowed myself to feel a surge of hope.

'Everyone pull back,' I ordered quietly. 'Stay under cover. With any luck we can disengage while they're too busy to notice us.'

'Confirm that,' Grifen said, with heartfelt relief evident in her voice. The other troopers began to retreat deeper into the safety of the cave, crawling backwards for the most part, keeping their weapons trained on the unequal battle in front of us.

While the two necrons had concentrated their fire on the orks behind the boulders they'd maintained their position, a big mistake, as I would have been happy to point out if anyone had asked me. Orks are remarkably resilient creatures, driven purely by rage and aggression, so I was scarcely surprised when the one left sprawling in a sorbet of its own blood suddenly grabbed the ankle of its erstwhile assailant and yanked hard on it with all its feral strength. Mortally wounded as it was it clearly had no intention of dying with unfinished business left behind, and the necron fell heavily, its right shin now detached from its knee joint.

Bellowing in triumph the ork began belabouring the fallen warrior with the stump of its own leg, raising a

clangour like a peal of cathedral bells (if they were horribly out of tune) and inflicting a remarkable array of
dents on its torso and skull. I was under no illusion that
this would be enough to incapacitate the hideous thing,
though, so I was unsurprised when it swung its combat
blade around with the same unhurried precision I'd seen
before and sheared through the greenskin's neck. A brief
flicker of bewilderment seemed to enter the creature's
eyes as its head detached from its shoulders, with the
concomitant geyser of gore, and it slumped across the
battered metal torso of its murderer.

Abruptly the distant firing we'd heard since just before
we first saw the orks ceased, to be followed at once by a
howl of barbaric euphoria. It seemed that the main body
of the greenskin force had won their battle, though no
doubt at a terrible cost. (Not that it would bother them
in the slightest, of course, they're not a particularly senti-
mental species by any stretch of the imagination.) The
two necrons before us stopped moving abruptly, as
though listening to something, and then simply vanished, along with the remains of their fallen comrades.
No doubt their departure was marked by the same crack
of air rushing in to fill the sudden vacuum I'd noticed
when Amberley was teleported to safety by her displacer
field, but if so I was unable to hear it over the howling of
the wind.

'Emperor's bowels!' Grifen shook her head, clearly trying to comprehend what we'd just seen. 'Where did they
go?'

'Straight back to hell, I hope,' Magot said.

'Close enough,' I confirmed. Even now they'd be
reporting what they'd seen, and drawing up their plans
for a major incursion, I knew that for a stone cold certainty.

The remaining orks were emerging from cover now,
stamping about where the necrons had vanished, and
looting the bodies of their fallen companions. Guttural

expressions of surprise and confusion drifted towards us on the wind.

'What about the greenies?' Simla asked. I hesitated. They weren't our most urgent priority now, and with any luck would divert any necron attention from us as we scuttled back through the tunnels to warn Kasteen and the others. But then again they'd already found the mouth of the cave, and would be too close behind us for comfort if they felt the urge to do any exploring.

Abruptly the decision was taken out of my hands. The biggest ork in the group, who I took to be the leader,[1] pointed straight at the mouth of the tunnel and bellowed an order of some kind. With a last look back at the bodies of the fallen, half a dozen greenskins started moving towards us. I had no choice; the security of the mission, and more importantly myself, demanded it.

'Kill them all,' I ordered.

---

1. *Generally a safe assumption.*

TEN

THAT WAS AN order the Valhallans were eager to respond to, and they did so with alacrity, opening fire on the greenskins while they were still caught in the open. We took them by complete surprise, the first couple falling under a hail of lasfire before they even had a chance to react.

The others were quick, though, assessing the situation with remarkable acuity for such imbecilic creatures,[1] and scattering again to make themselves more difficult targets. A couple of them went to ground behind a tangle of rocks, and began to shoot back at us. Fortunately their marksmanship was no better than usual so they inflicted no casualties, but they managed to come close enough to make us take full advantage of our own cover, their bolts bursting uncomfortably close to our position. Some-

---

1. *Though brutal and primitive by the standards of other races, orks have an instinctive understanding of combat second to none.*

thing stung my cheek, and I wiped away a smear of blood where a chip of stone had caught me. That was too near for comfort and I retreated further into the darkness of the cave, bracing my laspistol against a convenient outcrop of rock to improve the accuracy of my retaliation.

Seeing that we were effectively suppressed the four remaining in the open ran forwards brandishing their blades and screaming at the top of their voices in the way that they do. As they closed with us they fired their hand weapons sporadically, without even bothering to aim, which made a lot of noise but had little practical effect other than making even more sure that we kept our heads down.

'Lunt!' I yelled. 'Take the ones in the rocks!'

'Commissar.' His acknowledgement was crisp as he raised the barrel of his flamer cautiously over the outcrop he was sheltering behind. I directed a flurry of lasbolts at the snipers, if the perpetrators of such inaccurate shooting could be dignified with such a term, and to my relief Hail and Simla followed my lead. Grifen and Magot concentrated their fire on the charging orks in front of us, slowing them momentarily as the big ork in front with the horns on his helmet[1] took a las-bolt to the knee. He stumbled, falling face down in the snow, and a couple of his subordinates tripped over him. For a moment the hail of incoming fire dwindled as the fallen greenskins flailed at one another, exchanging guttural profanities and blows which would have stunned a grox, before floundering to their feet again.

The delay was enough for Lunt, however; he rose to his full height, and directed a searing jet of burning promethium at the tangle of rocks which concealed the shooters. With a roar which sounded more like rage than

---

1. *A common symbol of authority among the greenskins, apparently meant to prove that they've overcome something even bigger and nastier than they are.*

pain the two orks burst out into the open, like living torches, charging towards our position. Four lasguns spat as one, targeting them as they moved and the trailing one fell, but the one in front just kept coming, wreathed in steam from the snow which evaporated about him, charred bone becoming visible through the sizzling flesh.

'Emperor's guts!' Lunt swung the barrel, trying to line up another shot, then fell back, an expression of pained surprise on his face as a bloody crater exploded in his chest. I swung my gaze back to the main group of orks, who were now on their feet again, their crude weapons kicking up a flurry of snow and debris around the fallen heavy weapons trooper. Typically for their kind they concentrated only on the most visible threat, ignoring the rest of us for the moment; a fatal mistake.

'Jurgen!' I ordered, gesturing to the group which was now close enough to be a target for the melta. Smiling grimly, my aide took careful aim, sighting directly at the limping leader, who was still snarling in triumph at the death of our fellow trooper. (I'd seen enough bolter wounds in my time to know that such a hit would have been instantly fatal, smashing through the flak armour beneath his greatcoat to detonate inside his ribcage. There was nothing to be done for Lunt now other than avenge his demise.) The heavy weapon hissed once more, flashing the intervening curtain of snow into vapour, and reducing the ork leader and the two standing next to him to a rank pile of gently steaming offal. The sole survivor turned, blinking in what looked like stunned stupefaction, its left arm hanging limp and charred from flash burns, then turned and bolted (which just goes to show that at least a few of them aren't as stupid as they look.)

I rose fully to my feet and took careful aim, bracing the laspistol in my hand across my left forearm as though I were on the firing range, and trying to still the trembling which seemed to have taken control of my body. Whether it was a delayed reaction to the terror the sight of the necrons had inspired in me, anger at Lunt's sudden and brutal death, or simply my abused body starting to respond to the relative rise in temperature I couldn't say, but I was grimly determined to slay the foul creature myself in spite of it. I squeezed the trigger, thankful for the steadiness my augmetic fingers imparted to my aim, and was rewarded with a gout of ichor from between the greenskin's shoulder blades. Grifen and Magot joined in as it stumbled, bellowing in pain, and between us we dispatched it like the beast it was.

It was only as I stood there, exhaling slowly as the tension eased from my aching body and the trembling gradually came under control, that I noticed the burning ork was still stumbling towards us, its steps faltering now as it staggered drunkenly to the left and the right, but still forging forward, fixated on reaching its tormentors. It was a ghastly sight to behold, I must admit, and I was on the verge of ordering the troopers to finish it off when it dropped abruptly to the ground in a gout of steam from the melting snow around it and at last lay still.

Silence descended, save for the relentless keening of the wind, and the rasping of my breath in my throat.

'Lunt?' Grifen asked, the flatness of her tone already answering her own question.

'Dead,' Hail confirmed, standing over his broken body, the spilled blood and viscera already glazed with ice. I forced myself to join her, looking down at the dead trooper, feeling I knew not what. (Other than my usual sense of profound relief that it wasn't me lying there, as it so easily could have been, of course.)

'He did his duty,' I said, the highest praise I could think of, and everyone nodded soberly. Grifen gestured to Hail and Simla.

'Bring him,' she said. 'We'll take turns.' I shook my head, conscious of how she must feel losing a trooper under her command for the first time. It never gets easy, I can tell you that, but after a while you learn to accept it. Despite what they say, the Emperor can't protect everyone, which is why I take such good care to do the job myself.

'I wish we could,' I said, as gently as I could manage. 'But we don't have the time. We have to get back as fast as possible.' I half expected her to argue, but she nodded, reluctantly.

'We'll come back for him later then,' she said. I shook my head again.

'I'm afraid we can't,' I said, explaining as tactfully as I could. I was suddenly aware of four pairs of eyes boring into me. (Jurgen, of course, would simply go along with whatever I said without argument, his dogged and unimaginative deference to authority being foremost among his well-hidden virtues.)

'Why not?' She wasn't challenging my decision, I was pleased to note, just asking for an explanation, which I supposed they were all entitled to.

'We can't leave any trace of our presence here,' I pointed out. 'Right now, the necrons are only aware of the greenskins.' At least I hoped they were. 'Our best hope of making it back to warn the others is by sneaking past while they concentrate on the threat they know about.'

'The orks.' Grifen nodded in reluctant understanding. 'But if they find Lunt's body they'll come after us too. I see.'

'I'm sorry,' I said again. 'But it's the only way.' I motioned Jurgen forwards, and he readied the melta. I briefly considered trying to salvage the flamer, but it would be more trouble than it was worth; the tanks were too bulky for anyone to add to their kit, and the firing mechanism looked damaged by bolter fire anyway. I checked Lunt's pockets for any personal effects which his family back on Valhalla might want (if he actually had any, I had no idea really, just taking comfort in the familiar routine), and collected his laspistol as an afterthought, giving it to Jurgen to carry. He might as well get the benefit of something less dangerous to the rest of us in case we found ourselves in close quarter combat again. Then I nodded to my aide, stepped back, and he pulled the trigger. Lunt's body boiled into vapour in a matter of seconds, helped by the volatile promethium left in the flamer tanks, and I led the others in a few ritual words commending his soul to the Emperor.

We were a sombre group as we turned away, you can be sure of that, the drifting snow already beginning to obscure the scar in the rock where the heat of the melta had sent our comrade to join His Majesty. Sometimes, when I sit in my study here at the schola and watch the flames in the grate through a glass of amasec, I can't help thinking of all the brave men and women I've seen fall on a battlefield somewhere without even a grave marker left behind to show they were ever there, and reflect that I'm probably the last man alive who even remembers they existed, and that when I'm gone the last trace of them will fade with me. Then I thank the Emperor that I've lasted as long as I have, and that I've seen my last war, and I might just defy the odds long enough to die in bed after all (someone else's, with any luck.)[1]

We paused in the mouth of the cave, and Grifen started to take a quick inventory of our remaining stock of explosives.

'There's no time for that now,' I said, urging our party on without, I hoped, too obvious a show of impatience. 'Every minute counts.'

---

1. *Ironically this part of the archive appears to have been composed only a matter of months before the thirteenth Black Crusade engulfed most of the segmentum, and Cain found himself dragged out of retirement despite his advancing years.*

'Right.' She fell into step beside me. 'And there's no point in tipping off the tinheads, is there?'

'Exactly,' I said. Not only would collapsing the passage alert the next necron patrol to our presence, it would close them off from the orks, and the last thing I wanted to do was redirect their attention to the rest of the tunnel complex. Of course they could have found their way into the mines by now in any case, but I was betting that once they'd discovered an exit, and an enemy waiting beyond it, they'd ignore everything else until they'd exterminated the greenies; or at least as many of them as they could find in the vicinity. I explained this to Grifen, and she nodded.

'Makes sense to me,' she said.

'What I don't understand,' Jurgen said slowly, 'is how they got out of the tomb in the first place.' That had been worrying me too. I thought we'd brought down enough of the roof to keep them penned in for a great deal longer than this, but they had access to technosorceries which made the tau look like stone-age barbarians, so it never paid to underestimate them.

'We'll find out soon enough,' I said, apprehension settling across me like a shroud.

Normally I would have been profoundly relieved to have returned to the tunnels where I felt reasonably at home, but the knowledge that there were necrons abroad, possibly even sweeping the same narrow passageways we were so cautiously navigating, knotted my stomach with fear. I would have preferred to move on in the dark, relying on the eerie green glow given off by their gauss weapons to warn us of their presence, but none of the others had the advantage of my hiver's tunnel sense; they'd have been stumbling blindly in the darkness, and making more noise than a grox in a ceramics emporium to boot. So we moved at the double, the easy loping stride of the veteran trooper which eats up the kilometres without dragging you down with exhaustion, our luminator beams reflecting just as brightly from the frozen walls as before.

'There's something up ahead,' Simla said, a couple of kilometres later, taking his turn on point. My palms tingled with dread anticipation as the formation slowed, weapons coming to bear down the tunnel.

'What is it?' I asked.

'I don't know.' His voice on the comm-bead sounded puzzled rather than alarmed. 'There's a lot of blood.'

Well that was something at least: if it bled it wasn't a necron. We closed up into a tighter formation, moving ahead a couple of hundred metres to join him as he walked cautiously forward, his luminator playing on what looked like a large pile of butchered meat. The ice around it was crimson, slick with frozen blood as he'd said. Absently, I realised there was too much there for the body to be human, then as we got closer the full size of it became apparent.

'It's an ambull,' Hail said, surprise suffusing her voice.

'Not any more,' Magot added helpfully.

'Where did it come from?' Jurgen asked, as ever displaying his talent for the obvious question. Grifen shrugged.

'Cogboy must have got his head count wrong.' That much was clear, of course. I was more concerned with how it had died. I moved closer to examine the cadaver, and almost immediately wished I hadn't. Beneath its glaze of ice, raw, bloody wounds slashed across its body. Whatever killed it had done so in close combat, wielding razor-sharp blades with surgical precision.

'Where's its hide?' Simla wondered aloud. Grifen shrugged.

'Do necrons use hearth rugs?'

'Not that I ever noticed,' I said, getting everyone moving again. Something about the dead animal spooked me, I don't mind admitting it. The necrons I'd seen before had killed efficiently and dispassionately, but this mutilated carcase spoke of a refined and gleeful sadism of the kind I associated with the eldar renegades who prey on their own kind with as much abandon as they do upon humanity.[1]

As we left the grisly trophy behind us, all trace of it soon swallowed by the suffocating darkness which closed in around the tiny refuge of light cast by our luminators, my apprehension grew even greater. Every step we took was taking us closer to that hidden tomb, and whatever horrors it might conceal. (I had a better idea than most, after my experiences in the depths of their catacombs, so you'll have to forgive me if I confess that taking those steps became progressively harder as I had to exert every iota of willpower I possessed not to turn and flee, screaming, towards the daylight.)

At length a fatalistic numbness settled over me. Retreat was clearly impossible in any case, as the orkish armies would kill us just as surely as the necrons if we tried to go back the way we'd come, and our only hope of safety lay in returning to the refinery complex and the protection it afforded. (Meagre as that looked right now, caught between a gargant and who knew what terrors from the dawn of time.)

My sense of direction, reliable as always, was telling me we should be almost on top of the entrance we'd found by now, and I urged my companions to even greater caution. To my relief they needed little urging, the oppressiveness of the tunnels and the knowledge of what awaited us no doubt weighing on their minds as heavily as it did upon my own. I'd kept my laspistol in my right hand ever since the firefight with the orks, and I reached

---

1. *If not more so. The eldar corsairs appear to be touched by the Dark Powers in some way, and the enmity between them and their untainted kin seems to run as deep as that between the loyal subjects of His Divine Majesty and the traitors who seek to subjugate humanity in the name of their blasphemous gods.*

across with my left to loosen my trusty chainsword in its scabbard. Like the pistol I'd carried it for more years than I cared to remember, so long that it had ceased to exist in my mind as a weapon, or even an object in its own right; now when I drew it the humming blade was simply an extension of my own body.[1] Knowing it was there was curiously reassuring, and I breathed a little easier as we rounded the last bend in the tunnel before the roof fall we'd caused.

We'd doused all the lights except Simla's, allowing our eyes to get a little more used to the gloom and covering him from the concealing darkness as he advanced, and at first all seemed well: the tumbled heap of rock, stone and ice lay across the tunnel, narrowing it to half its width as I remembered. The palms of my hands were tingling though, usually a reliable indicator that something my conscious mind hasn't picked up on yet isn't quite right, so I slowed my pace, scanning the pile of debris in the light from Simla's luminator, and waited for my tunnel rat's instincts to provide the missing clue.

The rubble seemed undisturbed, however hard I stared at it, so it couldn't be that. My gaze flickered across a deep patch of shadow a few metres from it, and then on to the dimly-seen texture of the tunnel wall, where the light of our luminators bounced back in the sparkling reflections we'd grown so used to by now they scarcely registered...

---

1. *I can attest from my personal association with him that Cain was one of the most accomplished swordsmen in the sector, if not the entire segmentum. Even well into his retirement, and his second century, none of the combat instructors at the schola were able to match his skill, honed as it was by innumerable victories in the field. (Much to their chagrin, I might add.) Oddly, his memoirs give little detail about the actual techniques he employed in the mêlées he describes; probably because his fighting style was so instinctive he never bothered to analyse it.*

'Simla. Tunnel wall, about five metres from the cave-in,' I directed, and waited for our point man to swing his luminator round.

'Emperor's bowels!' Grifen brought up her lasgun, her shocked exclamation putting all our reactions into words. The shadow was no such thing, of course, the texture of the tunnel wall should have been visible there too, as my subconscious had been trying to tell me. A fresh passageway was now gouged out of the rock, leading off Emperor knew where. The work, presumably, of our butchered ambull.

'Claw marks,' Simla confirmed, shining the beam of his luminator around the mouth, and then into the depths of the new tunnel. His posture altered suddenly, the lasgun the luminator was taped to coming up into the firing position. 'Golden Throne!'

We ran forward to join him, anticipating Emperor knew what, and clustered at the tunnel mouth. At first it seemed no different from the other ambull runs we'd been travelling through. Then I followed the beam of light, saw what was illuminated by it, and swallowed hard.

'Orks,' Jurgen said, as phlegmatically as if he were handing me a fresh bowl of tanna leaf tea.

'You think?' Magot chipped in, with grisly relish. 'Kind of hard to tell without their skins.'

There were six of them in total, all dead, all flayed the way the ambull had been. Beneath their thin glazing of ice they looked for all the world like anatomical models, laid out for the instruction of apprentice medicae (if the greenskins ever bothered with such niceties as chirurgery, of course).[1]

'What killed them?' Hail asked, paling as much as she was able to. At that point I was past caring, to be honest. Their presence here was a strong indication that at least

---

1. *Actually they do, although not in any fashion we would recognise as good medical practice.*

one group had made it into the tunnels ahead of us, and that an indeterminate number of the brutes might even now be wreaking havoc behind our defensive lines. Not to mention standing between us and safety. All I knew was that the necrons must somehow be responsible, and that whatever tomb-spawned horror had killed them like this was something I didn't want to meet. With a premonitory tingle I realised that the new tunnel was running almost parallel to the necron one we'd blocked, and suddenly felt a violent urge to be somewhere else as quickly as possible.

'Look at this, sir.' Jurgen held up one of the crude bolters the orks had carried, an expression of mild curiosity on his face. It had been sheared clean through, the metal bright where a blade of unimaginable sharpness had sliced it in two, along with the hand that had held it if the amount of blood frozen to the stock was anything to go by. Automatically I scanned the scattered equipment around the bodies, looking for some kind of clue as to what their purpose had been. It was hard to be sure, but something about the weapons they carried and the few pieces of rag which hadn't been stained with blood reminded me of the scouts who'd shot down our shuttle.

That was a logical inference, of course, but quite disturbing in its way. It meant we could be up against orks who, untypically for their kind, were skilled at moving quietly and waiting in ambush rather than announcing their presence with loud voices and indiscriminate weapons fire.

'Shouldn't we see what's at the end of the tunnel?' Grifen asked, reluctance audible in her voice. I shook my head.

'No.' It took all the self-control I could muster to sound calm and collected, instead of screaming the word. 'Nothing's more important than reporting back what we've found.'

'Besides,' Magot chipped in, indicating the mutilated orks with a casual wave, 'that looks like a pretty definite Keep Out sign to me.'

'Then let's take the hint,' I said. Grifen nodded.

'You'll get no argument from me.'

'Hold it.' Hail had moved back to the main tunnel, and was now guarding our rear, standing next to the rockfall which had buried the entrance to the tomb. (And which, thanks to our stray ambull, had turned out to be a complete waste of time.) 'I think I can hear something.'

'Can you be a little more specific?' I asked, lowering my voice instinctively, even though no one else would hear it through the comm-bead in her ear.

'Movement. Beyond the rockslide.' Her voice was equally hushed. Simla scuttled forward to support her, dousing our last remaining luminator, and plunging us into darkness. I've never been prone to claustrophobia, a consequence of my upbringing I suppose, but at that moment the weight of the gloom around us seemed crushing. I found myself obscurely grateful for Jurgen's familiar odour, which reassured me that I had at least one ally down here I could trust, and drew my chainsword from its scabbard.

I strained my ears, listening for any change in the ambient noise around me, tuning out the sounds of my own breathing and my hammering heart. At first I heard nothing except the susurration of the lungs of my companions, and the faint rustling of their clothes as they moved into positions of readiness. Then it came to me, rising up out of the echoes: the sound of boots crunching on hoarfrost, and guttural voices whispering in orkish.

'Let them get close,' I sub-vocalised, hearing the reassuring murmur of response from the rest of the team, and hunkering down to present the smallest possible target. 'Take them when they come round the rockslide.'

It was a good strategy, and probably would have worked, except for my companions' inexperience of tunnel fighting and moving stealthily in the dark. I never knew if Hail or Simla was to blame, but as they settled into the shelter of the tumbled heap of rubble one of them dislodged a small piece of debris.

I held my breath as it skittered away across the ice, and the advancing footsteps halted. A loud sniffing sound echoed through the dark, followed by a muttered conversation in what, for greenskins, were hushed tones. I picked out the word, '*humiez*,'[1] which I'd heard often enough before to be sure of, and knew that our ambush had been discovered.

A glimmer of orange light was now visible behind the rockslide, flickering like fire, and a sick presentiment gripped me. One of the approaching greenskins apparently had a flamer, the pilot light providing illumination for the group as well as heavy support, and a vivid mental image of the immolated orks Lunt had killed rose up unbidden in my mind. I determined to make the bearer my highest priority target; of all the ways to die I'd seen on the battlefields of the galaxy, burning to death looked among the least pleasant.

'Stay back,' I sub-vocalised, probably unnecessarily, as I'm sure the others were all thinking the same. Then I levelled my laspistol at the constriction in the passageway where the greenskins must surely appear, and waited.

To my surprise, however, they didn't charge blindly forward into combat as I'd expected. A couple of small objects flew through the gap, bouncing on the frost-covered floor, and skittering wildly in random directions.

'Grenade!' Simla yelled, just before they detonated, and a storm of shrapnel ripped through the air. He fell backwards, ugly wounds peppering his body. Even the flak armour beneath his greatcoat couldn't stop all of the shards, and crimson stains began seeping across it as he

---

1. *The closest the orkish larynx can come to the gothic word 'humans.'*

tried to get to his feet. Hail was luckier, her partner taking most of the blast, but I could see her left arm was bleeding heavily and hung limply at her side. She leapt forward into the gap, screaming in anger, and fired her lasgun one-handed on full auto at the no doubt surprised greenskins beyond. She must have hit at least one, too, judging by the howls of rage and pain which echoed round the confined space.

'Hail! Get back!' Grifen shouted, but she was too late; a volley of bolts tore Hail apart in a rain of blood and viscera, and then the orks were among us. Simla tried to raise his lasgun as the first bounded through the narrow opening, but before he could pull the trigger a massive cleaver swung down to bisect his skull. The greenskin bellowed in triumph, but it was short-lived as Magot and I shot it almost simultaneously, and it dropped, most of its head blown away. Grifen kept up a steady suppressive fire against the opening through which they had to come, attempting to dissuade any more from following, but it was a futile hope. When the blood of an ork is up they have almost no sense of self-preservation, seeming happy to die if they can take a few of their enemies with them. Another greenskin dived through the choke point, spitting bolts from the crude pistol in its hand, and to my horror the flickering glow of the incendiary weapon was growing brighter, indicating that its operator would be the next to emerge.

'Jurgen!' I shouted, pointing, 'take out the flamer!' He nodded, and sighted the melta carefully. I had no more time to consider his actions after that, or anyone else's for that matter, because the greenskin was upon me, swinging its heavy blade at my head.

I ducked, bringing up the screaming chainsword to block it instinctively, and felt the sturdy mechanism shudder as adamantium teeth met crudely forged metal. Sparks flew, miniature orange suns melting tiny craters in the ice which coated the floor, before I turned my body, deflecting the brute's headlong charge into the wall. It roared as its head impacted with the unyielding ice-coated stone, and turned back towards me, thick ropes of drool hanging from its tusks. Now it was really hacked off.

Good. I cut at its leg, slashing a wound that would have disabled a human, but which seemed to affect it little more than a scratch. It brought its cumbersome blade down to block the strike, as I'd anticipated, and I slashed upwards, taking the loathsome creature in the neck. It looked startled for a moment, as if wondering where all the blood was suddenly coming from, and dropped heavily to its knees. With any other species this would have been a mortal blow, but I'd faced greenies too often before to underestimate their resilience. I swung the blade again, laterally this time, and took its head from its shoulders.

The whole fight could only have lasted a second or two. As I turned away my eyes were stabbed by the searing flash of the melta.

'Got him,' Jurgen confirmed, as I tried to blink my retina clear of the dancing after-images, and cursed myself for my carelessness. That degree of disorientation could cost me my life down here.

'Look out!' The breath was suddenly driven from my lungs as Magot dived forwards, catching me around the waist, and barging me out of the way of a large and unfriendly rock which had become detached from the ceiling. It crashed to the ground where I'd been standing less than a second before.

'Thanks,' I said, still trying to pick out the image of the redheaded trooper from the bright green haze which seemed to float between me and the rest of the world. I thought I could make out a grin, and realised she'd switched her luminator on again.

'Any time,' she said.

'The whole roof's coming down!' Grifen yelled, and I became aware of the creaks and rumblings which told me she was right. Apparently the explosion we'd touched off here earlier had left things even more unstable than we'd realised, something I suppose an old tunnel rat like me should have spotted if I hadn't been too busy being terrified of the necrons.

'Back!' I shouted, my childhood instincts kicking in at last; the worst of it sounded as if it was ahead of us. So we ran back to the shelter of the fresh ambull tunnel, and waited for the noise to stop.

'Emperor on Earth!' Grifen said, when the dust had finally settled. I can't say I blamed her. Of the nine troopers she'd set out with only Magot was now left, and she must have felt the loss of so many of her subordinates keenly. Scintillating ice motes danced in our luminator beams as we took in the full import of the sight ahead of us. Where half the passageway had once been blocked, an impenetrable wall of debris now barred our way. Of the orks, and our fallen comrades, there was no sign at all.

'We're frakked, aren't we?' Magot asked. I shook my head, afraid to speak. It looked to me as if she was right.

'I can try another shot,' Jurgen suggested. 'See if that might clear it.' More likely it would bring down even more rubble, and finish us off into the bargain. I shook my head again.

'Probably a bad idea,' I said, surprised at my restraint under the circumstances.

'We could go back,' Grifen suggested. 'Try to get to the refinery overland.' Over a mountain range, swarming with orks. In a blizzard. That would be suicide, and the dubious tone of her voice told me she realised that even as she spoke.

'We've got one chance,' I said, my mind skittering reluctantly away from the thought even as I voiced it. I tried to picture the map of the ambull tunnels Logash had been compiling on his auspex, and overlaid the mental image with the fresh one we'd just discovered. With a lot of luck it might intersect one of the others before too long, and allow us to bypass the blockage ahead of us.

On the other hand, it was also running more or less parallel with the passageway we'd been trying to block off in the first place, and it seemed pretty obvious that the necrons were already using it. If we went ahead we'd almost certainly die.

Well, almost certainly offers a bit more hope than definitely, which was what our other options amounted to, so in the end it was the only choice to make. It was a grim and silent group which started out, already half the size we had been when we passed this way before, and with the gravest peril we had to face still in front of us.

I averted my eyes from the mutilated orks as we filed past their silent and frozen bodies, and wondered if I'd doomed us all.

ELEVEN

BY THAT POINT we'd given up any attempt at maintaining a proper skirmish formation, advancing instead as a single group, huddled together for protection like the natives of some feral world scared of the daemons beyond the circle of firelight. The difference, of course, was that we knew the daemons were real, and that we were walking straight into their infernal realm. (And speaking as someone who's met a daemon or two in his time, I can assure you that the sensation was not at all dissimilar.)

We had by some unspoken agreement left all the luminators apart from Magot's switched off, so that only a single beam of light preceded us down that narrow and forbidding passageway. As a result, the shadows closed in around us even more suffocatingly than before, despite the reflective qualities of the ice which still coated the walls, intensifying the sense of brooding menace surrounding us. Moreover, my tunnel rat's instincts told me we were descending slowly once again, ever deeper into the bowels of the planet, and the deeper we went, the closer the enshrouding gloom seemed to wrap itself around us, until the air against my face seemed thick and warm, almost choking in its closeness.

Abruptly I became aware that the two phenomena were real, not psychological. The ambient temperature was gradually rising, and our single beam was reflecting less and less from the walls around us as dark rock began to emerge from behind its coating of translucent ice. The resultant humidity was making the air seem damp and thick, a faint mist rising from the floor ahead of us. It was still pretty chilly by any normal measure, you understand, but compared to the temperatures we'd been exposed to on the surface it began to feel almost tropical. The Valhallans certainly seemed to notice it, both women loosening their greatcoats and Jurgen removing his thick fur hat, which he stuffed into one of the equipment pouches he was habitually festooned with.

'Wherever we're going, I think we're here,' Magot volunteered, after an indeterminate period of silence during which we heard nothing apart from our cautious footsteps which seemed to ring like thunder with every pace, echoing all the louder in our ears for every pain we took to muffle them. I nodded, my mouth dry. A faint humming was discernable in the air now, hovering just on the edge of audibility, and a faint acrid tang tickled the membranes of my nose. All things I remembered only too well, and had hoped never to experience again.

'Move carefully,' I warned everyone, completely superfluously no doubt. I gestured to Magot. 'Kill the light.'

She complied, and with a sense of mounting horror I realised that the darkness around us was no longer absolute. A faint luminescence was visible from up ahead, percolating into the tunnel; a sick, gangrenous hue which turned my stomach.

'Down that way.' There could be no doubt at all now: whatever secrets the necrons had buried down here were waiting for us, and there seemed no way to avoid confronting them.

'I'll go first,' Jurgen offered, swinging the bulk of the melta up into a firing position. 'This ought to clear a way for us if we need it.' Frankly I doubted it, where we were going no amount of firepower would make a difference, but the thought that he might at least buy us a little time was a comforting one, so I nodded.

'Good man,' I said, somehow finding the time to enjoy the expression of perplexity on Grifen and Magot's faces. Jurgen was an easy man to underestimate until you got to know him, and few people ever bothered. I tried to look calm, but I'd be surprised if I fooled them for a second; both women looked almost sick with apprehension, and knowing what awaited us I have no doubt my appearance was even worse. 'Ready?' I asked.

'Ready.' Grifen gave Magot's upper arm an encouraging squeeze, and the redheaded trooper nodded.

'As I'll ever be,' she confirmed, and snapped a fresh power cell into her lasgun, more for the comfort the familiar action afforded than because she needed to reload, I suspected.

We emerged into a vast shadowy cavern, full of machinery of strange design and incomprehensible function. Vast geometric slabs rose into the gloom about us, leaking that rancid illumination from vents and thick pipes of stuff which looked like glass but undoubtedly wasn't, suffusing the whole space with shadows and flat, directionless light. In the pale green glow we looked like corpses, long dead and rotting, and I found myself wondering how I had ever hoped to come through this unscathed.

We probed forward cautiously, scuttling from one deep shadow to the next like mice on a cathedral floor, our minds assailed almost to the point of physical nausea by the sense of wrongness everything exuded. This was no place for the living, that much was plain.

'Emperor protect us,' Grifen breathed. We had come through a doorway high enough to admit a titan, hugging the walls of that vast chamber whose roof rose up beyond sight, and stopped short, our breath stilled by the prospect which awaited us. For those walls were composed of niches, each the height and width of a man, and in each stood a necron warrior, the sickly light gleaming from its metal surface. As we moved the shadows seemed to ripple across those blank, inhuman features, imparting expressions of utter malevolence.

For a moment we stood, transfixed by horror, until I realised with a surge of relief that this apparent motion was an illusion, and that each warrior stood utterly immobile.

'They're in stasis,' I breathed, as though saying the words aloud might alone be enough to wake them.

'Then they're harmless?' Magot asked, clearly not expecting the answer she wanted to hear.

'No,' I confirmed. 'Just dormant. If they were to wake...' I swept my eyes up and along that dizzying vista, seeing nothing but metal bodies receding to infinity, and gave up trying to calculate how many there were. Hundreds of thousands, at the very least, in this one chamber alone. I tried to envisage the havoc which such an army would wreak if it were ever unleashed upon the galaxy, and cringed inwardly at the scale of the carnage that would ensue. 'They have to be destroyed.'

'I think we'll need bigger guns,' Grifen said dryly, wrenching her eyes away from that all but infinite legion, and hefting her lasgun as though ready to fire. Nerves taut, we flicked our gazes left and right, alert for any sign of movement which might betray a threat, but the vast tomb seemed utterly empty apart from us.

'Then we'll get bigger guns,' I reassured her. Nothing in our inventory would even come close to doing the job, but an astropathic message to the nearest naval unit would bring a task force here within weeks, and a flotilla of battleships ought to be enough to level the continent. A couple of barrages from their lance batteries would be enough to excise this cancer, however deeply it was buried.

Of course the planet would be rendered uninhabitable for generations, but no one in their right mind would be willing to set foot here once the necron presence was known in any case, so the question was pretty moot. And if anyone were foolish enough to demur, I had no doubt that Amberley would bring the full force of the Inquisition to bear on the objectors the moment I appraised her of the situation.[1]

We pushed on cautiously, trying to keep the outer walls of the cavern in sight as much as we could; if there was indeed a way out of here I intended to find it. I simply refused to consider the alternative, that the ambull tunnel we'd come in by had been the only entrance left, as that way lay nothing but madness and despair.

'Movement!' Jurgen warned, melting into the shadows at the base of some vast mechanism which hummed away to itself oblivious of our presence. The rest of us went to ground too, finding what concealment we could. I crouched behind some metallic outgrowth which looked both regular and organic, and which felt warm to the touch. A moment later I saw it too, harsh angular shadows at first, presaging our initial sight of the necrons themselves as they rounded the corner of the metal canyon in the depths of which we lurked.

As the monsters themselves came into sight I could scarcely suppress a gasp of pure horror. I'd seen terrors enough on Interitus Prime, but these monstrous creations exceeded even those. At first I took them for ordinary necron warriors, fearsome enough in themselves as I

---

1. *He was not wrong in this assumption.*

knew only too well, but these were something far worse. Their fingers ended in long, gleaming blades, smeared with a substance which looked black in this pestilential light but which I had no doubt was truly red. Most terrifying of all, their metal torsos were hidden from view. For a second, as my appalled mind refused to acknowledge the sight before it, I found myself wondering why in the name of the Emperor these unfeeling automata would have donned clothing against the cold; then the realisation hit me, along with a spasm of nausea. They were draped in the flayed hides of the dead orks we'd found. (If one of them was wearing the ambull I failed to notice it, which believe me was quite easy to have done under the circumstances. If the Emperor Himself had tapped me on the shoulder at that moment it probably wouldn't have registered.)

'Golden Throne!' Grifen breathed, unable to contain her revulsion, and I froze, terrified that she might have been heard, but to my unutterable relief the hideous apparitions strode on oblivious,[1] with the inhumanly fluid motion I'd come to associate with all their forms, and after a moment they slipped away down a wide boulevard between arcane devices the size of a warehouse.'

'Should we follow them?' Jurgen asked, phlegmatic as always, as though he'd seen nothing more disturbing than my morning's messages, and I was instantly grateful for the sound of his voice in my comm-bead. It was a welcome touch of the ordinary which I seized on gratefully, and I felt my shattered sensibilities begin to stabilise. I

---

1. *Despite decades of intensive study by both the Ordo Xenos and the Adeptus Mechanicus the sensory mechanisms of the necrons remain a mystery. Sometimes they seem almost preternaturally able to detect an enemy, while at others, as in this instance, they overlook targets almost literally under their noses. At this time the Inquisition has no explanation to offer for this paradox; and if the Adeptus Mechanicus has one they're not sharing it.*

glanced across at Grifen, who was breathing shallowly, her face pale in the ghastly light, and Magot, who was muttering prayers to the Emperor under her breath, all trace of her usual cockiness gone. If I didn't do something to snap them out of it fast they were likely to lose it completely, or go catatonic on me, and neither was an appealing prospect at the moment. And Jurgen's suggestion at least had the merit of keeping the monstrosities in front of us, so I nodded.

'Good a plan as any,' I conceded, then turned to Grifen. 'Sergeant. We're moving out.' To her credit she responded almost at once, turning slowly to face me with wide eyes into which I could see a measure of hard-fought self control begin to return.

'Right,' she confirmed, and reached across to take Magot by the arm again. The trooper failed to respond. Grifen increased the pressure a little, forcing her to take a single step to retain her balance, and after a moment she broke off her muttering to look at the sergeant. 'Mari. Mari, we're going now.'

'We shouldn't be here,' Magot said, an undercurrent of hysteria too close to the surface for my liking. 'We have to get out.'

'That's just what we're going to do,' I assured her, with more confidence than I felt. 'But we need your help to do it. We need you alert, all right?'

'Right. Yes.' She swallowed, incipient panic still bubbling under the surface, but fighting it now. She took a couple of deep breaths. 'I'm on it.'

'Good. Because we're relying on you,' I said, in my most sincere voice. 'If we stick together we'll make it, you have my word.'

'I won't let you down,' she said, a hair's breadth from hyperventilation, and Grifen patted her on the shoulder, a brief, supportive show of human contact.

'I know you won't,' she said kindly. 'So get your arse in gear and let's try to make it back before hell thaws out, OK?'

'OK, sarge.' Whatever the bond between them it seemed to outweigh the terror of the necrons, at least for the time being, so I signalled to Jurgen.

'Move out,' I said.

How long we followed those ghastly apparitions for I had no idea, but it seemed like an eternity, time shifting and blurring until it had no meaning, a phenomenon I'd also noticed in the catacombs of Interitus Prime. At times we passed through forests of glowing tubes, uncannily reminiscent of plague-ridden trees, and at others we scuttled along in the shadows of blank-sided metal slabs the size of a starship. At least twice we passed through more stasis chambers, as full of dormant horrors as the one we'd first encountered, but looking back I find my recollections hazy, as though my mind was simply refusing to accept what it was seeing (probably just as well for my sanity). Abruptly I became aware of a fluttering of motion in my peripheral vision, and dived for cover again, with a sibilant warning to my companions.

And just in time, too. A group of ordinary necron warriors appeared from a side passage, which, like the one we travelled, seemed more like a street than a gap between warehouse-sized machines, and, turning as one with a precision which would have left any Imperial Guard drill instructor worthy of the name seething with envy had they been there to witness it, followed their charnel brethren towards whatever destination awaited them.

As I looked closer I could see faint traces of combat damage on their shiny metal torsos, the dents and craters left by the weapons of the orks already fading as the metal seemed to flow together, healing their wounds by some sorcerous process I was at a loss to understand.[1]

---

1. *An understanding which the Ordo Xenos would give a great deal to achieve, incidentally. It goes without saying that whatever inroads the Adeptus Mechanicus may have made into the problem, they're keeping to themselves.*

From somewhere up ahead, at the end of that cyclopean thoroughfare, we could now discern a glow brighter than the rest but no less repellent in its hue, and something about the shape of the mechanisms surrounding us seemed vaguely familiar. I began to feel a formless sense of recognition, which hardened into certainty as we approached that vivid corpse-light, and the source came into view in the centre of a broad open space the size of a starport landing pad.

'It's an active warp portal,' I breathed, making the sign of the aquila by reflex. Not that I expected to invoke any additional protection by doing that, of course, but believe me, under those circumstances every little helps.

'Are you sure?' Grifen asked, clearly awestruck at the prospect. Feeling this wasn't the time for lengthy explanations I simply nodded.

'Absolutely,' I said.[1] Ahead of us the flayed ones, as I later learned the Inquisition classified the trophy-takers, stepped into that eldritch glow and vanished, no doubt to some hell hole elsewhere in the galaxy. I must admit to wondering, for a panic-stricken instant, if they were merely teleporting to some starship in orbit, but a moment's reflection was enough to reassure me that no vessel could have emerged from the warp early enough to be here already without registering on the *Pure of Heart's* sensor array long before we set out on our ambull hunt, what seemed like a lifetime ago now. (But which my chronometer stubbornly insisted had been less than a day.)[2] A moment later the warriors followed

---

1. *Cain is almost certainly the only human in the galaxy to have survived a transit through a necron warp portal, during the adventures on Interitus Prime to which he has previously referred. His account of the incident is elsewhere in the archive, and need not detain us further at this time.*

2. *Cain is generally imprecise about the passage of time in his memoirs; it's usually possible to infer roughly how much time has passed between the incidents he describes, but this is about as specific as he ever gets.*

suit, evaporating from our sight like the vestiges of a nightmare on waking, and the warp portal dimmed back to the level of the ambient illumination.

'Emperor on Earth!' Magot said, a faint trace of her old bravado beginning to return. 'How's that for an exit?'

'It'll do me,' Grifen said grimly. 'Especially if it's permanent.'

'Maybe the greenskins were too much for them,' the redhead said hopefully.

'I wouldn't count on it,' I said. 'This was just a scouting party. They'll be back.'

'How soon?' Jurgen asked, his tone, as usual, no more than mildly curious. I shrugged.

'Emperor alone knows,' I said. 'Long enough for us to get the frak out of here I hope.'

'Amen to that,' Magot muttered. I stole a glance at the portal, which, though dormant now, seemed to pulsate with malevolence, as though ready to vomit a tidal wave of metal warriors across the planet at any moment. I thought briefly of trying to rig up something to destroy it from our remaining stock of explosives, but dismissed the idea at once. For one thing, if it was as robust as the equipment I'd seen on Interitus Prime we'd barely be able to scratch it with what little we still carried, and for another, the time it would take us to try would be far better spent looking for an exit. (If I'm honest, the thought of lingering for even a moment longer, certainly for the amount of time it would take to set the charges, was almost enough to start me running in panic; only the realisation that such a course would probably doom us prevented it.) And any attempt to interfere with the mechanisms here would most likely draw attention to us, which would be best avoided to say the least. Though many of the machines around us appeared to be powering down with the departure of the scouting party, which suggested we were alone down here now, there could be any number of alarms or sensors an explosion might trigger, and necron guards or their mechanical lackeys lurking in a corner somewhere prepared to deal with us if alerted to our presence.

'Which way, sir?' Jurgen asked, as though we were simply in the middle of a park somewhere looking for the quickest way back to the barracks. I hesitated. My instincts hadn't entirely deserted me, however arcane our surroundings, and after a moment's thought I pointed off to our left.

'The mines should be over that way, if I don't miss my guess.' Jurgen had been down enough holes with me to trust my sense of direction underground, and even if he didn't it was close enough to an instruction for him to follow without thinking about it, so he nodded, and began to move off in that direction. Grifen and Magot began to drift after him so I picked up my pace and fell in between my aide and the two women, feeling a little more secure (if that were even remotely possible considering where we were) now that I had armed troopers on either side of me.

Despite my growing conviction that we were unlikely to meet any more of the metallic monstrosities unless we did something to attract their attention I wasn't about to let my guard down, you can depend on that. In fact the closer we came to safety, or at least the promise of it, the more paranoid I became, starting at every minute sound, real or imagined. I scanned every shadow we passed, increasingly certain that every crevice concealed a swarm of scuttling metal insects or that a vast arachnoid construct lurked above our heads, but every time my apprehensions proved to be groundless.

'I can see the cavern wall,' Jurgen voxed, and we picked up the pace a little, an unspoken agreement sparking among us to quit this hellish place as quickly as we could. I began to see patches of smooth finished stonework ahead of us through the tangle of incomprehensible mechanisms and tried to estimate how far away we were, but my sense of perspective was confused by the strange geometries around us and I was still taken by surprise when we slipped through a grove of pipe-work the breadth of trees and found ourselves up against naked bedrock.

'It's completely smooth,' Magot said, running her hand along it, a tint of wonder entering her voice. She was right, the surface was sheer as glass, and I found myself trying to picture how the work had been done with such precision. The only explanation I could come up with was sorcery of some kind, which fitted right in with everything else I'd seen here since we arrived. I glanced to the left and right, hoping to find some sign of a tunnel, but in this I was predictably disappointed.

'Which way now?' Grifen asked. I didn't have a clue, to be honest, but I had a vague memory of the projected run of the ambull tunnels on Logash's auspex being more numerous off towards the right of where I estimated us to be, so I gestured in that direction with all the authority I could muster.

'That way,' I said. 'And pray to the Emperor for a miracle.'

'This whole place is a miracle, is it not?' a new voice asked. I whirled, bringing up my laspistol, and froze an instant away from pulling the trigger. The speaker sounded vaguely familiar, and a moment later I caught sight of a human figure in an emerald robe (which was actually white, of course, out of that ghastly illumination), whose eyes flashed dazzlingly green as they caught the light. 'All praise the Omnissiah, whose bounty has been revealed to the worthy despite the worst efforts of the unbeliever.'

'Logash,' I said, not quite sure if he'd gone barmy or not. 'We thought you were dead.' But he wasn't, worse luck; the treacherous little weasel had given us the slip in the snowstorm and come scuttling back here as fast as he could. Emperor alone knows what he was hoping to achieve with a couple of tonnes of rubble sealing the entrance to the tomb, but fanatics are like that, no common sense at all, and our stray ambull had solved the problem for him anyway. Of course he took that as a sign from His Divine Majesty, or the clockwork parody they worship, that he was intended to get in here all along, and didn't he just crow about that.

'The Omnissiah guided my steps,' he said, 'and the barriers were thrown down ahead of me. All praise the Omnissiah!' His voice rose, and I cringed inwardly, certain that he'd attract unholy attention. I hushed him with a gesture, and turned to find Magot's lasgun pointed straight at him.

'How come the tinheads didn't get you?' she asked, her finger a little too tight on the trigger for my peace of mind. Frankly, the way I felt now she could have shot him and welcome, but the sound of gunfire would echo around here like an Earthshaker barrage and I wasn't prepared to risk it. I deflected her aim gently with a hand on the weapon's barrel. Logash didn't seem to take offence, though, beaming broadly at the question.

'The holy guardians failed to notice me, as I would expect given my unworthiness. There are mysteries here far beyond my abilities to fathom, but no doubt those of greater wisdom can commune with the machine spirits of this wondrous place.'

'Assuming we ever manage to get out of here to tell them,' Grifen chipped in sourly.

'The Omnissiah will provide, you can depend on it,' Logash said, completely siggy beyond a doubt. (Even though with tech-priests it's often hard to tell.) I found it hard to credit that the necrons had simply ignored him, but I suppose it was a vast complex and it wasn't entirely unfeasible that they had simply failed to notice him as they had the rest of us, even though I had no doubt that he'd been wandering around in the open gawping like some hick up from the sump on his first trip to a guilder trade station instead of hiding like anyone with a micron of sense would have done.

'They certainly noticed the orks,' Magot pointed out. Logash nodded eagerly.

'Vile desecrators of these holy precincts. The guardians cut them down as they deserved.' There he went again, I thought, with a tingle of unease. Anyone who could use the word 'holy' to refer to this chamber of horrors had clearly become unhinged. I suppose the sight of all that technology lying around had overloaded his brain or something.

'Well that's good,' I said, a little too heartily, and prodded him experimentally in the back. To my relief he fell into step beside me. 'It'll still be safe when we tell the others all about it.'

'Oh yes, we must do that.' Logash nodded eagerly, and pulled out his auspex. It's probably a measure of how far gone I was that I was actually glad to see it. The rest of us clustered around anxiously as he called up the image of the ambull tunnels we'd mapped before, the ones in red extrapolated from the ones we'd actually walked.

'Is there another tunnel near here?' Magot asked, raising herself onto her toes to peer over the tech-priest's arm. He nodded, pointing off to the left.

'There should be another ambull run about two hundred metres in that direction.' Luckily no one said anything to me, although to be fair there did seem to be some other tunnels a bit further away in the direction I'd originally chosen. This wasn't the time to stand on my pride, however, so I nodded and patted the tech-priest on his shoulders (which were hard under the robe, and thudded dully under the blows).

'Good,' I said. 'Then let's find it.'

Editorial Note:

Despite my understandable reluctance to resort to this secondary source again I'm afraid it's necessary to fill a gap in Cain's narrative, which breaks off at this point only to resume after some time has passed. No doubt he felt nothing of significance had occurred in the interim, despite the passage of several hours.

As ever, my apologies for the style (or lack of it), and my assurance that readers with a refined appreciation for the Gothic language are perfectly at liberty to skip it.

It is, however, mercifully short.

Extracted from *Like a Phoenix From the Flames: The Founding of the 597th*, by General Jenit Sulla (retired), 097.M42.

VITAL AS THE task with which we had been entrusted undeniably was, it could hardly be described as challenging.

177

Once the miners had directed Captain Federer's sappers to the part of the workings where the flaws and stresses in the ice ensured our planned booby trap would work to best effect, there was little for us more practical soldiers to do other than fan out through the galleries to secure our perimeter against the remote possibility of infiltration by the orks. This we did, and although I have to admit that the task was a tedious one, to the credit of the women and men under my command they remained as alert after half the day had crawled by as they had at the commencement of our vigil.

This was disturbed at length by a vox message from deep in the lower galleries, so attenuated by the layers of intervening ice that I could scarcely discern it; and a moment's perusal of the tactical slate was enough to confirm what I'd already deduced. The source of the message was far deeper than the most far-flung of our patrols.

There could be only one explanation, and taking my command squad with me I made haste to respond, finding as we descended and the vox signal became clearer that my suspicions were correct; this was indeed a message from none other than Commissar Cain himself, returning with news of dire import, and demanding, as soon as communications became reliable enough, to be put through to Colonel Kasteen at once.

While my vox operator made haste to comply, his powerful backpack transmitter easily able to boost the tenuous signals of the commissar's comm-bead, I directed my troopers to his aid as rapidly as I could. Though the conversation had moved to a command frequency of a far higher level than those to which I, as a lowly lieutenant, had access, it was clear from the urgent tone of his voice that the tidings he brought were of such importance they must be disseminated as rapidly as possible.

The carrier wave was enough to lead us to the commissar's party, however, and I must confess to a moment of shock as I beheld the bedraggled survivors of what must surely have been a journey of epic endurance. Commissar Cain was, of course, the very picture of martial heroism he always presented, his bearing erect and eye steady, undaunted by whatever horrors he had faced, although his companions all too clearly showed the terrible ravages of the perils they'd fought their way through. The commissar's aide, in particular, looked as though he had come through hell, dishevelled in a way I had seldom seen in a trooper still living.[1] The other soldiers with him stumbled with exhaustion, horror written across their faces, and only the tech-priest at the rear of the party appeared to be in good spirits, doubtless because his augmentations had protected him from whatever had so afflicted the others.

'Help them,' I ordered, and my troopers made haste to obey, providing much-needed support for all.

It was only after I'd spoken that the commissar appeared to recognise me, looking in my direction for the first time, and I must confess to an overwhelming sensation of pride as he spoke my name, quite overcome at the confidence he so evidently had in my qualities as an officer.

'Sulla,' he said, in a voice clearly meant for no ears other than his own. 'Of course. Who else would it be?'

---

1. *Sulla had clearly had little prior contact with Jurgen.*

TWELVE

As you'll readily appreciate, all I wanted to do when we finally made it back to the refinery was eat, sleep, and grab a hot shower (preferably aboard the *Pure of Heart* while it was heading for deep space as fast as its engines would take it), but events were moving too fast to allow any such luxury. I managed to get rid of Sulla, who'd picked up my increasingly frantic attempts to contact the surface and been predictably unable to resist sticking her nose in, by asking her to make sure Grifen and Magot got to the medicae as fast as possible (which didn't hurt my reputation for taking care of the troops either, never a bad thing), and staggered off to meet Kasteen and Broklaw. At least I'd been able to get a tactical update from Sulla before she went, so I could concentrate on the immediate problem secure in the knowledge that the orks were still being held at our outer defensive line and the gargant was still too far away to open fire on us. For the time being at any rate.

'You look like hell,' the major said cheerfully as I entered the command post, but he held out a mug of tanna leaf tea as he said it, so I let him live.[1]

'You should see me from this side,' I told him, and dropped into a seat at the conference table. Now I was back in the warmth and relative safety of the refinery all the fear and accumulated fatigue of the last day or so bludgeoned me between the shoulder blades, and it was all I could do to keep my head from dropping onto the glossy wooden surface. As I tilted my head back to try and ease the tension in my neck something struck me as odd about the ceiling. 'Merciful Emperor! Did the greenskins get in here?' Broklaw followed the line of my gaze to the bolter holes filigreeing the plasterwork above his head.

'Just a small crowd control problem,' he said, smiling at some private joke. Well if he wasn't too bothered about it neither was I, and asking any more questions might complicate my life even further, so I returned my attention to the matter at hand.

'You should get some rest,' Kasteen said, looking at me with evident concern. I nodded.

'I should. Just as soon as we've dealt with the current situation.' I drank deeply, feeling the cobwebs lift a little from my mind as the tanna started to kick in. 'Did you get the old survey reports I asked for?'

'Right here.' She skimmed a data-slate across the surface of the table. I glanced at it, but the charts and technical data meant nothing to me. 'Scrivener Quintus has been remarkably helpful.' Broklaw grinned and winked at me, but in my dazed state I hadn't a clue what he was getting at.

'What does it all mean in plain Gothic?' I asked. Kasteen shrugged.

---

1. *Cain is, of course, joking here. Probably.*

'I ran it by a couple of the engineseers in the transport pool.' That had been a calculated risk; they were cogboys, of course, so their first duty would be to the Adeptus Mechanicus, but they were our cogboys, and had fought alongside the rest of us for long enough to feel at least as loyal to the regiment as to their tech-priest colleagues. So long as we didn't force them to pick sides they'd tell us what we needed to know, or so I hoped. 'It's not really their field, but they seem to think you're right. There are other deposits of refinable ice on Simia Orichalcae much richer than this one.'

'Then why build the refinery here?' Broklaw asked. I shrugged.

'The magos would undoubtedly reel off a dozen different reasons why this particular deposit was easiest to process, or the topography of the valley made construction simpler, or why it was the will of this clockwork Emperor of theirs. He might even believe it himself. But if it smells like a sump rat and it squeaks like a sump rat...'

'Someone in the Adeptus Mechanicus knew that tomb was there,' Broklaw said. 'Someone placed highly enough to make sure the mine was put on top of it.'[1]

'But why?' Kasteen was aghast. 'Surely they wouldn't be mad enough to think they could take on a planet full of necrons?'

I thought of Logash, who'd been driven all but insane by the desire to examine such a rich cache of archeotech, and tried to picture a cabal of high-ranking tech-priests pulling strings to set up the mine over so tempting a prize. It wasn't hard to do at all. If they even suspected

---

1. *The identification of those responsible for the decision wasn't difficult, but, as Cain surmised, hard evidence of conspiracy rather than an unfortunate coincidence continues to be elusive. Anyone with information which may prove helpful in resolving this matter will find an interested listener in Inquisitor Kuryakin of the Ordo Hereticus.*

such a thing existed they'd take any risk, however great, to get their sticky little mechadendrites on it. I'd learned that much at least from the Interitus Prime debacle.

'They probably assumed the tomb was abandoned,' I said. It wouldn't be the first time they'd made that mistake either, as I knew to my cost.

'The real point,' Broklaw said, 'is how many of the techpriests here we can trust. Whether or not there was a conspiracy to start with, they all know what's down the bloody hole now.'

That much was true. If I'd had my wits about me I'd have got Sulla to detain Logash as soon as she brought us back up to the surface, but of course she ignored him (only a civilian, and a tech-priest to boot), so by the time I realised what was going on he'd already disappeared. No doubt filling Ernulph's head with visions of sorcerous bounty unseen in millennia even as we spoke.

'None of them,' I said. My head was hurting, the grim, relentless migraine that goes with utter fatigue, and I wasn't looking forward to the next few hours at all.

I GOT THROUGH them, of course, due in no small part to Jurgen's skill at fending off unwanted interruptions. By the time Kasteen called a full meeting to discuss the situation I'd managed to grab a little sleep, a lot of recaf, and a hot meal (just soylens viridians again, but for some reason I'd gone off the idea of retrieving an ambull steak), and was beginning to feel tolerably human once more. A bath would have topped things off nicely but sleep was even more urgent, and I just had to resign myself to the fact that I was probably beginning to smell as bad as my aide. Jurgen, naturally, looked no worse than usual, probably as a result of a catnap somewhere. He accompanied me, partly to underline my status, and partly to take the blame if my suspicions about my personal freshness were correct.

Of course I'd done a lot more than take care of my personal needs. Even before I staggered off to the mess hall and bed, in that order, I'd roused the refinery's resident astropath and sent the most urgently-worded communiqué I could to both the lord general's office and the rather more guarded channels Amberley had suggested I use if I ever came across something which merited Inquisitorial attention. Well, a tomb full of necrons definitely qualified if anything did, but to my vague disappointment (though complete lack of surprise given the time lag inherent in even the most urgent interstellar communications) neither had responded by the time the briefing was scheduled to start.

The conference room was the most crowded I'd ever seen it as I entered the command post, the babble of conflicting voices almost loud enough to drown out the muffled explosions from the battlefield beyond the large picture window. My eye was drawn to it at once, searching for some sign of the gargant, and despite the ever-present snow whirling against the glass like a disconnected pict screen I was sure I could make out a dark, hulking shape against the mountains in the distance which hadn't been there before. Merciful Emperor, it was almost close enough to open fire on us, a handful of kilometres distant now. I thought of the havoc the massive belly gun would surely wreak, blowing apart buildings and storage tanks alike, and shuddered. Of course the greenskins would be trying to take the installation relatively intact, or at least the vast reserves of refined promethium it contained, so it couldn't really do its worst, but no one ever said orks were rational.[1] If the ork princeps, or whatever he called himself,[2] got

---

1. *Actually there have been a few xenologists who argued precisely this, claiming their actions make perfect sense in the context of their own barbarous society, but such views are generally considered eccentric at best.*

2. *Probably some variation of 'Nob' or 'Boss,' which appear to be the only major signifiers of rank and status their language possesses.*

over-excited this whole affair could end very loudly and suddenly.

'Commissar.' Colonel Kasteen looked up from her place at the head of the table, and indicated a vacant seat next to her. I dropped into it gratefully, while Jurgen went to find me some more tanna tea, and exchanged a nod of greeting with Broklaw who was seated on the other side of her. 'I'm pleased to see you looking so much better.'

'Thank you,' I said, as Jurgen materialised behind me with a large steaming bowl of the fragrant liquid. I glanced up and down the table, seeing all the faces I remembered from the previous meeting, and a lot more besides. 'Shall we get started?'

'By all means.' She nodded to Broklaw, who cleared his throat loudly, and to my astonishment everyone shut up and looked at him expectantly.

'Thank you for coming at such short notice,' he began, with barely a trace of sarcasm. 'As most of you are no doubt aware, the commissar's scouting trip has uncovered a much greater problem than the orks.' At this point he glanced meaningfully at the little knot of tech-priests clustered around Ernulph. Logash was sitting next to him, still wearing the imbecilic grin he'd been sporting ever since we found him in the tomb below our feet. I'd invoked my commissarial privileges to unlock some highly classified files, so that everyone who needed to would know precisely what we were up against, but now the seed of suspicion had been planted it was hard not to wonder if the magos had known most of it already.

'How sure are we that it's a problem?' Ernulph asked, an edge of eager acquisitiveness in his voice. 'If the necrons are in stasis we can surely concentrate our efforts on repelling the immediate threat.' Meaning let the poor bloody Guardsmen keep the orks off their backs while he and his cronies pillaged the tomb, of course.

'They are the immediate threat,' I said, as mildly as I could. I sipped my bowl of tea while the sudden flare of apprehension in my gut at the very thought of those mechanical killers subsided. 'If we were up to our armpits in orks, with a side order of kroot and eldar backing them up, I'd turn my back on the lot of them to take out a single necron. I've fought them before, and they're the biggest single menace in the entire galaxy.'

'Surely you exaggerate,' Pryke said, looking at me sternly, as though I was making the whole thing up. 'I've accessed the records of previous encounters with these... whatever they are, and reports of them are practically non-existent.'

'That's because they hardly ever leave any survivors to report anything,' I rejoined, feeling my hand begin to tremble as old memories came rushing back. A small gobbet of tea escaped the bowl to pool on the polished wooden tabletop, and Jurgen leant forward to mop up the spillage with a handkerchief that left the surface even grubbier than before. 'Everything else in the galaxy fights for a reason, whether it's for territory, honour, or souls for the dark gods.' I heard a satisfying intake of breath at that, having deliberately invoked the most shocking image I could think of to wrong-foot any objectors. 'Necrons don't. They exist purely to kill, and they know we're here now.'

'Are you sure about that?' Ernulph persisted. 'They certainly know about the greenskins. But you escaped unscathed, I gather.' He glanced at Logash for confirmation.

'The Omnissiah guided our steps,' the young techpriest declared, 'so that we might claim the bounty prepared for us.'

'The only preparation you'll get from the necrons is if one of them fancies your skin as a waistcoat,' I said, having the slight satisfaction of seeing him blench for a moment before his fanaticism kicked in again.

'The commissar is convinced that the party he encountered were simply scouts,' Kasteen said, determined to keep the business of the meeting moving. 'And while the warp portal remains active down there we can expect a full-scale incursion at any time.'

'What I don't understand,' Morel declared, cutting through the subsequent babble of consternation, 'is why now? They've been down there for Emperor knows how long. What got them so stirred up all of a sudden?'

'I think I can answer that.' As everyone turned to look at him, Quintus cleared his throat a little nervously.

'If you can make any sense of this mess I'd like to hear it,' Kasteen prompted after a moment. Quintus flushed even more, and stood, grinning nervously at the colonel. He produced a data-slate from the recesses of his robes, and projected a page onto the main hololith, which still jumped annoyingly as I tried to make sense of what I was looking at.

'These are the sensor logs from the traffic control system,' he began, before Ernulph interrupted.

'Those are technical documents which fall under the purview of the Adeptus Mechanicus. You have no business dabbling in theological matters!'

'I think you'll find,' Pryke rejoined, equally forcefully, 'that they are archive material, and therefore clearly the responsibility of the Administratum.'

'Their care and maintenance, possibly,' Ernulph persisted. 'But interpretation and consultation are the business of those appointed to commune with the numinous, not some jumped-up inky-fingered quill-pusher!' Pryke seemed on the verge of responding in equally trenchant tones, when Broklaw cleared his throat again. The room went suddenly quiet.

'Might I remind everyone,' Kasteen said mildly, 'that I'm in charge here and I decide who does what. And I want to hear what the scrivener has to say. Are there any objections?' Surprisingly there weren't, which might have had something to do with the way both officers had a hand resting casually on the butts of their bolt pistols; I began to suspect they'd been hanging around me a bit too much lately. She smiled at Quintus, who looked quite flustered for a moment, and nodded judiciously. 'Please continue.'

'Ah. Right. Yes.' Quintus cleared his throat again, and pointed to something in the middle of the display which looked like a stain of ackenberry juice. 'This is the flare of warp energy released when the greenskins' space hulk emerged into the materium.' Ernulph harrumphed disapprovingly at the young scrivener's use of the technical term, and a faint, fleeting grin appeared on Quintus' face just long enough for me to realise he'd done it on purpose to irritate the magos. 'And there was another one almost as strong when it dropped back into the warp.'

'We already knew this,' Ernulph said dismissively. 'Our instrumentation was practically overloaded. It's how we knew they were coming in the first place.'

'Precisely,' Quintus said. 'And because of the strength of the flare we missed that.' He pointed to something else with an air of triumph, undermined a little by the almost total inability of anyone else at the table to see what was hidden by his finger.

'Could you magnify it a little?' Kasteen asked. Quintus flushed, and complied, revealing another, almost imperceptible ackenberry stain. A murmur of voices rippled around the table, and Ernulph at least had the grace to look surprised.

'We missed that,' he admitted grudgingly.

'Quite understandably,' Kasteen assured him diplomatically. 'But can you tell us what it is?'

'I can guess,' the magos admitted reluctantly. Then he grimaced, as though biting into a bitterroot pasty someone had assured him was filled with sweetbriar,[1] and gestured to Quintus to continue. 'But I'm sure the young

---

1. *Cain was evidently still hungry at this point, judging by the sudden flurry of culinary metaphors; hardly surprising given the amount of energy he had expended over the last couple of days.*

man has worked it out already. He seems quite bright for a bureaucrat, and we'd never have noticed this anomaly at all if it wasn't for his diligence.' I suppose for all his bluster he was a fair-minded man, but it must have pained him to swallow his pride like that. His colleagues looked positively dyspeptic, and Pryke was gazing at him in open-mouthed astonishment. Kasteen just nodded coolly.

'Thank you magos. I'm glad to see we all seem to be on the same side at last. Quintus?' For some reason the young scrivener became flustered all over again as she looked in his direction, and stuttered for a moment before resuming.

'Well it's outside my realm of expertise, as the magos pointed out, but it seems logical to assume that the flare of warp energy somehow activated the dormant portal in the tomb.' Ernulph was nodding in agreement.

'That would be my interpretation,' he conceded.

'Of course!' Logash butted in with the single-minded enthusiasm of the obsessive. 'That's how the ambulls got down there! They came through the portal, and dug their way out of the tomb! That explains the anomalous habitat...' He trailed off, suddenly conscious of how very much nobody else in the meeting cared.

'And somehow the necrons noticed that it had reactivated.' Broklaw nodded. 'So they sent a scouting party through. That makes sense.'

'But where from, though?' Pryke asked, anxious to establish that her department was fully involved in things.

'Could be anywhere in the galaxy,' I said. 'Somewhere with ambulls, by the look of it, but that doesn't narrow it down much.'[1]

'That's not really the question at the moment,' Kasteen said, dragging everyone back to the point. 'What we need to decide now is what we do about them.'

---

1. *Indeed not. As yet the world or worlds at the other end of the necron portal remain unidentified, despite the best efforts of the Ordo Xenos.*

'There's only one thing we can do,' I said, as calmly and decisively as I could. 'Evacuate the planet, while we still have enough time to get clear.'

'Evacuate?' Kasteen echoed, clearly stunned. I nodded, conscious that I was risking my whole fraudulent reputation, but that it was precisely that reputation for heroism which might just do the trick now. I adopted an expression of barely-contained frustration.

'I know how you feel. I've never run from a fight yet,' (which was not entirely true, of course, but no one needed to know that), 'and it goes against the grain to start now. But there are wider issues at stake here. The necrons in that tomb outnumber us by hundreds to one, and that's assuming we could disengage from the orks cleanly enough to take them on in a stand-up fight.'

'They'd still know they'd been in a scrap,' Kasteen said grimly. I nodded again.

'I don't doubt the fighting spirit of anyone in the regiment. But if we stand and fight now we will all die. That's a plain, simple fact. They'll overrun us in a matter of hours.' More like minutes, if the ones I'd seen before were anything to go by, but if I told her that she'd never believe me. 'And that's just the start.'

'The portal,' Kasteen said, the coin dropping. I nodded again.

'Hundreds of thousands of them would be let loose on the galaxy. We simply can't allow that to happen.' I paused for a moment, letting the implications sink in. 'We have to call in the Navy to sterilise the whole site from orbit. It's the only way to be sure.'

'You can't do that!' Pryke and Ernulph both shouted at the same time, then broke off to boggle at one another, completely taken aback to find themselves in agreement for once.

'I can, and will,' I contradicted them. 'This facility is under martial law, which means the commissariat is the final arbiter of what can or cannot be done.'

'Have you any idea of the economic value of this installation?' Pryke asked, recovering first.

'None at all, and I care even less,' I said. 'So far as I'm concerned it's not worth the life of one soldier.' The soldier I had in mind being me, of course.

'But the archeotech!' Ernulph spluttered. 'Think of the knowledge, the spiritual advancement of mankind that you'd be sacrificing...'

'All we'd be sacrificing if we left that tomb intact is our lives,' I rejoined. 'Not to mention the millions of others who'd be slaughtered if the necrons down there revive and escape through the portal.'

'But they're in stasis,' the magos persisted. 'While they're dormant we can safely examine...'

'We don't know that,' Kasteen cut in. 'For all we know they're up and about by now. And even if they aren't, their friends could be flocking through the portal from somewhere else. We simply can't risk sending anyone back down there, and that's final.'

'On the contrary,' Ernulph replied. 'I don't think you can risk not sending anyone back.'

'Explain,' Kasteen said, although in a sudden agony of panic I realised what the magos was driving at. The worst of it was that he was right, damn it, and the spasming of my bowels told me who was by far the most likely candidate to get stuck with the job.

'You said it yourself,' he said triumphantly. 'The portal's still active. Even if you called in your naval strike it would be left intact and functioning for months before a flotilla could get here, possibly even years. The necrons would be long gone.'

'Emperor's bowels, he's right.' Broklaw looked more shaken than I'd ever seen him. 'We have to blow the portal before we pull out.'

I felt every pair of eyes at the table lock on to me like the targeting auspex of a hydra battery. The air grew tense with expectation, while my mind whirled frantically, trying to find some plausible reason why this was a truly terrible idea. But inspiration had, for once, deserted me. At length I nodded, my mouth dry.

'I can't see any alternative.'

'Neither can I.' Kasteen turned to me, solemnly pronouncing what I truly believed to be my death sentence. 'Can you lead a team back down to the tomb, commissar?'

THIRTEEN

OF COURSE I couldn't refuse, could I? Not in front of all those people. I'd been neatly impaled on my own rhetoric, and pulling out at this stage would have ruined the reputation I didn't deserve. More to the point it would have lost me the respect of the troops, which was probably the only thing I had left capable of preserving my miserable hide. So I made a few appropriately modest comments about appreciating everybody's confidence and hoping I wouldn't let them down before sinking into a torpor of absolute terror which, as luck would have it, was generally mistaken for fatigue.

As a result the rest of the meeting went by in a blur so far as I was concerned, and if anything else of consequence was discussed I must have missed it.[1] I did rouse

---

1. *Quintus's minutes of the meeting are singularly unhelpful in filling in this gap, concerned as they are chiefly with the way the overhead lighting struck highlights from Kasteen's hair.*

myself for long enough to listen to a progress report into some suicidal scheme for disabling the gargant, which Broklaw assured everyone would be effective if the orks in command of it were spectacularly stupid enough to blunder into an obvious trap, but given the intelligence of the ones I'd encountered before in my chequered career this seemed like a safe enough bet. Other than that I took no interest in anything apart from my bowl of tea, which Jurgen, attentive as ever, refilled at intervals.

So it came as something of a surprise when all the civilians stood up and filed out, the quill-pushers and cogboys predictably butting heads at the door over which of them had precedence while Morel and the miners guild delegation sailed serenely past them, and finally the room fell quiet.

'That went well,' Broklaw said, clearly not meaning it. Kasteen nodded.

'They've agreed to the evacuation, anyway. Not that they had a choice, but at least we won't have to waste any manpower herding them onto the shuttles at gunpoint.'

'Don't count on it,' I said. 'Once they've had time to think it over the tech-priests probably won't go without a fight.' At least most of the miners and Administratum staff had already gone, which only left a couple of hundred civilians still planetside. A couple of shuttle flights, no more than that, although lifting the regiment would be a lot more time consuming when the time came for us to pull out.

'Then they can stay and fight the necrons,' Kasteen said. 'I'm not putting any of our people at risk if they start playing silly frakkers.'

'Glad to hear it,' I said. Not that it would make any difference to me, with my molecules scrambled by a necron gauss gun. And that would be if I was lucky; I thought of the other monstrosities in their coats of ork hide, and hoped fervently never to meet them again. I turned my thoughts in more productive directions with an effort. I wasn't dead yet, and by the Emperor I didn't intend to be if I could find the slightest chance of weaselling out of the suicidal assignment I'd backed myself into. 'What's the tactical situation?' We hadn't discussed that in front of the civvies, of course, they were best being jollied along with vague generalities, and a resolute avoidance of phrases like 'we're frakked' which would only upset them.

By way of an answer Kasteen activated the hololith again and Mazarin appeared at her station on the bridge of the *Pure of Heart*, bobbing slightly in the current from a nearby air vent.

'None of this makes a lot of sense to me,' she admitted cheerfully. 'But you're the soldiers. What do you think?' Kasteen, Broklaw and I stared at the latest sensor downloads from the orbiting starship. The ork advance had unmistakably faltered, breaking against our battle line, and pulling back in places to cluster on their left flank. Broklaw frowned.

'The gargant's veered off,' he said. Well, thank the Emperor for that, I thought, at least I wouldn't have to worry about the booby trap they'd laid for it bringing the whole mine in on top of me while I was down there in the dark facing the necrons again... My hands began to tremble slightly as I thought about that, so I stuffed them into the pockets of my greatcoat and studied the hololith grimly. Something about the redistribution of the ork forces was nagging at my subconscious, and I felt my scalp prickling as I finally realised what it was.

'The tunnel entrance we found was about here,' I said, indicating a point on the opposite flank of the mountain from the valley we were so successfully defending. The bulk of the greenskin forces were moving in that direction, the gargant's unexpected diversion merely a part of the general drift. And there was only one obvious reason why the orks' attention would have been distracted from the ongoing battle with us.

'Frakking warp!' Kasteen breathed, coming to the same conclusion. 'The tinheads are attacking the greenies!'

'In some force, too, judging by the number of reinforcements moving up,' Broklaw said, studying the display in more detail. That wasn't necessarily the case, of course, orks will gravitate naturally to wherever they expect the fighting to be fiercest, but it was certainly suggestive.

'Perfect!' Kasteen said, to my absolute astonishment. 'You know what this means?'

'Nope.' Mazarin shrugged in the corner of the hololith, her image shrunk to the size of my hand. 'Not my department.' But of course Kasteen hadn't been talking to her in any case.

'It means the bloody necrons are awake!' I said, a strange mixture of terror and relief dancing down my spine. 'We haven't a hope in hell of getting to the portal now.' I tried to feign disappointment, while wondering how best to ensure I was on the first shuttle up to the freighter.

'Not necessarily,' Mazarin chipped in, and the flare of hope in my chest withered and died. Luckily it was only her image in the room with us, or I'd probably have throttled her with my bare hands. (Not that it would have done me much good, I suppose, given the amount of metal she seemed to have in what was left of her body.) 'If I'm reading these energy spikes right the portal's being activated roughly every seventeen minutes.'

'Which means what, exactly?' Kasteen asked, taking far too much interest in what the bisected woman had to say for my liking. Mazarin shrugged, unless it was the air conditioning behind her kicking up another notch and bouncing her around.

'The necrons here are probably still in stasis. The ones fighting the orks are being shipped in from somewhere else.'

'Securing the tomb before they wake the others,' Broklaw said. Kasteen nodded.

'Sounds plausible.' She looked across at me. 'And they still have no idea we're behind them. You can be in and out before they even know you're there.'

'Lucky me,' I said, clenching my fists in my pockets until the nails drew blood.

'I'M NOT GOING to lie to you,' I said. I felt a vague sense of disconnectedness after that, the reason for which continued to elude me for a while, until I realised that contrary to the habit of a lifetime the subsequent statement was actually true. The harsh arc luminators of the main staging area just inside the mouth of the mine flattened the colours of the scattered equipment around us, including the power lifter against which I leaned in what I hoped was a casual manner rather than revealing the weakness of my knees. 'Our chances of coming back from this assignment are practically non-existent. But it's also no exaggeration to say that the lives of everyone else on the planet, not to mention uncountable others, hang on whether we succeed or not.' I flicked my eyes along the impassive faces in front of me. Not one of them blinked. I ploughed on, feeling vaguely wrong-footed. 'I think you're the best team for the job, which is why I asked for you. But I'll only take willing volunteers. If anyone wants to pull out you have my word there won't be any disciplinary action taken or a word about it on any of your records.' Because I'd be too busy being dead to worry about it... I forced the thought away.

'We're up to it,' the storm trooper sergeant said, the unlit cheroot in the corner of his mouth waggling disconcertingly as he spoke. I gathered that it was some kind of tradition in his squad that he wouldn't light it until the mission was completed. The little knot of men behind him nodded in silent agreement. Not one of them broke ranks, which I would have found astonishing had I not spent a couple of hours combing the records for the most aggressive and disciplined squad in the entire regiment.

And Sergeant Welard and his squad were it: old school storm troopers (quite literally, they'd been together since the schola progenium assessors back on Valhalla had decided they were natural born cannon fodder). They were, accordingly, one of the few teams to have remained single-sex following the amalgamation of the two former regiments which now made up the 597th, since there was no point rotating in replacements for the casualties they'd taken on Corania[1] and wherever else they'd fought before. Schola-raised storm trooper squads generally fight better than most because they've been together so long and know each other so well that they share an instinctive rapport no outsider can ever fully share, but the downside of that is that once their numbers drop below a handful they become pretty much useless, and I've never understood why the Guard persists with the tradition.[2] Right now though, men who'd follow orders without thinking were precisely what I needed, and Welard and his team fit the bill nicely.

'I'm pleased to see my confidence wasn't misplaced,' I said. Apart from Welard there were five regular troopers left out of the original ten, so they were on the verge of falling below the critical threshold at which they would cease to be an effective fighting unit. Nevertheless, they would do. Numbers wouldn't help us on this mission, our only hope was to move fast and stealthily, and that, I knew, was something they were bound to be good at. (In the constant round of rivalries and practical joke playing between the different

---

1. *The system where a tyranid attack had decimated the imperial defenders, necessitating the amalgamation of the 296th and 301st to create the 597th in the first place.*

2. *Because the real reason for the practice is to provide properly indoctrinated foot soldiers for the Inquisition. Of course fewer than five per cent reach the exacting standards required, leaving the ones who don't make the grade to be palmed off on the Guard.*

factions in my days at the schola the storm trooper cadets were by far the most adept at sneaking into the other dorms and common rooms to make mischief, and always set the most inventive booby traps, although I still maintain we had the edge over them on the scrumball pitch. In fact the only team that ever regularly beat the commissar cadets were the novitiates of the Adepta Sororitas, who seemed to think the point of the game was sending the greatest number of opponents they could to the sanitorium rather than scoring goals.)

'We'll get the job done,' Welard said, moving the cheroot to the opposite corner of his mouth, and the quintet behind him nodded in unison. Their silence was unnerving, but I suppose it was a natural consequence of the rapport they shared. Not a word or a gesture was wasted, to the point where, swathed in their greatcoats and hats, their faces partly obscured, they seemed almost as emotionless as servitors. Or the necrons themselves. An aura of almost palpable lethality played about them, which I began to feel almost comforted by, until I remembered the odds stacked against us.

'Any questions?' I asked. Answer came there none, so I drew myself up, straightened my cap, and tried to sound confident. 'Good. Then let's go.'

THE EVACUATION WAS well under way as we set out for the lower levels, a steady flow of miners, Administratum drones and tech-priests walking towards the landing pads with the tense not-quite trot of barely-contained panic, lasgun-wielding troopers guarding the tunnels they thronged through. We strode against the tide, which parted almost miraculously in front of us, each step further from safety seeming like walking on knives to me. A babble of voices surrounded us like syrup, battering the eardrums but overlapping so much that individual words and phrases were indistinguishable.

'Comms check,' I said, more to distract myself than anything, and Welard and the other storm troopers sounded off one by one, although truth to tell, and I ought to be ashamed of it, I was so busy battling my own apprehension that none of their names registered with me. Everyone's comm-bead seemed to be working, though, so I nodded briskly. 'Very good.'

'General order.' Kasteen's voice cut in. 'Anyone in sight of Magos Ernulph report now.' There was an irritable pause, broken only by a faint hiss of static. 'Anyone with an idea of his whereabouts?' Another pause. 'Anyone seeing him, report at once.'

Great. It seemed the tech-priests weren't about to leave their prize behind after all, and were going into hiding until we'd left. Just so long as they stayed out of our way, though, it wasn't my problem.

The passageways we strode through were getting narrower now, the air cooler as we entered the mine workings themselves, and I told myself the shivering which seemed to be gripping my body was simply a result of the falling temperatures. Before long the walls around us were filmed with ice, and shortly after that there was nothing for the ice to coat; we were in the mine itself again.

Ahead of us a cavern opened out, harsh with the glare of luminators mounted on poles around its perimeter, the dark mouths of the main tunnels puncturing the walls at intervals. Equipment and storage crates littered the floor, and I recognised it as one of the main utility areas we'd passed through on our ambull hunt, little guessing the horrors we'd find in the depths below. Beyond this point our journey would truly begin.

'Movement.' One of the troopers raised his hellgun, and the others melted into the industrial detritus around us with breathtaking speed, leaving me feeling uncomfortably exposed. A lone figure was lurking at the mouth of the tunnel ahead of us, half hidden in the gloom beyond. After a moment to recover my composure, as the rational part of my mind kicked in to remind me that orks or necrons wouldn't be bothering with concealment, I strode forward unconcerned expecting to find some stray miner or tech-priest finishing off a last-minute job prior to joining the evacuation. As I got closer to the solitary figure I felt my spirits inexplicably lifting as I caught the faint whiff of a familiar odour.

'Jurgen,' I called out. 'What the frak are you doing here?' My aide stepped fully into view, and the storm troopers emerged from the cover they'd taken, looking mildly sheepish. 'I thought you were stowing our kit on the shuttle.'

'All taken care of, sir.' He produced a thermal flask. 'I thought you might like a bit of tea for later. And a sandwich.' He burrowed in one of his pockets for a moment. 'It's in here somewhere...'

'I see,' I said, silencing the barely audible snickering from a couple of the storm troopers behind me with a quick glance before turning back to Jurgen again. 'And the melta?' He shrugged, the heavy weapon slung across his back shifting as his shoulders moved.

'I couldn't let you carry your own provisions, sir. Wouldn't be fitting.'

'Quite,' I said, astonished yet again at the depth of his loyalty. For the first time I began to feel that I might actually get out of this ludicrous expedition in one piece after all. 'I suppose you'd better come with us, then.'

'Very good, sir.' He saluted as smartly as he ever did, which wasn't very to be honest, but more than made up for that in enthusiasm, and fell into step beside me. I motioned Welard and his men to the front and we set off into the darkness, towards the terrors which lay in wait for us in the frozen depths below.

Editorial Note:

As the attentive reader will readily appreciate, the overall tactical situation was now becoming increasingly complex. The unexpected necron attack on the orkish flank had thrown the greenskins into disarray, but, typically, they responded with the single-minded aggression of their kind, flinging themselves against this new and deadly foe with what can only be described as enthusiasm. The resulting carnage can barely be imagined.

However, the lessening of the pressure on the beleaguered Valhallans was undoubtedly of great benefit, enabling the evacuation of the Imperial forces to take place relatively unhindered, especially as most of the front-line units had already been given their orders to disengage in preparation for luring the gargant into the now abandoned booby trap.

As to the fate of this formidable war machine, the following extract from Sulla's memoirs may prove illuminating despite her best efforts to render it unreadable.

* * *

Extracted from *Like a Phoenix From the Flames: The Founding of the 597th*, by General Jenit Sulla (retired), 097.M42.

NOTWITHSTANDING THE FLOOD of rumours which had swept the regiment, most of them contradictory, but which all agreed in the main particular that Commissar Cain had discovered some new and potent threat in the bowels of the mine, I held fast to my duty and resumed my post at the front line. Whatever the truth of the matter I had my orders, and as a loyal officer that was enough for me. No doubt those better placed to evaluate the intelligence the commissar had so heroically gathered would inform us of whatever we needed to know to meet and overcome this latest vile stain on His Glorious Majesty's blessed dominions in the fullness of time, or so I told my subordinates, and until such information was furnished wild speculation about daemons, tyranids, or walking metal statues was merely a waste of time. This last flight of fantasy would, of course, turn out to have more than a grain of truth in it, but in the closing years of the forty-first millennium, with the true horror of the necron menace still unknown to all but a few, such talk seemed naught but the most febrile of fantasies.

My platoon had resumed its position in the forward line, with strict instructions to fall back at the specified time to draw the gargant into our carefully laid trap, and we had been engaging the main bulk of the greenskin army with a gratifying amount of success. So much so, in fact, that I began to fear that we were thinning them out too quickly, and that we would be forced to engage the towering war machine ourselves before the time came to disengage. The shadow of that grim colossus was falling across us as we gazed in awe at it, the shrieks of thousands of tonnes of unlubricated metal sliding across one another as it tottered forward on unfeasibly stubby-looking legs setting the teeth of every woman and man among us on edge, and I found myself comparing it most unfavourably to the swift darting elegance of the eldar walkers and the majestic nobility of our own blessed titans.[1]

I was on the verge of ordering those fortunate enough to be manning the forward trenches to engage those members of its crew who could quite clearly be discerned scurrying about on the main hull when the vast cannon nestled in the construct's belly spoke, the concussion sufficient to drive the breath from our lungs and cause cracks to appear in our stout fortifications even at this distance. I turned my head, expecting to see the most grievous havoc wreaked among the precious buildings of the refinery, only to see instead the distant gout of a vast explosion somewhere among the slopes of the mountains surrounding this vital outpost of the Imperium.

'It's veering off!' my communications specialist yelled, angling his head so I could read his lips, for the awesome sound of that titanic explosion had left my ears still ringing, and to my astonishment I beheld the truth of his words. It had clearly faltered, almost on the point of engaging our forward line, and was now turning ponderously towards the looming peaks it had so inexplicably attacked.

At that moment we received our orders to withdraw, so I cannot be sure of what I witnessed next, seeing it as I did at an ever-increasing distance in short, snatched glances over my shoulder as we ran, and through a curtain of falling snow. However, it seemed to me that the terrifying construct was surrounded by small structures, no higher than its knee, which had appeared by sorceries so arcane I

---

1. *Most unlikely, as at this point in her career she had yet to see either. Unless you count holopicts, of course.*

was at a loss to explain them. Blank metal pyramids they were, dully reflective, and surrounded by a crackle of lightning which blurred their outline still further; sorcerous lightning without a doubt, for it lashed forth to scourge the hull of that mountain of metal, striking sparks so bright they hurt to look upon. Chunks of metal larger than Chimeras fell lazily to the snow, and the burning bodies of its luckless crew pattered down around them, so that I cannot for the life of me conceive how it could ever have prevailed. But whether it did or not I cannot truly answer, for the snow whirled in around that epic confrontation, and I saw no more.

FOURTEEN

ONE THING I have to say for Welard and his storm troopers, they were as fast and stealthy as I could have wished for. Jurgen and I had to work hard at keeping up with them even though they advanced as cautiously as though the enemy were already in plain sight. Two or three of them covered the tunnel ahead while the others darted forward to conceal themselves in crevices or patches of shadow before taking up the duties of guardians themselves to allow their comrades to move forward in their turn. They did all of this with an eerie precision apparently unhindered by the bulk of the melta bombs they carried, communicating only by hand signals and eschewing the use of the comm-beads, for which I was grateful, starting in dread at every superfluous sound which might call attention to us. But as we hurried on, following the route which had etched itself indelibly on the synapses responsible for my ability to navigate underground, we saw none of the signs I so dreaded. No gleam of metal in the darkness ahead, no green charnel glow forewarning us of the presence of death incarnate.

We advanced in semi-darkness, our luminators shrouded, so that the dazzling highlights which had been struck from the ice surrounding us on my previous trip into the depths were almost entirely absent. Now, instead of the refulgent background glow I'd grown used to, the walls threw back no more than a slick, almost organic-looking sheen, as though we were passing down the gullet of some warp-spawned leviathan. The thought was hardly a comforting one, and I shuddered from more than the cold.

At length we reached the dead-end passage where Penlan had fallen, revealing the existence of the ambull tunnels below the mine, and we paused to regroup.

'This is it,' I warned everyone. 'From now on our chances of meeting a necron are greatly increased.' What I meant was 'practically inevitable,' but I shied away from pronouncing those words. Not out of deference to the feelings of Welard and his men, who I had no doubt would have responded with the same lack of emotion that they had displayed thus far, but because I didn't want to face that thought myself. Welard waggled his cheroot, which had by now acquired a thin scum of frost over the tightly-packed tabac leaves it was composed of, and which crunched irritatingly between his teeth as he spoke.

'We'll be ready for them.' He gestured with his left hand. 'Hastur.' One of the troopers stepped forward to cover the hole with his hellgun while the rest rappelled down into the darkness with display team precision. I heard a couple of clicks in my comm-bead, almost as if it were picking up some stray interference from somewhere but which I knew was the signal from the advance party confirming that it was all clear down there, and the sergeant grinned at me. For the first time it struck me that he was actually enjoying this. 'Coming?' he asked, and disappeared down the hole after his men.

Why I simply didn't shake my head and run for the surface, intent only on making it to the next shuttle out, I'll never know. There was still my fraudulent reputation to consider, of course, double-edged weapon though that had become in the last few years, dragging me into these ghastly situations almost as readily as I was able to turn it to my advantage, but even now I found myself reluctant to surrender it. And it couldn't be denied that my chances of survival would be marginally better with a screen of storm troopers between me and the necrons instead of wandering around these catacombs alone. I glanced round the narrow chamber, steeling myself, and met Jurgen's eyes. The sight of him was instantly reassuring, despite his usual unprepossessing appearance, a visible (and olfactory) reminder of all the perils we'd faced and bested together. He grinned at me, and hefted the bulk of his melta.

'After you, sir,' he said. 'I'll watch your back.' A task, I have to say, which he performed admirably throughout our years of service together. I forced a smile to my face.

'I don't doubt it,' I said, then before I could change my mind I seized the line and slithered down into the bowels of hell.

I landed heavily, but retained my footing, and was able to step aside as Jurgen lurched down the rope behind me. The storm troopers looked mildly disdainful at our performance, the awkwardness of which was underlined a moment later by Hastur's descent, which he managed with the dexterity of an acrobat.

'Where to?' Welard asked.

'This way.' I indicated the right direction and waited while the storm troopers went through the gap first, falling into place behind them. With every step we took the knot in my stomach wound itself tighter, the memory of where we were going insinuating itself into my forebrain, inextricably intertwined with images of the massacre I'd witnessed on Interitus Prime. This would be different, I kept telling myself. I wasn't fleeing in panic through an unknown labyrinth this time, I was heading for a known location, which, by the Emperor's grace, I had already entered before and escaped to tell the tale. Kasteen was right, the necrons would be concerned entirely with the greenskins, they didn't even know we were here...

'Found something,' the pointman said, snapping me out of my reverie and back to the claustrophobic confines of the ambull run. We closed up, the faint light from our shrouded luminators glinting from some detritus on the tunnel floor.

'What do you make of that, sir?' Jurgen asked, his feeble beam picking out something only he had noticed. Apart from myself, he was the only one of our party who had walked these narrow tunnels before, and would be able to notice any changes. The hairs on the back of my neck rose, something that happens in popular fiction far more often than it does in real life, and which I can assure you is a remarkably uncomfortable sensation. My aide was shining his luminator down a narrow cylinder punched into the ice lining the tunnel, about the width of my forearm and deep beyond the strength of the lamp he carried to pick out the end.

'They've been here,' I murmured. The only possible explanation was a stray gauss flayer shot striking the tunnel wall. I looked about us, finding several more of the sinister indentations.

'Then who were they shooting at?' Jurgen asked. That was a good question. If the orks had made it this far into the tunnels our job was about to get a great deal more complicated. I moved up to join Welard and the point man, who were staring in perplexity at a small mound of metal objects embedded in ice, ominously streaked with red.

'What do you think these are, sir?' he asked, the air of unassailable confidence taking a dent for the first time since I'd met him. I looked at the assemblage of tubes and wires for a moment, then the bile rose into my throat as I realised what I was looking at.

'They're augmetics,' I said, swallowing heavily. 'They've been ripped out of someone.' So that was where Ernulph had disappeared to. These might not be his remains, of course, but it was carrots to credits he'd led whatever foolhardy expedition this pathetic revenant had been a part of. I wondered vaguely if we'd find traces of any other victims, or if they'd all simply been vaporised.

One thing was certain, though. Thanks to these idiots the necrons would know there were humans on Simia Orichalcae now, and were most likely waiting in ambush ahead of us. This was just getting better and better.

Well, there was no point in standing around worrying about it, time was most definitely of the essence here, so I got everyone moving again and dropped back to walk beside Jurgen.

'Be ready,' I warned him, 'things could be about to get–'

I was interrupted by the dying shriek of our point man as he flared and dwindled to nothing in the necrotic glow of one of those hellish gauss weapons, and then the metallic warriors whose appearance I'd so dreaded were upon us.

'Place your shots,' Welard said calmly, and the surviving storm troopers unleashed a hail of hellgun fire against our attackers. The glare of the lasbolts impacting on the leading necron dazzled my eyes, then its chest gave way, seared and blasted by the precision volley, and it tumbled to the ice-slick floor revealing a fresh target behind it, already levelling another gauss flayer.

Credit where it's due, Welard and his men certainly knew their stuff. As I've mentioned before, the ambull tunnels were narrow, forcing the hideous automata to come at us almost in single file. But the storm troopers' discipline was excellent, and with the death of our first casualty they'd dropped into a practiced routine, the men at the front falling prone, those behind kneeling, and the ones at the rear standing up so that the whole squad was able to concentrate their fire as one. The second necron lost its head, quite literally, and fell heavily across the first with a sound not unlike someone kicking a bin full of scrap metal. As I watched it fall I realised, with a thrill of horror, that the first metallic warrior we'd all thought destroyed was rising slowly to its feet again.

'Jurgen,' I called, and my aide stepped forward levelling the melta. The storm troopers slipped easily out of his way, keeping up a barrage of hellgun fire to cover him while he aimed, and shielding their eyes as he squeezed the trigger.

The flare of actinic energy stabbed my retina, even through my closed eyelids, and the roar of ice flashing instantly into steam echoed all around us. The air against my face was suddenly warm and wet, as though I'd been teleported into a rain-forest somewhere. As I blinked my vision clear I could see nothing but puddles of molten metal surrounded by grotesque lumps of statuary, some of which still twitched, freezing almost at once into the rapidly-reforming ice. Then, in an instant, they faded away as though they'd never been, leaving behind nothing but drifting vapour and some oddly-shaped indentations in the tunnel floor.

'Clear,' Hastur called, taking the place of the disintegrated point man, and leading us on into the darkness. Welard nodded at Jurgen, an almost imperceptible tilt of the head as he passed my aide, the closest I suppose he could come to expressing thanks to an outsider, and jogged along in the wake of his men. I couldn't help contrasting the reaction of Grifen's team to the loss of Lunt with the storm troopers' matter-of-fact dismissal of the loss of one of their own, and mentioned as much to the sergeant.

'The mission comes first,' he said, his face hard, and that's all he would say on the subject. I wasn't exactly in the mood for idle conversation either, so I let it drop, and resumed straining my ears for the slightest sound which might indicate the approach of more of those monstrous guardians.

Luck or the Emperor must have been with us, though, as all too soon I beheld the baleful glow which forewarned us that we were about to reach our goal. We flattened ourselves against the ice-covered bedrock of the tunnel wall as we approached the entrance to that mighty cavern, through which I'd escaped only a few hours before, and strained our senses for any sign that we had been discovered.

All seemed quiet, except for that damnable humming and the artillery barrage pounding of my heart, so we crept out into the chamber I had so fervently hoped never to see again. My scalp crawled with apprehension, and I had to exert every micron of self-control I possessed to appear calm in front of Welard and his men. They kept their weapons trained on every patch of cover, every green-tinged shadow in the lee of those towering and incomprehensible mechanisms. If they were at all disconcerted by the sheer sense of wrongness surrounding them they gave no sign of it.

'Which way?' the sergeant asked, and I indicated the direction of the portal. He nodded. 'Move out.'

We scurried through that vast space as Jurgen and I had mere hours before, still sticking to the shadows of the towering machines, that ghastly charnel light bathing everything in a sheen of putrescence. Some of them were marked with the peculiar stick and circle hieroglyphics I'd seen on Interitus Prime, and you can be sure the memories the sight of them stirred up did little to calm my fears. By this time my nerves were stretched tighter than harp strings, and it was probably this sense of heightened paranoia which let me hear an almost inaudible sound, a faint scraping which reminded me of scuttling vermin. I signalled the sergeant.

'Five metres, two o'clock. Behind that... Whatever the hell it is.' Welard nodded, and gestured a couple of troopers to flank the gleaming tangle of green-glowing pipes. The rest of us closed up, ready to face whatever the threat was, and I drew my laspistol and chainsword. Not that I expected the latter to be much good against metal rather than flesh, but it had served me well on many occasions before now, and the weight of it felt comforting in my hand.

'Contact. No threat,' said one of the storm troopers, his voice slightly attenuated in my comm-bead, and fell silent again. I hurried forward to join them, cursing their taciturnity.

'Explain,' I said, equally terse, and afraid of transmitting for long enough to be triangulated on. If the trooper was surprised he gave no sign of it.

'It's a cogboy,' he explained flatly.

Not just any cogboy, of course, the Emperor has more of a sense of humour than that. Even before I joined them I had a sense of foreboding, which was amply justified as I looked down at the quivering bundle trying to wedge itself under the largest pipe.

'Logash,' I said. The young tech-priest must have recognised my voice, because he turned and looked up at me. Though his metal eyes made any expression hard to read, a sense of recognition began to surface through the expression of stark terror suffusing his face.

'Commissar Cain?' His voice trembled, wavering in pitch like a boy in early adolescence. If he wasn't bonkers before, I thought, he certainly was now. 'You were right, you were right. We were unworthy to trespass on the sacred mysteries of the Omnissiah–'

'Where are the others?' I interrupted, squatting down to his level, and keeping my voice calm. I haven't had that much experience with madmen, give or take the odd Chaos cultist, but I've seen enough cases of combat fatigue and his symptoms seemed similar; overwhelmed by the horrors he'd witnessed he'd simply retreated inside himself. 'Where's Magos Ernulph?'

'Dead,' he moaned, his blank eyes roving aimlessly, 'struck down by the guardians for our hubris. We should have listened to you, we should have listened...'

Resisting the temptation to say 'told you so,' albeit with some difficulty, I raised him to his feet as gently as I could manage. (Which wasn't very, to be honest, he was all but catatonic, but I succeeded in the end.)

'You're bringing him with us?' Welard asked, in tones which left me in no doubt what he thought of that idea. I nodded.

'We can't just leave him here,' I said. The sergeant looked dubious, and for a moment I wavered, thinking our mission here was hanging by a thread as it was, and adding a babbling lunatic to our number wasn't likely to help any. Then again, Logash had been down here longer than any of us, and might have information which could save our lives, or at least help us blow up the portal. As so often in my life it was an almost impossible decision to make, and one which no one else could, but that's why I get to wear the fancy cap. I pulled on the tech-priest's arm, reminded of Grifen's attempt to snap Magot out of her stupor not far from this very spot. 'We have to go,' I said. To my relief Logash nodded, and fell into step beside Jurgen and myself.

'I take it Ernulph asked you to guide him down here?' I asked, and the tech-priest nodded.

'I remembered the way. The Omnissiah guided–'

'Yes, quite,' I interrupted. 'Then what happened?' His face twisted.

'We entered the temple, and the guardians fell upon us. Some were cut down where they stood, in the very act of making obeisance to the machine god, while others fled. But the guardians pursued them without mercy.' That explained the remains we'd found in the tunnel anyway, a few of them must have made it that far out of here before they were cornered. Logash turned a pinched, anguished face to me. 'They were swift and terrible,' he whispered, 'and shrouded in horror.'

Well that sounded pretty much like every form of necron I'd ever encountered, and I dismissed his words as a figure of speech at the time, although I was soon to discover how right he was.

'Contact,' Hastur said, and opened fire. The other storm troopers followed suit, and I dived for cover, dragging Logash into the shadows with me. A moment later an acrid odour of unwashed socks indicated that Jurgen had joined us.

I levelled my laspistol, seeking a target, and was gratified to see that the storm troopers were doing sterling work in engaging the advancing party of metallic warriors. They were the skin-hunters we'd seen before, or identical copies of them, advancing with terrifying speed, their long blades whispering through the air as they swept back and forth. Instead of ork hides, though, the leading ranks were swathed in human skins, still wet and leaking, thin runnels of blood turned black by the corpse-light, which illuminated everything here, veining the metal torsos beneath. As I tracked the leading one, placing a las bolt squarely in the centre of its forehead, I realised with a shudder that the obscene covering it wore still had the vestige of a face; a face, moreover, which I recognised.

'Ernulph!' I whispered, revulsion twisting my stomach, as the creature inside his skin staggered backwards. I made sure of it with a flurry of follow-up shots, then turned my attention to the monstrosity behind it. The magos had been a pompous fool, it was true, but no one deserved a fate like that.

'They're behind us!' Hastur warned, before his voice rose in a throat-rending scream. I turned just in time to see him borne down by one of the razor-wielding automata, eviscerated in seconds, his blood left streaming down the sides of the bulky metal cabinet from behind which, a heartbeat before, he had been pouring hellgun fire into the main body of our vile assailants. A moment later the flayed one rose from a crouch, the still wet skin of the deceased storm trooper clinging to its metal torso by the stickiness of its own blood.

'Frak this!' I shouted. 'Jurgen!' On cue my aide unleashed another blast from his melta into the centre of the group, cutting a swathe through them as efficiently as before. Once again the necrons caught by the full force of the blast were simply annihilated, flashing into vapour as thoroughly as the victims of their own terrible weapons, while the ones at the fringe of that ravening burst of energy staggered, limbs and torsos seared and softened like candle wax. For a moment I expected them to rally, restoring themselves in that unnerving fashion I'd seen before, but the survivors simply vanished into thin air. For some reason Hastur's body went with them, but why they would want it was a mystery I was sure I would never want to know the answer to.[1]

'How far to the objective?' Welard asked, as the surviving storm troopers regrouped. Beyond a single glance at the coating of blood on the metal surfaces marking the spot where Hastur had died he seemed utterly unperturbed by the terrible fate which had befallen his comrade, and the rest seemed equally focussed on the outcome of our mission, scanning the halls around us for any sign of renewed necron activity. I was grateful for their vigilance, but I was beginning to find their complete lack of emotion somewhat unnerving.

'About three hundred metres,' I said, forcing my mind back to the issue at hand. Welard nodded, and waved to his remaining squad mates to move out. Jurgen and I fell in behind them as before, although I was now acutely

---

1. *Presumably for the same reason their harvester fleets abduct the populations of isolated colony worlds. Whatever that is.*

aware that an attack could come from any direction, and you can be sure that I scanned our surroundings with even more diligence than before. I got Logash moving again with a relatively light tug on the arm, and he trotted along with us, apparently perfectly happy to follow whatever orders I gave now I'd been proven to be right about the inadvisability of being here in the first place.

After a few moments I caught sight of a bright glow from beyond the concealing bulk of one of those vast machines, and indicated it to the sergeant.

'That's it,' I said, watching it pulse like the beating of a diseased heart, and fighting down the surge of dread which suddenly suffused me. 'The portal.' The glow intensified for a moment, with an accompanying thunder crack of displaced air which rumbled and echoed through that city-sized cavern as though presaging a tropical downpour. 'And it's active.' I tried not to think about how many reinforcements had suddenly arrived; rather too many, judging by the amount of air that had been elbowed out of their way as they materialised.

'Not for long,' Welard said, his confidence apparently undiminished by the loss of a third of his squad already.

'Movement,' one of the troopers cut in, as blandly unemotional as before. 'Eleven o'clock, thirty metres.' We turned to face this new threat, the quartet of storm troopers raising their hellguns, while Jurgen lifted the melta into a firing position. Logash was trembling violently.

'Omnissiah protect thy circuits,' he mumbled, 'let this unworthy relay speed the electrons of thy great computation, preserving us from burnout...' and other tech-priest gibberish. I glanced back at the storm troopers, and was astonished to see them quivering almost as badly.

'Emperor be with us,' the closest was muttering under his breath, 'protect us with the shield of thy will...'

Something was seriously wrong, I thought. After everything they'd already shrugged off it was hard to credit that they would be spooked so badly by a single group of warriors who barely outnumbered us. But Willard's jaw was clenched, bisecting the cheroot, most of which had fallen unnoticed to the floor. The hellgun jittered in his hands, wavering almost too wildly to aim, and he was muttering too, one of the catechisms of command which had evidently been drummed into him by the schola tutors, and rather more effectively than it had been with me judging by his demeanour up to this point.

He began firing wildly at the approaching warriors, and as if that were a signal the others opened up too, badly-aimed las-bolts detonating all round the necrons with barely a single hit scored, almost as inaccurate as orks. There was something about these warriors which was different from the others we'd seen, a more resolute, self-aware quality, which sent shudders down my spine as I took in more of the details of their appearance. Less skeletal than the others they seemed composed of ceramics as much as metal, and with writhing pipes and cables corded around their metallic bones which flexed like living muscles as they moved. Thin tendrils of despair seemed to wrap themselves around my very soul as they approached us, bringing not mere death but annihilation in their wake. Fear I was used to, could master and control at least to some extent, but this was different, a primal terror which rose up from somewhere deep within me, and threatened to swamp my very sense of self. Levelling the laspistol in my hand, and ironically grateful for the augmetics which steadied my grip in spite of the treachery of my own body, I fired at the leading one, gouging a neat crater in the centre of its forehead.

'The horror! The horror!' Logash was going foetal on me again, clinging to my ankles, and the storm troopers were breaking, fleeing in all directions with cries of terror. 'The horror returns!'

'Jurgen, get him off me!' I yelled, restrained from following only by the dead weight of the gibbering tech-priest. I fought against that rush of primal emotion, feeling my very sense of self under threat in a way I hadn't experienced since the Slaaneshi witch tried to sacrifice my soul to her perverted deity on Slawkenberg over a decade before, and shooting entirely by instinct now. The green lance of a gauss flayer beam missed me by a couple of centimetres, and punched a neat hole through the smooth-sided cabinet beside me. I shot back, taking my assailant in the chest, and making it stagger for a moment before resuming its unhurried advance.

'Come along, sir.' My aide was at my side now, prising Logash's fingers away from my boot, which wasn't easy given that they were closed by a rictus of terror and augmetic into the bargain. The pressure against my soul eased abruptly, as though cut off by the slamming of a door. I hustled Logash to his feet, and moved behind Jurgen as he aimed and fired the melta.

Once again the powerful weapon did its work, taking down our most immediate assailants, but this time there was to be no reprieve from them teleporting out to lick their wounds. The group had scattered to hunt down the fleeing storm troopers, and we only got a couple of them. As I looked around for some sign of our erstwhile companions I saw two of them taken down with gauss flayer shots, screaming into vapour even as I watched. Welard was backed into a corner between two blocky structures the size of Chimeras, eyes unfocussed, his mind clearly gone, hellgun hanging forgotten from his hand, babbling incoherently. He was still crying out to the Emperor for help which never came when the leading automaton swung the heavy blade of its polearm-like weapon and took his head off cleanly with a single sweep, spraying itself with a thick coating of his blood.

'Come on,' I said urgently. 'We have to get out of here!' Logash was beginning to recover whatever was left of his wits, and shook his head slowly.

'What happened?' he asked. I was beginning to understand, but there was no time now for lengthy
explanations, and at our last meeting Amberley had
impressed on both Jurgen and myself the paramount
importance of not revealing his gift to anyone, so I just
grabbed him by the arm to get him moving.

'Stay close to Jurgen,' I instructed, and we went to
ground between a blank-faced metal cabinet about three
storeys high and a loop of conduit which resembled a
glowing green intestine. A faint shriek, abruptly cut off,
confirmed the loss of the last storm trooper.

With pounding pulses we stayed put for some time, as
Logash had undoubtedly done before, while those
ghastly apparitions began what had every appearance of
a methodical search for us. To my relief, however, they
seemed to become mildly disorientated every time they
approached our hiding place, veering off before they had
come within a handful of metres of us, a deliverance I
could only attribute to Jurgen's peculiar qualities.[1]

At length, when everything seemed quiet again, I
decided it was time to move. The evacuation must be
well under way by now, and I meant to be on a shuttle
and safe aboard the *Pure of Heart* before anything else
had a chance to go wrong.

'What about the portal, sir?' Jurgen wondered aloud. I
shrugged.

'Nothing we can do about it now.' Which was actually
true, as the storm troopers had been carrying the melta
charges which were the only things which might have
stood some chance of destroying it, and they'd been

---

1. *Perhaps correctly. The aura of terror projected by necron pariahs appears to
be at least partly a psychic phenomenon, so it's quite reasonable to assume that
a blank would repel them and mask the effect. However, since no other record
exists of a blank coming into such close proximity to a group of pariahs, and
they're far too rare and valuable to risk in deliberately testing this hypothesis, it
must remain conjectural.*

vaporised along with the soldiers. 'We'll just have to call in the Navy after all.' Tough luck on the galaxy, of course, but it's a big place, and even a necron army couldn't put that big a dent in it. I hoped. So we made our cautious way back to the tunnel we'd come in by, scurrying from cover to cover as we had done before, and freezing into immobility at every sign of movement.

To my immense relief we encountered no more of those terrible apparitions, catching sight of the more common warriors only at a distance. The aperture left by the ambulls was unguarded, to my delighted surprise, and I regained the sanctuary of the ice tunnels with a lightness of spirit which was almost intoxicating.

It was too good to last, of course, and inevitably it didn't.

Editorial Note:

As Cain began to make his way back to the surface, things were begin-
ning to take an unfortunate turn there too. The tech-priests' incursion
into the necron tomb had indeed, as he feared, drawn their attention
to the existence of the human colony above their heads, while the orks,
outmatched as they were, had begun to break, only to find the Valhal-
lan defences weakened or abandoned altogether as they fell back. Not
unnaturally many of the routing greenskins took advantage of the new
line of retreat thus opened up, and began to threaten the refinery itself.

Under this renewed pressure the evacuation began to falter. Even
though almost two full companies had thus far been ferried up to the
orbiting starship the converted civilian shuttles aboard the Pure of
Heart *simply weren't up to the challenge of embarking an entire reg-*
iment in a matter of hours. As the following extract from Captain
Durant's log makes clear, the loss of well over half the men and
women deployed just a few days before seemed almost inevitable.

* * *

+++*Vox-log record of Captain Durant,
Merchant fleet freighter* Pure of Heart, *651.932 M41.*+++

STILL STUCK IN orbit around this miserable iceball. At the last count we had most of the civilian staff and their families stowed away somewhere, only a couple of hundred still cluttering up the corridors with their carcasses and personal effects, but Bosun Kleg has promised to sort that out so I'm leaving him to it.

The Guardsmen have started arriving back up here too, although at least they've got somewhere to bunk. The officers are having a hard time keeping order, as most of them seem concerned about the majority still stranded planetside. Can't say I blame them, as Mazarin says there's no way our shuttles can get many more runs in before the refinery's overrun by the greenskins or these metal creatures, or possibly both. She keeps checking the sensor net and calling the surface with updates, but so far she says the gropos[1] keep losing ground, and I can't see any way of stopping that.

But then I'm only a starship captain, thank the Emperor, so what I know about soldiering you could write on the back of a holocard. I told Mazarin not to worry, that colonel looks as though she knows what she's doing and their commissar's supposed to be some kind of hero, but I can tell she wasn't convinced...

---

1. *A contraction of 'ground pounders,' a Navy term for the Imperial Guard units sometimes billeted aboard their warships. Less common among merchant crews, Durant's use of it here implies that this wasn't the first time the* Pure of Heart *had been pressed into service as a fleet auxiliary.*

FIFTEEN

AFTER MAKING OUR way through the ambull tunnels without so much as a sniff of the necrons I began to think we might just be lucky enough to rejoin our comrades without further incident, and I must confess to a sensation akin to euphoria as we scrambled up the rope to emerge into the lower galleries of the mine itself. After the cramped ambull runs the high ceiling and the wide tunnels of the man-made workings seemed as broad and open as a city boulevard. We made good time back towards the surface, proceeding in line abreast at a rapid trot. Logash seemed to be a little more rational now we'd left that hive of the damned behind us at last, although being a tech-priest that was only relatively speaking of course, and he kept up with Jurgen and myself without any obvious difficulty.

Jurgen and I had set our luminators to full refulgence now we were back on what I fondly imagined was safer ground, and the beams were lighting our way some considerable distance in front of us. The surrounding ice was bouncing the light as it had before, throwing back the photons in the shimmering blues and star cluster sparkles I remembered so well, so it was a second or two before I realised that the gleam up ahead had come not from the walls but from a reflective metal surface.

'Kill the lights!' I shouted as the coin finally dropped, and twisted to the side as I did so, a reflex which undoubtedly saved my life. A bilious green beam cut through the space in which I'd been standing an instant before, illuminating for an instant the darkness which now enshrouded us, Jurgen having followed my lead, and throwing the three of us into sharp relief before it vanished again, evanescent as lightning. The situation was as grim as any I'd faced; to remain where we were would make us sitting targets as the necrons advanced, whereas the slightest glimmer of light would betray our position. A couple more dazzling green flares flickered past us to emphasize the point. Fleeing blindly down the tunnel would merely ensure we were shot in the back, if we didn't simply slip and fall on the icy surface. Our only option seemed to be to stand and fight, although judging by the positions of their weapon flashes the metal warriors were too spread out to make an obvious target for Jurgen's melta, negating the only advantage we had.

I had just drawn my laspistol, preparing for a bit of speculative fire myself in the no doubt vain hope that the necrons would think twice about rushing us (from what I'd seen of them before they didn't strike me as being easily intimidated), when I felt a light tap on my arm.

'This way,' Logash whispered, and I heard the faint scurrying sound of rapid crawling movement to my left. A moment later I heard the same murmur from somewhere in Jurgen's immediate vicinity (which wasn't hard to pinpoint, as my sense of smell was still unimpeded), and I realised with a thrill of hope that the young tech-priest's augmetic eyes were somehow able to function in the darkness which enveloped us.

Having nothing to lose I crawled rapidly in the direction of his voice, guided by occasional murmurs of 'straight ahead,' and 'left a bit... No, the other left, I meant mine...' until I found myself against the frozen surface of the wall. I was just about to ask what now when a gloved hand accompanied by Jurgen's unmistakable odour reached out to seize my arm.

'In here, commissar,' he whispered, giving me the full benefit of his halitosis, and I found myself squeezing through a narrow crevice in the ice. After a few metres it angled sharply, concealing us completely from the main shaft, and we held our collective breath as a clatter of metal feet echoed past our hiding place.

'Well spotted,' I said, when I was sure it was quiet out there, and adjusted my luminator to minimum refulgence. My companions' faces emerged out of the gloom, Logash's pale, and Jurgen's as impassive as ever. The techpriest nodded.

'Praise the Omnissiah for our deliverance...' he began, and I hushed him quickly.

'Yes, good, thanks very much,' I said. 'Any idea where this goes?' It wasn't on the chart I'd seen before, but that was hardly surprising, showing as it did every sign of being a natural fault rather than having been dug.[1] Logash pondered a moment.

'It seems to be bearing towards the main processing area,' he said at last. 'Assuming it doesn't just peter out.' Well that was a risk I was willing to take, since the alternative was be facing Emperor knew how many necron patrols. I hoped they were simply scouting the mine rather than invading it in force, but I wasn't keen to hang

---

1. *How Cain came to this conclusion he doesn't bother to explain; it was probably something to do with his affinity for underground environments.*

around and find out one way or the other. At least this way we stood a better chance of avoiding them.

An hour or so later I was beginning to think we'd have done better taking our chances playing tag with the necrons. The fault was narrow and jagged, so we were climbing up slopes or slithering down them more often than we were walking, and chunks of ice kept catching at our feet or projecting from the walls at heights and angles calculated to bruise or worse. On several occasions we had to crawl, as the ceiling descended too low for us to walk, and once we were forced to worm our way forwards on our stomachs as the passage became too constricted even for that. Jurgen's bulky melta became wedged with monotonous regularity, requiring some laborious chipping away of the ice with our combat blades before we could free it. (My chainsword would have done the job in a tenth of the time, of course, but in that confined space one of us could all too readily have lost a limb by accident, so it remained in its scabbard.) Each time it happened I considered simply abandoning the cumbersome weapon, but it had proven its use too often to be lightly discarded, so I simply gritted my teeth at the delay and carried on.

My sense of direction was no less sure down here than in any other underground passageway, so at least I had the consolation of knowing that we'd come almost a kilometre from our encounter in the main gallery and were moving in the general direction of the centre of the complex, when Logash paused. He was continuing to lead us simply because the passageway was too narrow for any of us to change position, which had left me trailing in Jurgen's wake, uncomfortably aware that if the metal warriors found the entrance to the cleft and came after us I'd be the first one to know about it. The thought was an unpleasant one, producing an itching sensation between my shoulder blades, so I tried not to dwell on it.

'What's the matter?' I asked. The tech-priest shrugged.

'Dead end,' he said. I could have throttled him, but fortunately Jurgen was in the way. I shook my head, unwilling to believe it.

'It can't be.' The words were a reflex denial, but as I said them I was sure that I was right, all of my tunnel rat's instincts told me so. I wondered for a moment why I was so sure, then realised I could feel a faint current of air on my face. 'There's a draft in here.'

'The passage seems to continue,' Logash agreed. 'But it won't do us any good unless you can get through a five centimetre gap.' That really was hard to believe. The passage had constricted before, of course, but that it could narrow so much, so fast, went against all my experience in such an environment. I said so, possibly a little more forcefully than necessary, and Logash squeezed against the ice wall to let me see for myself. Our way was indeed blocked, by a regular convex surface which curved down to just above the floor. Something about the shape struck me as familiar, and then I realised that it was the lower part of a vast cylinder some three or four metres in diameter.

'What the hell's that?' I asked. Logash thumped it with his hand, producing the unmistakable dull thud of thick metal.

'One of the main extraction pipes,' he said. 'Runs up to the processing plant on the surface.'

'And what's in it at the moment?' I asked, an idea so audacious I could barely acknowledge it beginning to form even as I spoke. Logash shrugged.

'Nothing now the plant's shutting down...' His voice trailed off as he evidently came to the same conclusion as I had. I reached an arm out towards him, past my aide.

'Can you get behind Jurgen?' I asked.

'I can try.' It wasn't easy, I can tell you that, but after what seemed to be an eternity of wriggling and swearing he and I were crouched behind what little cover we could find, and Jurgen was aiming the heavy weapon at the pipe. As before we were engulfed in a roar of steam as he fired, so it was a moment or two before our vision cleared enough to show us the metre-diameter hole he had successfully blasted in the wall of the conduit.

'That'll have to be logged for the repair crews,' Logash remarked conversationally, as if the place would ever be back in operation now the necrons were here, and after a moment to let the metal cool Jurgen hoisted himself through the hole and into the pipe.

I followed suit, the tech-priest bounding up ahead of me, to find myself in an echoing metal tube at least twice my own height floored with rapidly-refreezing slush where the metal had conducted the heat of the melta blast away. Stalactites of ice descended from the curved ceiling, where the uniform coating of rime had been disturbed by our blazing entry.

'This way,' I said, taking the lead again, and moving as rapidly up the gentle slope as I could manage on the treacherous surface. Jurgen had no trouble matching my pace, of course, having been born to conditions like these, and Logash apparently had some sort of augmetic balance enhancer, as he seemed as sure-footed as the Valhallan. Despite my tendency to slip unnervingly from time to time, and the faint curvature underfoot doing nothing to make the job any easier, I found the wide, unhindered passageway almost exhilarating after the cramped confines of the defile and set a good pace if I do say so myself.

After a while I became aware of a faint susurration in my ear, and realised that my comm-bead had come within range of the regimental vox net. We were closer to the surface than I'd realised, and a flood of relief almost knocked the breath from my lungs. If someone was still here I wasn't too late to get a shuttle out.

Not that they'd wait if they all thought I was dead, of course, so I lost no time in contacting Kasteen and passing on the status of our mission.

'Commissar!' She sounded surprised and pleased in almost equal measure. 'We were beginning to think you hadn't made it.'

'I nearly didn't,' I admitted. 'They were waiting for us. We never got close to the damn portal.'

'I see.' Resignation tinged her voice. 'How many survivors?'

'Just me and Jurgen.' No point in going into lengthy explanations now, so I glossed over Logash's presence. 'The necrons are moving through the mine. Have they broken out onto the surface yet?'

'No.' Her voice faded for a moment, as she presumably turned her head away from the voxcaster to talk to someone else, then returned with an edge of urgency. 'Wait one...' The link went dead.

Absorbed in my conversation with the colonel I'd hardly noticed that the pipe had come to an apparent dead end. As I craned my neck and shone my luminator upwards, I could see that it had made an abrupt turn to the vertical, soaring away out of sight.

'What now?' I asked. Logash grinned, and indicated a set of metal rungs protruding from the frost, slick with a coating of ice. 'You have got to be kidding.'

He wasn't, of course. He just grabbed a bar and started climbing, sure-footed as a Catachan up a tree, and after a moment I shrugged and went after him. Jurgen followed, as always.

'Why are these here?' he asked.

'The maintenance servitors use them when the pipes shut down,' Logash explained. 'There should be an access panel up here somewhere...'

Concentrating only on maintaining my grip on the treacherous, ice-slick rungs I was startled by the sound of Kasteen's voice suddenly in my ear again. I almost slipped, hanging on purely by the Emperor's grace and the strength of my augmetic fingers.

'We've lost contact with two of the pickets in the middle levels,' she said. 'We're reinforcing...'

'No!' I cut in, a little too loudly. 'Pull everyone back out of the tunnels! It's the only chance they have!'

Bottled up in a confined space, unable to concentrate their fire, they'd be picked off easily. I'd seen that all too clearly before. 'Cover the entrances with everything you've got, and engage them as they emerge.' It probably wouldn't do us any good in the long run, but at least that way they'd be the ones held up by the bottleneck. I tried not to think about their ability to teleport, or move through walls...

'Acknowledged,' Kasteen said, clearly willing to defer to my greater experience with these hideous foes, and cut the link. I considered what she'd just told me, not liking the conclusions I was drawing. It was obvious the necrons were moving through the mines in considerable force if they'd been able to take out two of our squads before they even managed to get a vox message off. Maybe the ones in stasis were beginning to revive, and join the new arrivals...

'Found it,' Logash said above me, unnaturally cheerful under the circumstances, and began scraping the covering of frost from the wall, sprinkling me with a light dusting of powdered ice as he did so. He evidently knew what he was doing though, extending a thin metal probe from one of his fingers, and prodding hopefully at an indentation in the side of the pipe. 'Ah. That should do it...'

A section of the wall next to his hand withdrew suddenly, with a loud hum that set my teeth on edge, letting a blast of light and warm air into our frigid enclosure. The tech-priest vanished from sight, and after a moment of scrambling upwards I followed gratefully, heaving myself out onto a metal mesh floor illuminated by a dim electrosconce in the nearest wall. Despite its feebleness the yellow glow seemed incredibly welcoming as I turned to reach down and haul Jurgen up after me.

The chamber we stood in was small, barely large enough for the three of us, and glancing around I realised that it was merely a landing on a vast metal staircase which rose dizzyingly above us as well as descending to a vertiginous depth below. Logash glanced at some runes stencilled on the outside of the access panel we'd exited the pipe by, and nodded in satisfaction.

'Good,' he said.

'What is?' I asked suspiciously. Given his level of mental stability that could have meant just about anything by this stage. The young tech-priest indicated our surroundings with a casual wave.

'We're in one of the primary maintenance shafts. We should be able to get into the main control shrine a few levels up.'

'Best news I've had all day,' I said. 'Lead on.'

IT WAS MORE than a few levels, of course, we must have been climbing for almost half an hour before Logash stopped at another access panel in the plain metal wall, and I'd lost count of how many flights of stairs we'd climbed. My knees hadn't though, and ached abominably, but it's surprising how motivated you can be with an army of murderous automata at your heels and I kept going. Jurgen, of course, showed no sign of strain or discomfort, even lugging the heavy weapon.

'This should be it.' Logash hesitated, and I noticed the door was larger and more elaborate than any of the ones we'd passed on the way up, decorated with the cogwheel symbol of the priesthood.

'Good,' I said. 'Then let's get out of here.'

'I'm not sure I should open it,' the tech-priest said slowly, eyeing Jurgen and myself with a speculative expression on his face. 'This is a holy place. Only ordained and sanctified personnel are permitted beyond this point...'

'Fine,' I said. 'We're on a mission for the Emperor. Can't get much holier than that, right?' Logash looked confused.

'That would be an ecumenical matter,' he said. 'I'm not sure I'm qualified to judge...'

'Don't worry,' I said. 'I am. Now are you going to open the frakking door or will Brother Jurgen do it?' My aide stepped forward, raising the melta, and Logash hit the activation rune with almost indecent haste.

I'm not sure what I expected to find inside, but my first impression was one of overwhelming technological sophistication. Unlike the necron tomb below us, though, whose incomprehensible sorceries pulsed with palpable malevolence, this was a shrine suffused with the benevolence of the machine spirit, harnessed for the good of humanity and blessed by the tech-priests who normally worked here. I made an automatic gesture of obeisance to the large stained glass window depicting the Emperor (in His aspect of the Omnissiah, of course, but the Emperor still for all that) which spilled patches of colour across the serried ranks of dark wood and polished brass lecterns, each one inlaid with a pict screen displaying some aspect of the plant's function.

'Try not to touch anything,' Logash warned, brushing past Jurgen, who was making the sign of the aquila, his jaw even slacker than usual. No fear of that, I thought, shying away from the nearest lectern, when my eye was caught by the image on the pict screen. It showed a blurry, flickering image of what looked like one of the mine galleries, and to my horror the unmistakable shadow of a necron warrior passing swiftly out of sight. A moment later another of the metal monstrosities appeared, then a third.

'Logash,' I called. The tech-priest left off genuflecting to the alter in the corner with every sign of annoyance and ambled over to join me. I indicated the pict. 'Where's this?'

'Sector five, level fourteen,' he said after a moment spent consulting some runes on the lectern. He adjusted the controls, and the picture changed, showing another gallery. After a moment the leading necron appeared there. 'Moving towards sector three.'

'Can you see the whole mine from here?' I asked. He nodded.

'The rituals of focusing are very similar to those of your hololith. You may use this lectern if it will help.' After a few moments of instruction, the lighting of an incense stick, and muttering a few prayers over me he left me to it with an air of evident relief.

The picture I started to build up was grim, to say the least. It didn't take me long to establish that the lower levels were crawling with necrons, hundreds at least, and that they were systematically combing the tunnels, moving ever higher as they went. I voxed Kasteen.

'By my estimate we've got about half an hour before they reach the surface,' I said. 'If we're lucky.' At least the few troopers I'd found were already in the upper levels and pulling back, so she'd heeded my earlier advice. An external pictcaster had shown me the landing pad, already crowded with hundreds of our men and women, not to mention vehicles, waiting patiently for their turn to board one of the shuttles. With a sudden sinking feeling in my stomach I began to realise that the vast majority of them would still be there when the necrons emerged.

'We'll be ready,' Kasteen promised, but I already knew how hollow that promise was. They'd be massacred, no doubt about it, and more to the point I'd never make it to the safety of the starship either. There had to be something we could do to hold them off, if only I could think of it...

'Logash,' I called, but this time he ignored me, intent on some task at one of the other lecterns. I walked over and seized his arm. 'Logash, this is important.'

'So is this,' he said, a trace of irritation in his voice. 'The stabilisation rituals for the storage tanks have to be performed every six hours, and are already overdue. You must realise how volatile refined promethium is...'

'Oh yes,' I said, an idea so audacious I could hardly credit it myself beginning to form. I glanced past the glowing glass Emperor to the complex outside, where the huge storage tanks squatted, bulky as hab blocks. 'How much is in the tanks at the moment?'

'Roughly eight million litres,' he said. 'Since the tankers can't land with the orks about it's built up rather. But still within acceptable safety parameters, I can assure you.'

'I was rather hoping it was unsafe,' I said, and if he had any eyebrows I'm sure he would have raised them at that point. I pointed to the tangle of pipe work around the storage tanks. 'Do any of those pipes connect directly to the mine?'

'Not directly, no.' He looked at me quizzically. 'Why do you ask?'

'Because if we could dump all that liquid down the shaft it should really give the necrons something to worry about,' I said. A slow smile began to spread across the tech-priest's face.

'It would mean overriding a number of safety rituals,' he said, considering the idea. 'But it can be done.'

'Excellent,' I said, feeling a flare of optimism returning at last. 'Then you'd better get to it.'

'Indeed.' He huddled over the lectern, muttering gibberish, and what sounded suspiciously like an occasional high-pitched giggle, as he manipulated the controls. The chance to strike back at the creatures who had massacred his friends was obviously stirring up a lot of emotion, and I began to wonder if his fragile sanity would hold for long enough to implement our plan. Still, there was nothing to do but watch in silence while the minutes dragged by, and the automata in the pict screen moved ominously closer to the surface.

'Tanna tea, sir?' Jurgen materialised at my shoulder, proffering the flask he'd brought as a transparent excuse to join the expedition, and I took the fragrant liquid gratefully, suddenly aware of how tired and hungry I was.

He still couldn't find the sandwich he'd stowed some-where, to my barely-concealed relief, so we contented ourselves with the standard ration bars which tasted reassuringly of nothing particularly identifiable.

'Ready!' Logash said at last, another giggle rising to the surface. His face was preternaturally flushed, and his fingers trembled over the controls of the lectern, the first time I had ever seen augmetics do so. I nodded.

'In the name of the Emperor,' I said solemnly.

'In nominae Ernulph!' The tech-priest squeaked vindictively, and flicked a switch.

For a moment nothing seemed to happen, then I became aware of a low rumbling sound which seemed to suffuse the complex. Runes on several of the lecterns began to glow red, and a powdering of snow dislodged itself from the rim of the window outside. Then, for interminable moments, nothing seemed to happen at all.

'Look, sir!' Jurgen pointed to the pict screen, which I'd left tuned to one of the upper levels. A torrent of liquid became momentarily visible, filling the width of the gallery, sweeping all before it, tearing chunks of ice the size of Baneblades from the walls as it came and tumbling them casually ahead of itself. Then the pictcaster was ripped from its mounting, and the screen went dark. I switched to another just in time to see a party of necron warriors, far closer to the surface than I would have thought possible, trapped by the onrushing tsunami, picked up and thrown around like so many rag dolls. If I believed them capable of emotion I might have thought they stood dumbstruck before it before turning to flee, but it engulfed them all the same. I wondered if they'd fade away, smashed to pieces by that irresistible tide of pure promethium. Much good would it do them if they did; their tomb was at the lowest point of the tunnel complex and would surely flood in time, even though Logash had calculated that it would take the torrent around twenty minutes to seep down that far. Not that they needed to breathe, of course, but at the very least it should stop them using the portal until they found some way to pump the chamber out, by which time with any luck the Navy would be here to sterilise the planet.

All in all, I felt, a rather satisfying result.

I WAS STILL feeling pretty pleased with myself as I joined Kasteen and Broklaw on the landing pad a short while later, so buoyed with euphoria that for once I didn't even mind the bone-biting cold. The plain of ice was swarming with activity, Chimera engines rumbling as the engineseers marshalled them for embarkation and commenced the services of mothballing, and platoons marshalled by squads ready to take their place on the outgoing shuttles. A blur of motion in the corner of my eye resolved itself into a Sentinel, trotting eagerly round our flank, keeping an eye out for hostiles.

'Well done, commissar.' Broklaw shook me firmly by the hand. 'I don't think anyone else could have come close to achieving what you did today.'

'Well the next time we run across a necron tomb you're welcome to try,' I told him. He grinned, taking the remark for a joke, but any reply he made was drowned by the scream of a shuttle engine as one of the utility vessels from the *Pure of Heart* rose into the sullen air. Kasteen gestured at it as it howled over our heads and began to diminish into the leaden sky above.

'That was the fifth one,' she told me, raising her voice slightly over the ringing in our ears. 'Two full companies embarked already.' Which still left well over half our number, around six hundred troopers, stranded on the ground. Another half dozen flights still needed. I estimated the time that would take, and didn't like the answer. Even if the necrons had been dealt with, there were still plenty of orks around...

'What's the situation with the orks?' I asked Broklaw, but before he could respond a titanic explosion detonated among the refinery buildings, reducing the main Administratum block to rubble in an instant. Debris pattered down around us, mixed with chunks of ice and what looked uncomfortably like fragments of human tissue.

For a moment I was at a loss, my ears still ringing, and cast around for some sign of damage to the storage tanks, convinced that something must have touched off the leaking promethium. Then I saw it, tall as the building it had just destroyed, lurching forward through the rubble. Its hull was seared and breached in a dozen places, its main gun gone, but at least one of the secondaries was evidently still capable of wreaking havoc. Despite being delayed by the necrons, the gargant had arrived at last.

SIXTEEN

So HORRIFYING WAS the sight of that gigantic war machine, battered, scarred, but still lurching forward almost unstoppably, that for a moment none of us noticed the ant-like scurryings around its feet. Only as the ear-splitting cry of 'WAAAAAARRRRRGGGHHHH!' forced itself through the echoes of the explosion still fuzzing up the inside of my skull did I become aware of the horde of greenskins racing across the frozen ground ahead of it. They were afoot mostly, with just a handful of bikes and trucks bouncing forwards to pull clear of the main pack, and I was pleased to see our Sentinels peeling off to engage the light vehicles. Their lascannons cracked repeatedly, punching holes in the crudely welded armour, and a gratifying number of the ramshackle vehicles slewed to a halt leaking smoke.

But my attention remained fixed on the gargant, which loomed over everything like a shadow of doom. Despite the great rents in its metre-thick armour plate and the fused wreckage of its primary armament it still looked unstoppable, lurching forward uncertainly with a shriek of tortured metal, the left leg dragging slightly as though limping from its wounds.

'Fire at will!' Kasteen roared, suiting the action to the word, and hundreds of lasguns crackled repeatedly, sending echoes booming like surf from the structures still standing. The orks replied enthusiastically, but, praise the Emperor, no more accurately than usual, so our casualties remained light in comparison to the scores who were falling and being trampled underfoot by their comrades.

'Target the gargant!' Broklaw ordered the Chimera crews, and dozens of heavy bolters began to hose down the looming tower of metal which continued to plod towards us, cracking the ice of the landing field under its weight with every tottering step. They didn't seem to be bothering it much, but at least they were keeping the crew's heads down, and the open galleries on its shoulders clear of the heavy weapon crews who would otherwise have been adding a hail of supporting fire to its own formidable armament.

'They're consistent at least,' Kasteen muttered at my elbow. True to their nature the orks were attacking us directly across the landing field, sweeping down the length of it parallel to the line of storage tanks, now shimmering behind a haze of promethium vapour from their rapidly-draining contents. At the sight of that wavering shroud my blood ran even colder than it already was. It would only take one stray round landing next to them for the entire complex to be engulfed in an explosion almost impossible to imagine. And us along with it, of course.

'Keep our fire directed away from the storage tanks,' I cautioned, and she nodded grimly, perceiving the danger too. Not that it would make a lot of difference in the long run, I thought. The gargant was swinging its remaining gun around to target the centre of our formation, which of course meant me along with the senior officers, and I began to think we only had moments left if that. The ork advance seemed almost unstoppable, for every greenskin that fell another dozen continuing to charge forward slavering with bloodlust.

'Shuttle three requesting landing co-ordinates.' A new voice cut into the comm-net, and I became aware of the roar of a powerful engine becoming audible even over the din of the ongoing battle. A flare of hope rose within me...

'Shuttle three, abort your approach.' Mazarin's voice cut in abruptly, shattering it, her tone calm and authoritative. 'The greenskins are all over the pad.'

'I can still make it,' the unseen pilot argued, and the blocky shape of the shuttle suddenly appeared over the refinery, banking sharply round to run in over the main bulk of the ork army. Something about his voice sounded familiar, and I wondered if it was the same one who'd got us down here in the first place. Sporadic small arms fire bounced off his hull, and I stilled my breath remembering our abrupt arrival here, but the orks didn't get lucky this time and he came in low over our heads, his landing thrusters screaming. A few of the troopers waved and yelled, but most kept firing grimly into the onrushing horde of blade-waving barbarity. Another couple of moments and they'd be on us. I drew my chainsword, preparing for the shock of impact, and continued spitting las-bolts into the wall of screaming ork flesh bearing down on us almost as fast as the tidal wave of promethium still scouring the mine beneath our feet.

The gargant lurched forward again, and impelled by panic or instinct I finally noticed the deep gash in its leg. It was a slim chance, but...

'Target its left leg!' I yelled, and the Chimera crews switched their aim, pouring a concentrated barrage of heavy bolter rounds against that single, vulnerable spot.

For a moment I thought the desperate gamble would fail, but as the torrent of explosive fire chewed away at the torn and overstressed metal the towering leviathan began to sway alarmingly. The damaged limb seemed to seize up entirely, then failed altogether with a crack of rending metal which echoed like thunder between the encircling hills, audible even over the din of battle surrounding us.

Abruptly it lost its equilibrium entirely, toppling absurdly slowly at first, then faster and faster as more of that titanic bulk neared the ground. The orks around it scattered in panic, like ants beneath a descending boot, and a gratifying number of them failed to make it.

The impact shook the ground beneath us, cracking the ice for hundreds of metres around the huge wreck, swallowing almost a third of that vast bulk and opening chasms which engulfed the vast majority of the fleeing greenskins. From deep within that mountain of metal the dull thud of secondary explosions going off echoed like bronchitic coughs, and the lurid red glow of spreading flames began to join the smoke I'd seen earlier.

'Finish them off!' Kasteen ordered, and the Valhallans responded with a will, surging forward to engage the stunned survivors. After a short exchange of weapons fire it was all over, the few remaining orks fleeing beyond the effective range of our lasguns and Kasteen reining in the more enthusiastic platoon commanders who seemed on the verge of going after them with a display of profanity verging on the pyrotechnic. I'd expected Sulla to be leading the charge, but it turned out her company was the first to have been shuttled back up to the ship, so for once she didn't have the chance to do something stupid, which made a refreshing change.

'I think we should board as soon as we can,' I said, feeling our luck had already been stretched far thinner than we had any right to expect, and Kasteen nodded.

'I think you're right,' she said. 'Simia Orichalcae's rather lost its charm for me.'

'You and me both,' Broklaw agreed, and hurried off to organise the next stage of the embarkation as the incoming shuttle grounded at last.

I have to admit that the surge of relief I felt as I hurried up the cargo ramp and heard the comforting clang of metal beneath my boot soles once more left me almost giddy. Nevertheless I couldn't shake a strong sense of foreboding which intensified with every extra minute we remained on the pad, and continued to hover by the open hatch as a steady stream of Guardsmen and women made their way on board. Kasteen joined me there after a while, her face pensive.

'Looking for something?' she asked.

'Hoping I don't see it,' I admitted. 'It'll take more than a bath to see off the necrons if I'm any judge.' All the time we spoke I kept an amplivisor trained on the edge of the complex, dreading the sight of a flash of moving metal. Kasteen nodded ruefully.

'Shame you couldn't blow up the portal,' she said. I echoed the gesture.

'Shame you never got the chance to blow up the gargant,' I echoed. We looked at one another, the same thought occurring to us both simultaneously, and went to find Captain Federer.

'WE WERE GOING to detonate it by vox pulse,' Federer confirmed. He was a thin-faced, dark-haired man, whose enthusiasm for problem-solving was matched only by his lack of social skills. Rumour among the regiment had it that he'd once aspired to become a tech-priest but been expelled from the seminary for his morbid fascination with pyrotechnics, and he certainly seemed to have an almost instinctive understanding of the arcane technologies of the combat engineer. If the rumours were true, the Adeptus's loss was very definitely our gain.

* * *

WE FOUND HIM in the shuttle's main cargo bay fussing over the stowage of the small amount of equipment he'd been able to salvage; under the circumstances Kasteen had decided to abandon our vehicles and stores and use the space we saved to bring up another couple of platoons at a time. Riding back here would be hideously uncomfortable, but far better than still being around if the necrons stirred again.

'So you could still set the charges off from here?' I asked, raising my voice slightly to carry over the babble of voices from the troopers beginning to file in to the echoing hold. A few of them had evidently been in a similar situation before, unfurling their bedrolls into improvised acceleration couches as they settled. Federer nodded. 'Oh yes. You'd just need a sufficiently powerful transmitter. You could even do it from orbit if you wished.'

'That might be safer,' Kasteen suggested. 'After all, it's going to be a pretty big bang.'

'Oh yes.' Federer's face lit up with what I can only describe as unhealthy enthusiasm. 'Huge. Massive in fact. On the order of gigatonnes.' His eyes took on something of a dreamy quality.

'We didn't place anything remotely that powerful,' Kasteen said, looking vaguely stunned. 'We'd have blown ourselves to pieces along with the gargant.' Federer nodded, his voice taking on something of the quality of Logash discussing ambulls.[1]

'That was before the commissar flooded the mine with promethium,' he explained. 'The liquid will have settled to the bottom levels by now. That means the

---

1. *This is the last time Cain mentions the tech-priest in his account of these events. His subsequent career in the Adeptus Mechanicus can best be described as unspectacular, rising to the rank of Magos without doing anything further to draw attention to himself. His last known assignment was at the Noctis Labyrinthus mine complex on Mars.*

upper galleries would be full of vapour. In effect you've created an FAE bomb several kilometres wide.'[1]

'Assuming the explosives you placed weren't washed away by the flood,' I said. Federer shook his head.

'We anchored them pretty firmly. We were expecting a gargant to tread on them, don't forget. We allowed for stresses in the region of...'

'Never mind,' I said, cutting him off before he could get properly started. Once enthused, as I knew from experience, he was hard to bring back to the point. 'If you say it'll work I'm sure it will.'

'Oh yes,' he said, nodding eagerly.

I MUST CONFESS that, despite the uneventful journey back to the orbiting starship, I didn't feel entirely safe until I heard the docking clamps engage at last and felt the reassuring solidity of the *Pure of Heart's* deck plating beneath my feet.

'You're back, then,' Durant greeted us as we arrived on the bridge. It was much as I remembered it from our last visit, except that the hololith was now showing a panoramic view of the snowscape outside the refinery. From the height and angle I judged that the pictcaster was mounted somewhere above the main hull of the last shuttle to leave that benighted place, the final few pickets withdrawing to the safety of its cargo hold even as I watched. The refinery complex still seemed as deserted as ever, but I kept an apprehensive eye on the distant line of structures nevertheless.

'You seem pleasantly surprised,' I said. Durant made the almost-shrug I'd noticed before.

'Yes, well. The Munitorium might have argued about our charter fee if we'd left you behind,' he said, a little too gruffly to have meant it.

---

1. *Fuel/Air Explosive, a type of bomb which releases a volatile gas before detonation to magnify its power and area of effect.*

'Shuttle one preparing to lift, captain,' a junior officer called from a lectern somewhere to our left, and a palpable air of relief swept the whole chamber.

'Good,' the captain said. 'We've been sitting next to this damned planet so long I'm beginning to put down roots.' He gestured to Mazarin, who was huddled over her workstation with Federer, deep in discussion about something. 'Take us out of orbit as soon as they dock.'

'Aye aye, captain,' she responded, and hummed across to another console, where she busied herself with the rituals of engine activation.

'Better make it fast,' I said. As I'd feared, a glint of moving metal had appeared among the refinery buildings, moving rapidly towards the pictcaster. As it got closer I was able to discern a squadron of speeders, each one with what looked like the top half of a necron welded to it. All of them had a heavy weapon apparently incorporated into their right arm, and as I watched, dazzling green beams of malevolent energy lanced out to strike the hull of the slowly-rising shuttle.

'They're scratching the paintwork!' Durant roared, outraged. Truth to tell they were doing rather more than that, scoring visible channels in the metal. They were a long way from actually breaching it, shuttle hulls are sturdy to say the least, but the fact that they were able to inflict any damage at all spoke volumes for the power of the weapons they carried.

'They're going after the shuttle,' Kasteen said, her eyes on the skimmers which began to rise after it, wheeling about the slowly-climbing slab of metal like flies round a grox. They were growing in number too, I noticed with a quiver of unease, more and more of them rising to the join the swarm.

'They're not going to make it,' I said, alarmed. The pilot was making what evasive manoeuvres he could, but the craft was built for durability rather than agility, and several more of the deadly beams struck home. It could only be a matter of moments before something vital was hit...

'Don't be too sure,' Durant said. A moment later the main engines flared into life, vaporising any of the skimmers unfortunate enough to be behind the craft in a burst of superheated plasma, and lifting it cleanly away on an escape trajectory.

'They're falling behind,' Mazarin confirmed, and the projection obligingly rotated to show the remaining skimmers tumbling aimlessly in the wake of the shuttle's passage. A few moments later the image showed the reassuring refuge of our docking bay, and everyone breathed an audible sigh of relief. (Except for Mazarin, possibly, who may have had her lungs augmetically replaced.)

With our shuttle out of danger Durant had retuned the hololith to the aerial view of the refinery complex which he'd treated us to when we first made orbit.

As he magnified the tangle of buildings and storage tanks, now reassuringly far below us, my breath caught in my throat. A glittering tide of moving metal was emerging from the mouth of the mine, more warriors than I could count, blurring into a single amorphous entity which flowed between the buildings like flood water.

'They've woken!' I gasped, a spasm of fear gripping my bowels. They'd prevented the tide of promethium from flooding their temple, Emperor knew how, which meant their portal was probably still active...

'Broklaw!' I yelled, blessing the hurry that had left the comm-bead still in my ear. 'Stand to! Prepare to receive boarders!' Everyone looked at me as though I'd gone mad. 'They can teleport, remember?' I snapped, and Kasteen nodded grimly.

'They can swim, too, by the look of it.'[1]

---

1. *More likely they simply waded through the flooded levels until they broke the surface.*

'Federer!' I called. 'Now would be a good time!' The sapper grinned happily, exchanged a few more words with the hovering tech-priest, and prodded a rune with his finger. All eyes remained fixed on the cluster of buildings in the hololith. Nothing seemed to be happening.

'It didn't go off...' I began to say, then a gout of ice erupted from the plain at the mouth of the valley. Mazarin did something to enhance the clarity of the image, and in front of our eyes a vast, growing crater spread to engulf the nearby metal warriors. They tumbled into it like broken toys, more and more of them as the ground crumbled away faster than they could flee, and Federer punched the air as though he'd just scored the winning goal of a scrumball match.

'That would have seen off the gargant,' he said cheerfully.

'That it would,' I agreed, awestruck at the amount of devastation he'd wrought. But that had only been the prelude. Deep in the bowels of the pit a sudden flare of light erupted as the promethium vapour trapped in the caverns below ignited. A gout of flame fully a kilometre in height burst from the rupturing ground and raced across the snowscape at the speed of thought, melting the fleeing warriors in an instant, throwing blazing fissures ahead of itself as it went.

There were other explosions now too, the entire surface of the valley erupting like pyroclasts, vaporised rock, ice, and necrons forming a low, looming cloud riven with thunderbolts as electrostatic discharges of incredible power jumped between the particles. The refinery disappeared, sliding into the hellish inferno below, and vanishing as though it had never been...

'Brace for impact!' Durant called out, as though this were just a minor inconvenience, and the *Pure of Heart* was suddenly picked up and shaken like a child's toy by the titanic shockwave as the very atmosphere of the planet bulged under the force of the energies released. Even the crew grabbed for handholds, and I found myself bracing Kasteen, who had fallen back against me (something I had no complaints about at all).

'Just a minute,' Mazarin called, playing the controls in front of her like the keyboard of a forte, and the shuddering gradually ceased. She grinned again, and I began to suspect she enjoyed the chance to push the limits of her engines. 'Lucky we were so high. If we'd been down where the atmosphere's thicker it would have been a bit trickier.'

'Is that it, then?' Kasteen asked, her eyes riveted on the scene of destruction below. Even from orbit the dust cloud could still be seen staining half the planet, and in spite of all the horrors I'd endured down there I couldn't help feeling a spark of regret at the scar across the face of the pristine world I'd first looked upon from this very spot a few short days before.

'I hope so,' I said, although the twist of apprehension in my gut didn't fade entirely until we'd dropped back into the warp and were well on our way back to the safety of the Imperium.

Although, of course, where the necrons are concerned nowhere is ever remotely safe, as we now know to our cost. At least that particular nest appears to have been dealt with, even if no one can ever go back to check; the first thing Amberley did when my message finally caught up with her was to place the whole system under Inquisitorial quarantine.[1]

If there was one bright spot in the whole affair it was that I got to spend a little free time with her, after the interminable debriefing sessions were finally over and

---

1. *Subsequent examination of the site showed no signs of an active necron presence, although if anything was left of their installation it would have been buried far too deeply to have left much trace of anything. I for one would not be at all keen to start digging holes to find out for sure.*

she'd finished going round every trooper in the regiment who'd seen or heard anything of what we'd found on that miserable iceball and threatened them with the wrath of the Emperor if they ever breathed a word of it again. Or the wrath of the Inquisition, which, trust me, is even scarier.

AMBERLEY WAS IN an uncharacteristically sombre mood on the last night we spent together, the occasional table in her hotel suite covered in data-slates as she collated all the witness reports, and looked up with a wan smile as I entered.

'You were damn lucky,' she said, the blue of her eyes clouded with fatigue. I nodded, and stood aside to let the room servitor trundle in with a tray of food. She saw it and raised an eyebrow.

'I took the liberty of ordering,' I said. 'You seemed busy.'

'Thank you,' she said, stretching, so I wandered across and massaged some of the tension from her shoulders as the servitor set out dishes and cutlery on the dining table. She smiled as the covers came off.

'Ackenberry sorbet. One of my favourites.' That hadn't been hard to remember, so I smiled in return.

'You did say you'd live on the stuff if you could the last time you ordered it.'

'So I did.' The smile widened as the main course came into view. 'What's that?'

'Ambull steak,' I said. 'I think they owe me that much.'

[Cain's narrative continues for several more paragraphs, but since it only covers personal matters of no interest to anyone else I've chosen to end this extract from the archive right here.]

ABOUT THE AUTHOR

Sandy Mitchell is a pseudonym of Alex Stewart, who has been working as a freelance writer for the last couple of decades. He has written science fiction and fantasy in both personae, as well as television scripts, magazine articles, comics, and gaming material. His television credits include the high tech espionage series *Bugs*, for which, as Sandy, he also wrote one of the novelisations.

Apart from both miniatures and roleplaying gaming his hobbies include the martial arts of Aikido and Iaido, rifle shooting, and playing the guitar badly.

He lives in a quiet village in North Essex with a very tolerant wife, their first child, and a small mountain of unpainted figures.

More Warhammer 40,000 from Sandy Mitchell

FOR THE EMPEROR

'STAY BACK. WE'LL handle it,' I told Crassus, and leaned over the driver's compartment to call to Jurgen. 'Take us in!' I shouted.

As usual, where anyone else might have hesitated or argued, he simply followed orders without thinking. The Salamander lurched forwards, accelerating towards the blazing building as rapidly as it could.

'There! Those loading doors!' I pointed, but my faithful aide had already seen them, and a hail of bolter shells ripped them to shreds an instant before we hit.

COMMISSAR CIAPHAS CAIN – *renowned across the sector for his bravery and valour – is sent to help maintain order on an outpost world on the borders of Tau space. But when the alien ambassador is murdered, Cain and his regiment of Valhallans find themselves in the middle of a war. As the Imperial Guard struggle to contain worldwide civil insurrection, can the wily Commissar Cain identify the real villain before the planet is lost to the Imperium forever?*

Available from all good bookstores and Games Workshop outlets, or direct from www.blacklibrary.com